IRIS OF THE CROWNED FLAME

ORACLES OF THE GELID

OLIVIA TILDON

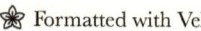

For everyone who's ever been told their love was too strange, their dreams too loud, their truth too dangerous.
Burn the script. Break the rules. Love without apology.

Your heart is not too much. It is revolutionary.

CHAPTER 1

Something was wrong, the thought repeated in my head over and over. My stomach twisted as I walked down the dimly lit hallways from Mother's locked office to her chambers. Courtiers stopped talking and averted eye contact, casting their heads down and away as I passed. The only noise I heard came from my slippers smacking against the marbled floors as I moved as quickly as I could without abandoning my training in formality. Each step felt heavier, and the air thickened, as if the castle itself was holding its breath. I turned the corner of the hallway to find many people had gathered before her chambers. I flinched at the swell of voices ahead, my shoulders tensing as I spotted the crowd. One of the castle guards recognized me, and started elbowing people, forcing them to move out of the way for me.

"What's going on?" I demanded, my voice wavering more than I wished.

"Princess, His Majesty is in the room, best you hear from him." The guard who first spotted me informed me. He gently pushed a handful of my mother's maidens out of the way. I followed, murmuring customary apologies. Their bickering blurred into meaningless noise, my ears straining for a familiar voice instead.

Nothing but chaos greeted me inside her chambers.

1

Courtiers, maidens, and guards, standing or sitting all around, talked or argued, creating such a loud noise that I couldn't hear any coherent words. I pushed through the crowd, finally laying eyes on the doorway to her bedroom. Two guards flanked the closed door. Between us, people tried to push to the door, but the guards blocked them. I was only a few steps from the door when a hand touched my elbow. My breath caught, the pressure halting me. Touching me was too improper, no one outside of my ladies dared to do that. I turned, my heart beating faster, relief stole my breath as my brother's familiar face came into view.

Ethan's crystal-blue eyes, so much like our father's, held a sharpness that suggested more than he let on. Most of the time, they twinkled with mischief. His chestnut curls were uncharacteristically tousled, the way they got when he had been running his hands through them—his habit when thinking through something dire. Broad-shouldered and effortlessly confident, he moved through life with the easy charm of someone who had never had to try too hard, whether he was twirling a goblet of wine at a feast or flashing a disarming smirk after narrowly avoiding trouble.

"Ethan! What's going on?" I searched my older brother's face for any sign of the answer. His firm jaw and lips gave nothing away, but his eyes—glossed over, rimmed red—held my attention, betraying his calm exterior. I couldn't recall a time I'd seen him this distraught.

"Lyla, come, father will tell you." He said nothing more. His voice fell flat, his tone left no room for argument, telling me whatever I was about to find out needed the privacy found behind that door in front of us.

The guards bowed their greeting to us before knocking. After a pause, a muffled voice called through, and one of the guards opened the door for us, Ethan entering close behind. The voices were hushed now, the tension quieter but more pressing—like waiting for bad news. The court physician, my father, and a handful of advisors for both Mother and Father were in the room. They had all paused, watching to see who was entering.

I saw father first. His jaw clenched, then his hand rose to cover his mouth, a quiet sob slipping through his normally steely resolve. Tears fell from his crystal blue eyes. The physician placed a hand on his shoulder in comfort but glanced at Ethan and me.

The door clicked shut behind us, then the physician said, "I'm sorry, Princess, the queen has left us."

A hollow ache punched through my gut; my eyes widened and my breath stilled. I looked around the room at all the people standing, none were mother. My eyes landed back with my father, then followed his gaze down to the bed he was standing over. There she was, under the covers, like she was sleeping the morning away. But I could see it in Father's eyes, the physician spoke true. Father stared down at her, motionless, his breath shallow. The longer I stared, the more tears I saw falling from his face to her blanket. His hands held hers, but her lifeless skin looked almost translucent against her black hair.

"No, it can't be, she can't be," I whispered, my knees buckling. Ethan reached for me, catching me before I fell, someone else carried a chair and helped me into it. Ethan sat on the arm of the chair next to me, one arm on my back so I could lean into him, clinging to whatever privacy we could find. He offered me his handkerchief, and I buried my face in it, resting my head against his chest.

'*A ruler must always remain in control*,' Mother had drilled into us. Her words echoed, but did little to hold me. I sobbed into Ethan's chest, hiccuping as my breaths hitched. How could I control myself when this had happened? She was too young. We were supposed to be meeting this morning to discuss suitors for me. She wasn't supposed to go yet.

After several minutes, my emotions finally tapered, allowing me to find the control I needed. I raised my head, finding only Ethan and Father staring at me. All others in the room busied themselves, giving us the space we needed to grieve.

I inhaled deeply, trying to find my voice. "What happened?"

My eyes pleading for answers to anyone who would make eye contact with me.

Behind me, the physician spoke up. "Can we have the room?"

I turned my head over my shoulder, watching as the others pushed each other out of the room.

Once the room cleared, he started again.

"Nothing is immediately evident. She had no complaints over the last few days and had been perfectly healthy, not even a cold in recent years. I did notice this mark though." He paused, easing to the bedside opposite Father, and motioned to a small scorch mark on her collar bone, almost imperceptibly small, jagged pink lines, like a fresh scar, and connected to look like lightning. "This is quite unusual; I haven't seen it before. I will need to investigate it further prior to her burial."

"What is it?" Father's voice cracked.

"Nothing good, Your Majesty. It doesn't sit well with me." The physician's gaze flicked toward the door, then quickly back to me, unable to hold steady. His features were composed, but the tension in his brow betrayed him. This wasn't the usual quiet worry he carried when someone fell ill. No, this was deeper, more raw, as if even he didn't trust the calm he was trying to offer us.

Ethan cleared his throat, providing an unspoken request to speak. "I don't mean to interrupt, but while I was in her sitting chambers waiting for Lyla to arrive, I received a message from the Council. It seems that word of this had already reached them, and they are demanding a meeting this afternoon."

Father snarled. "They can't allow us to grieve for one moment before their power-hungry leaches call a meeting."

He took a breath, calming himself before continuing. "You two better come. This will undoubtedly be about which of you will take the throne."

Ethan and I glanced at each other. Her body hadn't even moved. We only just found out she's gone, and they're already trying to push forward as if her passing was just a hiccup in their plans.

Wait. Succession? Not even I knew which of us would take the throne. While other countries do have traditions about a first born or the first of a specific gender, we didn't. The throne simply stayed within a family, passed down to any child the previous king and queen felt were most worthy.

Both a king and a queen have also always ruled Elthas. Upon the death of one monarch, the other must marry again or cede the throne to their heir. After decades with her, there's no way Father would want to replace Mother. Not when Ethan and I were old enough to step in.

I could hear Mother's voice again, *'We do not rule alone, because the Gods didn't. How could we be so arrogant as to think we can handle running the kingdom better than the Gods ran theirs? We don't have one god to show the way; thus, we cannot have one person leading us there.'*

"Who... which one of us is it?" My voice quivered. Ethan had been considering offering a betrothal to a Lady of the court, but neither of us were ready. Me least of all. It was the last thing I wanted to do.

Father looked between us, concern etching in his face. "Your mother and I were just discussing last week. We both wish for Lyla to ascend to the throne." Father's eyes remained on Ethan. "Your mother hoped that you would advise your sister until you found an advantageous union of your own." His eyes shifted to me. "And she hoped that you would find a suitable husband quickly."

I nodded, hearing the underlying message. Nausea hit me as I realized what they were doing. I had always been so very against marriage, and Mother knew it. She hoped to fix me of my beliefs about marriage, and about men, by putting me in a position that required me to marry. Plus, Ethan had never been one for any form of leadership, preferring to enjoy time in gambling houses and with courtesans. He might have been my older brother, but he was always the one goofing off, playing pranks, and teasing the ladies of the court over any form of responsibility. This was her way of bringing us both into the roles she expected of us.

When I glanced at Ethan, I could read the irritation. His

5

emotions were always on full display, and this time was no different. The newly placed expectation angered him.

"I need to go back to my chambers." My voice was clipped as my fists clenched.

"Will you accept all that comes with this, Lyla?" Father pointedly asks.

"Yes." I gritted out with more anger than I intended.

Father nodded, expecting my response. "Expect the meeting to be immediately after lunch. You know where the Councilors meet, yes?"

I nodded once more, not trusting my voice to cooperate anymore.

"You are expected as well, Ethan."

I stood, trying to overcome the weakness grief caused. I couldn't bring myself to ask Ethan how he felt about also attending, so I quickly fixed my hair and face in the room's mirror before rushing to my chambers. I knew my best friends would be there, and I desperately needed their support.

CHAPTER 2

By the time I reached my chambers, I was out of breath. While it was never proper for a Lady to run, I'd pushed the limit to get there, hoping to look too rushed to be stopped by anyone I passed in the hallways.

My knees buckled the moment the door clicked shut.

Ivy and Amyra were in my chambers, tidying up from the morning as they normally do. I tried to make it to the sitting area just as a fresh wave of tears spilled over.

"Lyla! What's wrong?" Amyra's voice felt distant, like it reached me through thick fog. But I knew that sound — the warmth beneath her panic. Her pale blue eyes widened, searching my face as she pulled me into her arms. Her long, wavy black hair brushed against my cheek, falling around me like a curtain. I inhaled deeply, taking in the familiar scent of warm apple cider, and it nearly undid me. Her lips grazed my temple, and even through my shock, I caught the faint sweetness of raspberries and honey, a reminder of safer moments.

Ivy's eyes sharply flicked to the window, gauging the time of day. "You're supposed to be in the meeting with the Queen. Why are you here?" she asked, her voice tight but steady. Always steady. Her gold eyes locked onto me, bright and sure. She crossed the room in a few fast steps, her red curls bouncing, and without a second thought, she took my hand. Ivy had always been my compass in moments of chaos, and now I clung to her like she could point me back to solid ground.

Before I could speak—before I could even think what to say—they were both there, steadying me as the world tilted. The sobs came hard and fast, my whole body shaking with them, but they didn't let go. They held on, and I let myself fall apart in their arms.

After several minutes, I could finally breathe again.

"It's Mother, she…" The words stuck in my throat.

"Is she forcing you too hard on this suitor business? You only just turned 20. Surely she doesn't expect you to get betrothed this summer?" Ivy was always ready to defend me, and I couldn't help but love her so much for it. She had been my best friend since we were children, and my Lady-in-Waiting since Ethan and I came home from our study abroad, 5 years ago.

"Ivy, stop, let her talk!" Amyra chided.

While Ivy might be ready to start fights for me, Amyra had always been the one I could count on for emotional support, for comfort, and for rationality. Even now, as my world crumbled, Amyra's calm steadied the air between us—and made me ache for what we couldn't have. Amyra, with her pale blue eyes that could see straight through me, and her long, wavy black hair that always seemed to catch the light like polished obsidian. She smelled of warm apple cider, even in summer, and her pale skin, so soft beneath my fingertips, never failed to draw me in. When we came home from studying abroad, she had moved into the castle to join her father, one of the Councilors, after growing up on an estate along the coastline.

Ivy had introduced us. Fiery Ivy, with her gold eyes sharp as blades and her untamable red curls that always seemed to bounce in rhythm with her energy. Her pale skin was a canvas of freckles, scattered like constellations across her nose and cheeks. From that first meeting, the three of us had formed an inseparable trio. But Amyra and I had something deeper, a love too precious to lose. We could never be caught. Her father would disown her, and I would be forced into exile, never to take the throne. But the tension from staying apart was more unbearable than the fear of losing everything. Ivy was the only one who knew what we were to each other, and it needed to stay that way.

Instead of talking, I shook my head. The words stuck to my tongue; I couldn't get them out. "She... gone." I choked out in a whisper.

"Gone? Like she left? Why would she schedule this meeting with you if she were traveling?" Ivy, Gods, I loved her, but I couldn't take this.

"No." I sniffled. "She didn't wake up this morning. She..." The words wouldn't come. I couldn't admit it. Let me try a different way. "I have a new meeting this afternoon. With the Council. Father is going to tell them I've been chosen to take the throne."

"Take the thr..." Ivy trailed off, finally understanding.

Amyra held me tighter, her arms strong and warm around me. "Oh Gods, Lyla, I'm so sorry."

Both women started crying as well. Mother had always invited them to any social event she needed me to attend and had grown to know them over the years. She had become as much a mother to them as their own could be. Well, as much as the queen of a country could be.

Through sniffles, Amyra asked, "How did it happen?"

I could only shrug. "The physician didn't know. There was a funny burn mark on her chest, right here," I pointed to the spot on my own. "But it didn't look like anything that was fatal. I don't know."

"And those rat bastards are calling a meeting now? Today? They couldn't give you time to grieve the loss of your own family?" Ivy was seething as she realized this.

"Wait, are you going to be the queen?" Amyra asked. She pulled on my shoulders so she could face me.

I nodded.

"What about the marriage law?" Amyra questioned the age-old tradition of always having a king and queen ruling over the kingdom. We have never had the throne held by one person before, except during these transition periods. This council was too focused on returning to the past to allow me to be the first. They might let Ethan, maybe, but they would sooner start a war than allow a queen to sit alone... let alone to sit with a second queen.

"I... I think that's part of why they chose me. They know I don't want to marry, ever. And Mother always found my refusal horrifying." It's not that I don't like men. It's just that men are always so busy with finding new ways to subjugate their wives, so I never wanted to be tied to one. Besides, I loved Amyra. We could have made it if only the throne had gone to Ethan.

I reached for her face with both hands, gently holding her as we stared into each other's eyes. "I don't know what's going to happen, but I do know I can't live without you. I promise I'll find a way for us if you are willing to stay, but I will never stop you if you decide you can't do this."

Her crystal blue eyes glistened with her love, tears threatening to spill down her pale cheeks. "Promise me, Lyla, you will never risk exile for me. I can't bear that burden."

Her smile betrayed the promise she wanted me to make. She didn't want me to announce her as my love to the world. I understood why. Elthas was not kind to unwed women, and it had only gotten worse in recent years, as Councilors from the richest districts put more conservative men in their seats.

Ivy interrupted my thoughts. "No, Amyra, please, don't make her promise to leave you behind. You two have a love so rare. I'm sure we could find a way to modify the expectations. Do we know the law says it must be one man and one woman? Maybe it's just any marriage to anyone that is required."

I broke my stare with Amyra to face Ivy. She meant well, but was only making this harder. She knew that marriage between women wouldn't fly for our regular citizens, let alone for the future Queen. "It is explicit. I checked when I first realized I love Amyra. There is no legal way..."

"But there are illegal ways! So many of the men take their mistresses. Half the halls are filled with mistresses and ladies of questionable origin. Surely, you could take one too?" Ivy pointed out.

I hadn't dared to think this way before. Men always had the freedom to visit other beds. Only when these situations produced children did they ruin lower-standing men and cause high-ranking men to take leave for their farms, bribing their wives into silence and hiding illegitimate children. Amyra and I couldn't meet that ending. Maybe there is an idea there.

I turned back to Amyra. If I asked her to be my mistress, I could ruin her ability to have her own family. We had shared many dreams about our children running and playing together, raising them as siblings together.

She didn't let me ask. "Lyla, I will stay by your side for all of eternity. You are my heart, my everything. I would give everything up for your happiness. I just won't give up your reputation. Please don't ask me to sacrifice you. If you take this throne, and you marry a man, you could change the Council, and then change the laws, and allow others to live more freely than we have ever imagined. You are the change the country needs."

I nodded, too moved to speak. She was too good for me. They both were.

I took a few breaths to compose myself. "I love you too, Amyra. And I need you to have your own life. If you won't let me give up mine, I can't let you give up yours."

Amyra grasped my hands and pulled them to her lap. "We will find a way, as long as you rule the country."

Ivy jumped up. "Well, that's it. Now we need to find a way to pick a husband that won't mind being second fiddle. Should be easy, right?"

"As easy as putting out a fire with my mind," I replied with a dry smile. Nothing about this would be easy. But finding a way to keep Amyra in my life, and maybe to set her up to have her family, would always be worth the effort.

Ivy made her way to my closet. "Well, you have an important meeting to go to after lunch, so let's talk strategy while we get you ready to show those Councilors that you will be a Queen worth following."

Amyra crossed to my vanity and started digging through the cabinet next to it where all of my accessories were stored. The two of them moved with such efficiency. Within minutes, Ivy had picked out a deep navy dress, made with capped sleeves and minimal decoration, one of my only dresses within the acceptable mourning colors. She came back into the room just as Amyra turned around with two pieces of jewelry. She had picked out a delicate gold necklace with a small crescent pendant made from lapis lazuli, which always stood out stunningly against my warm ivory skin. She also held a golden circlet, with matching lapis lazuli chips sprinkled through it. She had given me this set when we first visited her hometown.

The two helped me to dress, and then I sat down at the vanity while Amyra started arranging my straight brown hair with braids to secure the circlet in place.

All the while, they fired off increasingly ridiculous ideas about how to find a man who wouldn't limit my relationship with Amyra. Most of the ideas they had were quite impractical, ranging from death battles to sending them on quests to find mythical objects from our fairy tales. Two ideas struck me as possibly useful, though, and I tucked them into my proverbial pocket, ready to use them if needed. As they bustled around me, hands threading through my hair and clasping delicate metal at my throat, I knew—I didn't deserve either of them.

By the time a courtier brought lunch to my chambers, I was ready for the meeting, and even comfortable seeing all the nobility in the castle, knowing the gossip and hushed whispers that accompany them.

CHAPTER 3

Father and Ethan were waiting for me in the hallway outside the Council's conference chambers. The halls were otherwise empty, the silence confirming they were already gathered inside. Father's crystal-blue eyes, so much like Ethan's, held none of their warmth, now distant beneath the weight of grief. His short black hair, always neatly groomed, added to the severe lines of his face, sharp and imposing, like a man carved from stone rather than flesh.

Father was wearing what he called his working crown, a simple metal band made of silver leaves. It was the least ornate type for men, and the one he wore any time he had to decide for the kingdom. He always told us the weight of the crown helped him to remember that his choices shaped the future in ways we can never fully predict. Both men were otherwise dressed in simple black clothing, wearing long sleeves despite the heat of the day.

They stood there in deep, but particularly quiet, conversation. I paused in front of a mirror near them, checking my appearance. I hated that I had to care about how I looked right now, hated that this moment demanded poise instead of mourning. Nevertheless, I straightened my shoulders and took in my reflection with a hard, hollow gaze. My long, straight brown hair, streaked with golden highlights, had been braided and pinned neatly beneath the gold circlet, the chips of lapis lazuli catching the light like tiny shards of sky. The deep navy dress Ivy had chosen contrasted against my warm ivory skin, giving me the somber appearance they all expected of me. Around my neck, the delicate gold necklace sat like a chain, beautiful but binding.

My eyes, brown with just a hint of red beneath the surface, caught the light in a way that made the crimson glint show more clearly. Mother used to say she loved that about me, how the red in my eyes always burned brighter when my emotions were strong. I swallowed hard, the memory sharp and unwelcome, but I couldn't look away. Now, all I could see was the fire of my grief, the anger simmering just beneath the surface. I looked too composed for someone whose world had just been ripped apart. Maybe that was what they wanted to see. A queen in waiting, already hardened, already shaped by grief into something useful. I swallowed down the bitter taste rising in my throat and forced myself to stand taller, wrapping my sorrow and my fury tightly around me like armor.

This meeting would determine whether the Council supported my ascension, and I needed their support to delay the wedding. The law didn't allow for coronation until after I was married, and we had never gone more than three months without both a king and queen. Three months to find and accept a man to be my husband was far too fast for my liking, no matter who the man might be.

"Are you ready?" Ethan asked, trying to break the silence between us.

I nodded. "As ready as I can be. What about you?"

I caught his reflection in the mirror as I pretended to adjust a tendril of my hair. His dark brown brows furrowed and his jaw clenched. He pressed his lips together, trying to hold back his emotions.

"I'm always ready to support you, Lyla. Always." He gave a tight nod.

I turned to face Father. "Any last words of wisdom?"

"You look so much like your mother when we went into the

Council for the first time to claim her throne." His eyes watered, threatening to spill for a moment, before anger replaced his nostalgia. His back stiffened, jaw clicked into place, and he cleared his throat. "We will go in, I'll announce you as the next queen. They will question you about the suitors you have and expect a timeline for marriage. Remember your history and provide them with a proposal they can't refuse. Do you have a plan?"

I nodded, hoping I projected confidence. But the truth twisted in my gut. This was the last thing I wanted to do. I didn't even know what I could even propose.

"My Ladies helped me to brainstorm with some options." Not quite a lie, anyway.

"May I offer a plan? I talked with my lord as well, not sure how much time you'd be able to spend thinking about this," Ethan offered. I nodded silently, giving him the space to speak. "A ball to meet the suitors, and then another council meeting to announce who you will marry. You could invite them to bring their best options, so they feel they have some say in the matter. But of course, you'll have final say."

Mulling the plan through, I realized this was not the worst idea. "A ball may be the best plan yet."

Ethan smiled. Father nodded; his lip twitched briefly before he mastered his expression again. "Your mother would be proud of both of you."

The doors to the chambers opened with a flourish, interrupting us. Two courtiers announced they were ready for us to join. Father led the way, striding in with confidence and not a sign of any emotional distress. I followed, hoping to convey the same with my movements, and Ethan was behind me.

We found three seats left open for us at the head of the long oak table. The councilors occupied the rest, one representing each region of Elthas. Most of them were men I knew nothing about, but I could identify the only female Councilor, Lady Juniper Mallard, sitting at the far end from where my seat was. We had never talked, but I had heard how she was the only one rumored to challenge Lord Luther without flinching. Next to her was Amyra's father, Lord Greenhow.

Next to us, unfortunately, were the two lords I least enjoyed by reputation alone. Lord Patrick Luther was the most conservative man in the room, and the one most vocal about the need to assert male authority over their feminine counterparts. His strong misogyny often enraged Mother after meetings with him. Across from him, next to the seat Ethan was to take, was Lord Eric Denenbaum. He was the father of Ethan's girlfriend, Katelle. His reputation was slightly better than Lord Luther's, but he still supported many of the measures Luther proposed, which left me feeling distrustful of him. He may be more charismatic, but that didn't make him a better man.

The Council rose as we entered the room and waited for the three of us. Once we were standing next to our designated seats, the courtiers moved in to pull the chairs out in a synchronized motion. We took our seats, which signaled to the Council to take theirs. I looked at each face, taking them in as they studied me. When I got to Lady Mallard, she offered a wink. I didn't know what that could mean. We had never met before, let alone shared a secret.

As I reached the last councilor, Father cleared his throat. I looked at him as he nodded towards Lord Luther. The councilor thumped a gavel on the table. "Session shall resume."

He stood and read the list of items they planned to handle during this meeting. It sounded like a regularly scheduled meeting, rather than one called to order just for Mother's death. Glancing back at each person, I wondered how many knew the queen was dead. This certainly was a bizarre way to honor her memory. It felt so callous, so cruel, to sit here and listen to them act like just an unfortunate accident occurred to some irrelevant person, a minor bump in the road. I clasped my hands around each other, flattened in my lap, and took some deep breaths to soothe the irritation I held.

Finally, he finished his list. "We shall commence with the matter added this morning. As you all are now aware, the

Queen of Elthas was found deceased earlier today. Our King is here to provide you with what we need to know."

Lord Luther sat down as Father stood. "Good afternoon, councilors. It is with profound sorrow that I confirm the passing of my wife, Her Majesty, the Queen of Elthas, earlier today. The royal physician has initiated a thorough investigation into the circumstances of her passing and has enlisted the support of select members of the royal guard. We expect gaining further clarity in the days and weeks ahead and will provide updates as more information becomes available."

Father paused, and I could have sworn I heard an almost imperceptible sniffle.

"As established by our longstanding laws and traditions, the monarchy must be led by both a king and a queen in service to the people. Given my advancing years, I find myself unable to take a new consort and fulfill this duty as required. Therefore, I will abdicate my position and entrust the throne to its rightful successors, while remaining available to serve in an advisory capacity to the new king and queen."

Father paused once more, though this seemed more intentional, as he watched the councilors take notes about his announcement. After a moment, he continues.

"Over the years, the queen and I have engaged in extensive discussions regarding the future of the realm. As such, I can say with certainty that the selection of our next leader reflects not only my judgment but also the queen's expressed wishes. It is with full confidence that I announce Princess Lyla will ascend to the throne and lead Elthas with strength and wisdom for many years to come."

The councilors paused their writing to offer a polite applause. I didn't know what to do, so I stood to accept it. Father placed his arm around my shoulder, an unexpected gesture of warmth in such a formal moment, and one I clung to.

Moments after standing, Lord Luther stopped his clapping, which caused the rest to stop almost instantaneously. It felt almost rehearsed. His influence was palpable. As the applause died, Father sat down, leaving me the only one standing.

"Princess Lyla, my congratulations are yours," he began, his tone measured. "As you must be aware, traditions dictate that your marriage coincides with your coronation. We want to ask about the status of your courtships, since there has been no formal betrothal announcement. Might you provide us with an estimation when we may expect both your betrothal and subsequent nuptials to be completed?"

Seriously? Despite the lack of proper mourning for Mother, he demanded I discuss my marital prospects. I expected the callousness, but it was still jarring to witness. I felt my eyebrows raised for a moment and worked to straighten my face and remove any signs of emotions.

"Thank you, Lord Luther, and everyone else, for your warm welcome to the Council, especially under such tragic circumstances." I noticed Lady Mallard's expression flickered; a small smirk lifted the corners of her mouth for only a moment before she composed herself. "As I had only just reached an age where courtship is welcome, I have only started to meet with potential suitors. I understand the urgency with which the Council must feel, as an open seat of the throne can be an invitation to instability. If the Council would be so kind as to consider a proposal that I had the briefest amount of time to prepare, I would appreciate it."

I paused here, waiting for signs of assent. Several councilors briefly nodded before ducking their heads, focused on the paper in front of them, prepared to take notes on what I was about to say. My heart stuttered for a moment, and I felt a sudden rush of warmth to my cheeks. My hands became clammy as I clasped one hand over the other in front of my hips, as a sign of the composure I wished I had. I forced myself to speak once more.

"I believe that the best course of action would be to host a ball, perhaps a month after the Queen's funeral, to allow suitors to come present themselves. The ball can be open to all nobility from Elthas and neighboring countries, and I would even invite all of you to select a suitor that you feel is a worthy match. I expect this would not only help my search, but offer an opportunity for our local economic growth."

Father offered me a slight nudge from his leg, which I took to indicate approval. I hoped so, anyway.

"This is certainly an interesting proposal, Princess. Our yearly budget does not support such an event. How would you suggest we approach the funding for this?" Lord Denenbaum asked.

I felt the panic return for a moment. How would I know how to pay for this?

Father cleared his throat and stood. "Lord Denenbaum, while I acknowledge your observation as quite perceptive, I must remind you that the passing of Her Majesty, the Queen, was an entirely unforeseen event. We could not prepare for such a situation until mere hours ago. Traditionally, we have kept financial discussions closed, so we haven't introduced Princess Lyla to them yet. The allocation of funds will require a separate meeting, allowing the planning committee ample time to assess this matter thoroughly. At this moment, I would suggest we redirect our conversation to a more strategic, brainstorming level. We will convene the financial and planning committees in three days to address the fiscal concerns."

Lord Denenbaum's posture stiffened, and his face flushed with embarrassment. His eyes dropped to the table, shoulders tightening, like he hadn't expected Father's sharp rebuke. I tried to keep my face neutral as I felt gratitude for Father stepping in.

Lady Mallard raised her hand. I nodded in her direction, to allow her a chance to speak. "My deepest condolences, Your Majesty and Your Highnesses. The Queen was a beloved ruler, always just and fair. Princess Lyla, I look forward to helping you learn the role, so that you can make your mother proud as the ruler she hoped you would be."

She bowed her head briefly, and I returned the gesture. "I would like to offer support for the ball. I think this is a great way to hasten introductions to several suitors at once. As a member of the budget committee, I can assure Lord Denenbaum that we will find funding for this venture."

Relief bloomed in my chest. I hadn't been wrong to hope she'd be the one to back me. Lady Mallard was the youngest councilor by almost a decade, only just a few years older than Ethan. She came from a northern mountainous region called Frosted Forests, not very well populated, but a hardy and egalitarian region all the same.

Over the years, when imagining running away with Amyra, I had often wondered if we could find a small community there and hide from bounty hunters and others who would come looking for a crown princess so we could just live out our lives openly. The fantasy was charming, if impractical.

With her input, the other councilors that supported the idea started offering ways to make this ball happen. Father sat down and tapped my arm, indicating I should as well. I watched as the various men argued the finer points of the idea. Father leaned over and whispered, "You did well, Lyla. This discussion shows they will adopt the idea once they satisfy Denenbaum's tight ass."

I nodded, satisfied this first meeting had gone well. Ethan reached for my hand and offered a squeeze. He then leaned in and said, "Great job. You handled them better than I could have hoped to do. You're a natural at this."

If I had nothing else, at least I had the support of my brother and father. The discussion of a ball to find me a husband had reached a fervor I hadn't expected. Men twice my age talked about my marriage like a sport. My gut twisted as I imagined a parade of smug smiles and veiled threats, each suitor more power-hungry than the last. This was the last thing I wanted to do.

CHAPTER 4

The next two weeks flew by in a whirlwind of emotions. Each morning, I woke every day with the weight of it pressing into my chest—the choice, the grief, the knowledge that no part of my old life was coming back. My earlier life offered more freedom, privacy, and self-determination. After Mother died, I felt everyone was watching me, and it felt like it was for all the wrong reasons. No one cared about me, the real me. Every interaction felt like a costume fitting—tight, uncomfortable, for someone I didn't recognize. Sure, their concern extended to my attire, my gaze, the mystery man I might be involved with, and the future King. I couldn't say I blame them, but I didn't feel comfortable with all the speculation and gossip.

Although the Council hadn't invited me to any further meetings, my father confirmed with Ethan and me that the ball was scheduled for one month after Mother's funeral. They chose the date to allow for travel from several kingdoms that were the farthest trading partners we could reasonably support.

The event coordinators had me pick out lots of colors and decorations. They believed the ball would define my reign as queen, as if my future choices would always reflect these decisions. Thankfully, it was summer, and with so many flowers in bloom, the choices were relatively easy. They chose pinks and purples—my mother's favorite orchid tree and my love of irises reflected in every bloom. I appreciated the nod to her memory. Eliza, my seamstress, saw the color scheme and promised to make me a gown worth being the center of the show, but refused to let me know her inspiration. The secrecy in it even made me look forward to the ball a little.

Most of all, Ivy and Amyra helped me learn about the suitors that got invited. Father knew where Mother's list of best suitors was, because of course she was thorough in her efforts to marry me. He ensured invitations went out to everyone on it, regardless of their past attempts to attract my attention. Eight men were on that list and thus invited, along with their courts. Each of the councilors provided additional options. The four most conservative men added four more men from their estates. It was overwhelming to have to choose among twelve men, and to have only one evening to talk with all of them and get to know them. Thankfully, Amyra is nothing if not an expert at getting details about people, so she spent most of the time leading up to Mother's funeral compiling information on these men.

Following the funeral, Amyra, Ivy, and I discussed the men when someone knocked at the door. We each looked at each other, as if that would tell us who it was. People rarely came to my chambers, even now in this transition. I got up to answer my door and found Ethan on the other side. "Lyla, I really need to talk to you about this ball."

He didn't wait for me to invite him in, pushing past and rushed to close the door. I'd never seen him behave this way before. Ethan's voice dropped to a whisper as his eyes darted across the walls, scanning for shadows that weren't there, "Is it just the three of you? No one else? These walls have ears, you know."

Ivy and Amyra nodded while I replied, "Of course it's just us. What's going on? This is so unlike you!"

I quickly returned to my seat, pointing to an empty chair to invite him to join us. He reviewed the scattered papers listing suitors' names and information.

"It's the suitors. I know you've been looking into them to understand their motives. Have you ruled out any so far?"

The look of concern on his face was intense. My fingers froze over the page. I narrowed my eyes, waiting for him to get to the point.

"We haven't yet. We are still trying to understand them. What is troubling you?"

Ethan glanced at Ivy and Amyra again. It seemed like he was worried about trusting them. He's never doubted my judgment on friends before, not that I've had many to doubt. "Ethan, you can trust them as much as you can trust me. Ivy and Amyra are trying to help me find someone good, not just for the kingdom, but for me."

I watched his face relax a bit, and he continued.

"Katelle's dad invited a suitor from Scoria Bay that he is going to insist you focus on during the ball. He's been urging me to increase your interest in him before the ball comes. He's given me an entire list of information he wants me to share with you. But it feels weird Lyla, I don't like it. I can't tell what his angle is. His duchy doesn't trade with Scoria Bay. I couldn't see any reason he would benefit from this suggestion."

Katelle was Ethan's girlfriend, and her father was Lord Denenbaum, who certainly wasn't anyone I trusted. I ruffled through the papers, looking for the information on this suitor. We had little on him. The people of Scoria Bay were notoriously secretive about their affairs. All we could confirm was that he would arrive the next day, after the funeral.

"OK, I see here. This says his name is Egan, he's the third born son of the King... they are a kingdom that decides succession by birth order, right?" I glance up to see Ethan nodding. "Hm, ok, so he's potentially power hungry. That's not unexpected in this group. We haven't had strong trades with them in the last five years. They export mainly fish and ice, and we have very little need for either. I don't see why this would be a politically helpful choice. What does Lord Denenbaum want me to know about him?"

Ethan pulls his list out of a breast pocket. "He wants me to talk up his affinity for musical theater, the arts, and sailing."

The Lord had to know I treasured a good performance, or a painting that really captured emotion in a new way. Sailing seemed like an odd choice; I didn't really care for the water, and it was easy to assume he would like that, living in a kingdom of islands.

"There's nothing truly suspicious about this. Could Denenbaum have a familial connection? Maybe he is trying to position his family to gain from this? What are your senses telling you?" I scanned the pages, confused, yet Ethan possessed a reliable instinct for this. It was really a shame that he goofed off during lessons, that sense would have helped him a lot with navigating life as a king.

Ethan shook his head. "I can't really find a reason for this, either. Katelle says she has no family outside of this country. Her mother hails from a small estate two-days-ride from here. They're completely landlocked. She doesn't know much about her dad's side, but she's positive that this isn't a relative. Something feels off by this. I can't quite tell, but I want you to be aware of him and this deal. He wasn't on Mother's list, nor was anyone else from the Scoria Bay, and I'm not sure if that's because she knew something was off with them. Mother and Lord Denenbaum didn't always get along. She hid it from others, but he used to make remarks."

My eyes widened, and my thoughts raced. "What remarks? Do you think he...?" I trailed off, but we knew the physicians remained baffled by Mother's death. We were still waiting for the official report, but so far, nothing made sense.

Ethan abruptly shook his head. "No, no, I don't think he was involved in that. I know he was disappointed to find out I'm not taking the throne. He really thought I would be the heir, but he hasn't wanted Katelle and I to get married yet. It makes little sense for him to do something now. I wonder if he's taking advantage of the situation, though."

I glanced at Ivy and Amyra. Both looked pensive. "What do you two think?"

Ivy sighed, and Amyra was the one that spoke. "I think we need to strategize. We have four weeks until the ball, and not much information on these men. I don't want you to marry any of them. I wish we could convince the Council to allow you to rule alone. But this is the path we must take, and in that respect, I think choosing one person at the end of the night isn't the way to go. We need to determine the Council's other invitees and devise a plan. Maybe we could use this to our advantage. Select a handful of these men and invite them to stay and prove their value to you as a king for our country."

Amyra had a sly smile on her face. "Maybe, just maybe, you can make them fight for you. Might as well have some fun with this, right?"

Ivy giggled, "Oh, yes, Lyla, do this! It would be so much fun! We could have trials! We could have them do a fencing competition, or maybe we could try archery, or maybe you can have them wrestle with each other to prove their worth."

Her eyebrows raised, telling me exactly where her mind was going. I smiled at her implications.

My mind raced. This wasn't a bad idea. I could narrow down to three choices before the ball even gets here, I'm sure. I could even spend a couple more months after the ball getting to know them, and this could be the way I select someone that I trust. And if we got some show boating along the way, through some old-fashioned competitions, I could even gauge how my people felt about them. This wasn't a bad idea at all. I could already picture the headlines. A competition. A test. Delays that might hopefully lead to a way out. My eyes fell upon Ethan; he too seemed lost in thought. "What do you think, Ethan?"

"I think that if you do this, we could get to know Egan a bit better and select one or two others who are strategically important or capture your interests. It could be smart and certainly take the pressure off of your choice with this ball. I don't see any downsides."

I smiled, and Amyra and Ivy jumped up. They knew my smile meant I was on board, and they immediately started throwing ideas back and forth on what trials they would want to see the men go through. *Trials* were a generous description; their ideas kept getting more ridiculous — and far less proper — with each new suggestion.

"What about a test of stamina?" Ivy said, her grin wicked. "We could have them run the palace grounds until they collapse — or make it something a bit more... private."

Amyra laughed, eyes glinting with mischief. "Or a test of endurance," she added. "See how long they can last at a dance. Or in a sparring match. Or..." Her voice dropped lower, playful and teasing. She didn't finish the thought, but her smile said enough.

I gave them a look, fighting back a laugh. "You two are terrible."

"That's why you love us," Ivy shot back with a wink, already onto her next scandalous thought. "We could have them wrestle. No shirts allowed, naturally. We need to see their... form."

Amyra laughed, covering her mouth like she might actually be scandalized by Ivy's boldness, though her eyes gave her away. "Or swimming in the palace baths," she said, struggling to keep a straight face. "It's not improper if it's for strategy."

"Of course not," Ivy agreed, with a mockingly serious nod. "Purely for the good of the kingdom."

Their laughter filled the room, bright and a little wild, cutting through the heavy cloud that had been hanging over us all day. And despite their teasing, there was a spark of something real beneath it. Maybe, just maybe, this could be more than a game. Maybe it could be my way out.

I walked my way through the choices again. I could lead with any of these men, if they wanted what was best for my people as much as I did. But I just didn't know how I could get into the romantic side of the relationship. One step at a time, I supposed. First, find someone I could trust with my kingdom. And second, just as important, find someone who wouldn't dare stand between me and the woman I loved. I didn't need a husband to rule me. I needed a man smart enough to know he never could.

CHAPTER 5

The castle quickly became teeming with people as more and more arrived for the ball, which would happen the next evening. I was grateful to have the chance to dine with old friends I hadn't seen since our lessons had to get more serious. But I was constantly pulled into meetings to settle issues these last few weeks. Father meant well, trying to get me acclimated to these issues, but it was all overwhelming. I wished he had waited until after this ball to defer to me on all these decisions. On the other hand, I appreciated not being pulled into some of the bickering the guests kept starting. So many of these men wanted to show off to me, and almost none of it helped them.

I had already decided on two of the three men I wanted to keep around. Prince Egan, of course, was one. Lord Luther's choice, Prince Frederick, was the second. Ivy kept fawning over him, and Amyra even endorsed him. He appeared to be a safe choice. He was a second-born son in another country with birth order establishing order of succession. His older brother was already married and had a son, so he was unlikely to sit on their throne. However, he had been important to many new pacts with his homelands and had proven to be a great diplomat. I worried about his disposition, though. To be sponsored by Lord

Luther, he likely wasn't one to see me as an equal. Amyra insisted many of the ladies in his country wished they could be with him, and that he was very kind and generous, so I was open to looking deeper into him.

The third choice eluded me. Part of me wished to choose Spencer, but I worried it was just because of familiarity. He wouldn't be the most strategic choice, but he would be someone I knew I could get along with, and I didn't feel entirely grossed out by the thought of having romantic relations with him, so that was a bonus, I supposed.

I needed to get one more measurement for Eliza on my dress. She really had a way of getting me excited for this ball by playing this secret dress game with me. I found myself intrigued, since she had never kept her ideas from me. She had planned to meet me in my room for the measurements and had already spent some time there with Ivy. The two of them were planning the accessories to use. I wouldn't wear a crown yet, as the coronation hadn't happened. But Ivy insisted on a tiara, and today they intended to choose which of them I would wear.

I opened my door, and I could hear them both abruptly stop talking. I watched them as they glanced at each other, the table between me and them, and tiaras everywhere. They dissolved into giggles, which were so infectious that I also let loose a small laugh as I asked, "What's going on?"

"Nothing, Lyla! But hurry, let Eliza measure you so that you can return to your official queen life, and we can get back to planning your outfit!"

Their excitement for this was infectious, and I could shrug off the worries of the day and engage in their banter for a few minutes. Eliza grabbed her last couple of measurements when someone knocked on my door. This business of coming to my room needed to stop. I had to talk to someone about establishing boundaries.

Ivy opened the door and announced the visitor with the same excitement she had with Eliza about the tiaras. "Spencer! I'm so glad to see you. Please come in!"

I shot Ivy a look. She had never invited people in without checking with me. This whole ball business must be getting to her head. Still, I was grateful it was just Spencer, and that I was dressed well enough. "Spencer, it is a pleasure, but also a first to see you in my room."

As he stepped inside, Spencer's gaze drifted over me, pausing for a heartbeat too long before settling on my face. His emerald-green eyes held something bright and steady, something that caught me off guard. His dark hair curled neatly above his brow, and his skin, a warm, honeyed bronze, seemed to glow in the afternoon sun. He was striking, really. Somehow, even more so than I remembered. He had been at the castle since Mother's funeral, but we'd barely spoken. I wish we had.

Mother had included him on her list, so, naturally, he received an invitation to the ball.

"Lyla, I have been most looking forward to talking with you, and it's been near impossible to get time with you," he said, his voice warm and easy. "I hope you forgive me for coming here, but I wanted to catch up before tomorrow evening's festivities."

When he smiled, two dimples carved into his cheeks, deep and endearing, softening the sharp line of his jaw. Had he always had them? Why hadn't I noticed before? His eyes seemed to twinkle too, like emeralds catching sunlight. Little butterflies inside me seemed to dance to the silent beat the twinkles created.

"I'm sorry I've been so busy." I returned the smile and noticed Eliza had disappeared, along with the tiaras. Ivy was hiding near the door. She knew the scandal of leaving us alone in my chambers would cause serious problems, and I suspected she wanted to have some juicy gossip to share with Amyra. We caught each other's eyes, and she nodded towards him, silently telling me to focus on him. "Please, let's sit and chat. Ivy, could you have dinner sent here?"

Ivy cracked the door open and made the request for three plates. Grateful she made it obvious she was staying; I turned my focus to Spencer. His eyes seemed to have never left my face.

I blushed with the attention. "Tell me, how have things been for you? We haven't seen each other in five years. I'm sure there's so much to catch up on."

Spencer and I spent the next hour reminiscing about our lives since we last saw each other, and then recalling some of our misadventures. It was nice to reconnect and to share these stories with Ivy. Spencer enjoyed sharing some of the more embarrassing stories with her, too, much to my chagrin. And the whole time, I kept catching him staring at me with a look I couldn't recognize. I suppose he might have been catching me staring, too. I couldn't quite put a finger on it, but while he was exactly the same boy I remembered with such fondness from my childhood, he was also so much more. He really grew into his body. I last saw a gangly, lean teen with a face still sporting chubby cheeks and knees so bony that he sometimes resembled a foal trying to navigate the barn for the first time. He had grown into high cheekbones, an angular jaw, glistening emerald eyes, dimples that accented his smile, and the quiet confidence of a leader.

His gaze caught mine again, and this time he didn't let it go. "Lyla, some people would say that staring is impolite." He bit his lower lip to hold back a smile, and my eyes darted to Ivy. I could feel my cheeks heating and Ivy didn't do well at holding back her giggle.

"Some people probably would. And what would you say?" I couldn't say why I got so bold, but I rolled with it. I returned my gaze to his, this time holding it.

He let his smile free as he said, "I'm flattered that you can't take your eyes off of me. I've been struggling to keep mine off of you. You've grown since we last met, and I think it's been only the best of enhancements that have graced your beauty."

Oh. Oh, he went there. My heart raced, and my blush deepened more. My hands instinctually covered my chest as if to hide, and I felt at a loss for words. For a moment, I could even see him wearing my father's crown… and not much else. The image did not help me regain my composure. Ivy used the opportunity my silence gave to rescue me. "Alright, you two, let's give the other eligible men half of a fighting chance tomorrow evening. Spencer, I thoroughly enjoyed the stories tonight and look forward to what I hope will be many more nights of sharing stories and perhaps even creating a few. I hope you enjoy the rest of your evening."

She got up and headed to the door, with Spencer nervously standing to follow, turning to me just before he left. "Lyla, I apologize for crossing any lines. I thought I sensed more of a connection from you. Please know I hold nothing but respect for you and our history."

"Spencer, you have only behaved with grace. I look forward to seeing you tomorrow and shall reserve a dance with you." I smiled, hoping it would soothe his fears. He returned the smile and offered a small bow of his head as he pulled the door shut.

Ivy leaned against the door, audibly counted to ten to make sure he was out of earshot, and then let out a squeal as she rushed back to the table. "He is so very dreamy! How could you not just select him right at this moment? He is so into you, too!"

I smiled at her energy. As handsome as he might be, and as charming as he was, I still didn't know if marrying him was right. "We practically grew up together, Ivy. He feels just as much of a brother as Ethan is." I scrunched my nose, imagining marrying my brother. "Besides, his kingdom and Elthas have always had strong ties. It might not be the best step politically. I need to make sure I make the right decision for our people. This is about more than me."

I got up and moved to the vanity to remove my hair pins. Ivy followed to help, reaching for the ones I'd never hope to find. "You know, it's ok to marry for yourself and to improve diplomatic relations in other ways. You don't have to sell yourself for the good of the country, and I'm certain our people wouldn't want you to be miserable on their behalf."

Ivy had such a good point. Wasn't one of the reasons I was so opposed to the idea of marriage because of how it's been used to subjugate the women of our kingdom? Why was I following the same path? I knew I couldn't escape marriage, but why couldn't I marry for love, for true companionship? Why did I feel the need to sell my kingdom's security with my body and my family's future? What if I just asked the Council to allow me to take a bride instead?

This really was the last thing I wanted to be doing.

CHAPTER 6

Footsteps echoed through the corridors, overlapping with shouted orders and the sharp clatter of trays being delivered. The castle pulsed with motion as everyone rushed to prepare for the evening. Thanks to Father's interference, the usual parade of advisors had been turned away. For once, no councilors demanded my attention, so all my attention could be on the ball. Father stood by, ready to intercept any issues. The event planner was running through the list one last time with me to ensure the timing of the various announcements and festivities, while Ivy and Amyra helped me with my hair. They had wet my long, normally straight chestnut hair before dawn and twisted it around dozens of thin ropes. Since the ball was just two hours from starting, they were taking the twists out so that my hair had a tight curl. After releasing the twists, they took my hair and wove it into a waterfall style, pinning the face-framing strands to the back to hide the tiara's edge. This was always one of Mother's favorite styles on me, but it was so much effort to create, especially since the twists never stayed overnight in my hair, so we always needed to wake up early to start the process.

The tiara they chose was not just beautiful — it was breathtaking, almost painfully so. A pink morganite gleamed at its center, soft yet commanding, set in an intricate weave of gold filigree that curled like flames caught in a frozen moment. Brilliant sapphires, crimson rubies, and gleaming amethysts scattered down the sides, catching the light with every movement like bright embers trapped in metal. It looked like something plucked from a fairytale; a crown meant for a queen beloved by her people.

But I knew better than to be swept away by its beauty. The weight of it pressed heavy on my head, not just in gold and gemstones, but in expectation, duty, control. A silent warning of the role they needed me to play — the queen they wanted me to become. I didn't know if I was being adorned for celebration or sacrifice. Maybe both. Maybe neither. Maybe it didn't matter, because I wouldn't let them decide for me.

I couldn't deny its beauty, nor the strength it symbolized. But I could refuse to let it cage me. Even as the gold circled my head like a noose disguised as a crown, I let my chin lift just a little higher, daring it to tighten.

Just as they finished securing the tiara, Eliza entered the room. Amyra jumped up, "Oh perfect, Eliza, we are ready for the dress now! What do you think of Lyla's hair and tiara?"

Eliza sized me up and nodded. "It is magnificent. I'm afraid, Princess, that I may have set the bar too high. Please forgive me." Opaque white paper hid the dress she held, preventing me from seeing any details. Eliza unwrapped it using delicate, practiced movements, and I could finally lay my eyes on it.

My breath caught. My fingers hovered above the fabric, afraid to touch it. It didn't look real. The fabrics were a mixture of the pinks and oranges that Eliza had heard me discussing with the planners throughout our many fittings. Before I could even say a word about it, all three women were eagerly helping me to step into it. Once it was on, they helped me up onto my stool so that Eliza could evaluate for fit, and Amyra and Ivy helped me into my shoes for the evening. The dress looked even more stunning on me. The structured bodice fit snugly to my torso, providing a sweetheart neckline that accentuated my chest perfectly. A twist of sparkling orange and pink tulle wrapped around my upper arms in an illusion of sleeves. The skirt of the dress seemed to be made entirely of layers of pink tulle, with pale pink fabric orchids delicately hand-sewn throughout. Eliza had pulled out a bouquet of real irises and started pinning the delicate flowers into the dress. I had never seen anyone wear real flowers in their dress before, and the effect was stunning.

As I stared at my reflection, a tear rolled down my face. My mother would have loved to see this. I was never much for getting dressed up like this, but she lived for this type of excitement, and this dress would have floored her. I could almost hear her voice behind me. *'Tilt your chin higher, Lyla. Royalty doesn't slouch.'*

"Eliza, it truly is perfect. I am so glad you had this vision."

Eliza smiled, mouth full of pins, as she attached another iris along my waist. Amyra noticed my tear and wiped it away with a peach-colored square of cloth. She passed the square to me. "My sweet Queen, you are stunning. I adore this on you and know that you will find the perfect princely consort tonight. Here, take this square. You have pockets on your sides. Stick this in there, in case you need it. I have seen the ball room today, and I suspect you will continue to be moved to tears. The Queen truly surrounded your family with people who understand you and want to celebrate you in ways I don't think you realize yet."

Many aspects of this evening felt like the end of my life, but it sounded as if our court was full of people determined to make it memorable. A flicker of something stirred in my chest. Hope, maybe. Anticipation, certainly.

At that moment, a knock sounded at my door. Ivy stepped back and surveyed me, then provided a firm nod. "You are ready to receive people. Shall I check?"

I nodded, and she turned to the door, cracking it open.

Ethan strolled inside like he owned the palace — which, if I hadn't been the heir, he probably would have. He looked annoyingly handsome in his usual choice of formal wear: black on black, a flat black shirt with silky matching pants and coat. His only pop of color was a crisp white satin bow tie, which somehow made the rest of him look even more dangerously charming. This had become his unofficial uniform for palace balls, and it suited him far too well.

"About time," he teased, flashing a grin as he caught Ivy's eye. "You let her wear all this and didn't save me a preview?" He let his gaze sweep over me with exaggerated flair, then turned to Ivy, giving her a playful once-over. "And you look far too composed for a night of mischief, Ivy."

She arched an unimpressed brow at him, but I didn't miss the faint twitch of a smirk at the corner of her mouth.

"Ethan," I interrupted, fighting the urge to roll my eyes, "I'm glad you're here. It's almost time to head to the ball, and I want to review my choices before we go."

The teasing faded from his expression, replaced by focus as he shifted smoothly into his role. Whatever else Ethan was, he never failed me when it mattered.

"Of course," he said, stepping closer. "I know we discussed choosing Prince Egan and Prince Frederick, but who's the third in your sights?"

I took a breath, steadying myself. "Please, I need you to be on board with this one. It's personal, but Ivy made a strong case for it last night."

His brows rose, curiosity flashing in his eyes. "Go on."

"Spencer."

A flicker of something crossed his face — a brief, almost imperceptible flash of distaste, maybe even surprise. And then, as quickly as it came, it was gone, buried beneath his careful neutrality.

"What benefit does Spencer provide?" he asked, his voice measured but not dismissive.

Dammit. He wasn't convinced. But at least he wasn't outright rejecting it. I clenched my hands in my lap, willing myself not to fidget, as I pressed on.

"I know his kingdom and ours have strong relations, and that won't change. But more than that, we know Spencer — as a person. He's kind. Thoughtful. And I trust him. Our existing friendship could help us manage the Council and push for the progress we need. And I like him," I admitted, quieter now. "On a personal level, he's someone I can be comfortable with, someone I can trust alone. None of the others can give me that. I want to feel safe in my own home."

My mouth tightened, my brows drawing together as I waited for his answer. If I couldn't convince Ethan, I'd never convince the Council. And I couldn't claim love — not when there'd been no courting, no declarations from any of these men.

Ethan's eyes softened. He took my hands in his, the warmth of his grip steadying me.

"I think those are all powerful reasons," he said, his voice gentler now. "And, Lyla? You don't have to choose any of these men if you don't trust them. Your safety matters more than trade deals or alliances. We can always negotiate for what our people need, but we can't trade for your peace of mind."

His lips quirked into a small, roguish grin. "Besides, if anyone makes you uncomfortable tonight, Ivy and I will have a lovely excuse to start a scene."

"You'll have an excuse to start a scene regardless," Ivy replied dryly.

Ethan's grin widened. "Now that's the spirit."

CHAPTER 7

We quickly made our way through the castle to the ballroom. Ivy, Amyra, and Ethan were all expected to enter ahead of me. Father agreed to meet me near the entryway, and we would enter together; the outgoing king escorting the soon-to-be queen, to an event designed to choose the new soon to be king. Over a dozen men were here, their eyes followed my every move, hopeful and hungry, each one offering forced smiles or stiff bows as if a glance from me might tip the scales in their favor.

I quickly filled Father in with my three preliminary choices and then selected two more that I randomly recalled from our hours of research. He intended to have conversations with these men this evening, to evaluate their commitment to our kingdom. He would tell me the next morning what his take was on the men prior to a council meeting to announce the selection. Father and the Council believed I intended to choose one man at the meeting in the morning. I didn't think telling them differently would go well. They might have said no, giving me a bigger problem. But I hoped that by presenting the list of three men in a way that felt spontaneous to them, they might have agreed to a time to get to know them longer.

The band played the queue we knew to listen for, causing

Father to glance at me. "Ready?" He asked, reaching for my hand on his elbow.

"As ready as I could be," I replied. The question and reply had been our little ritual for these events. It was comforting to go through it one more time. I blinked back another tear. As we turned to the doors, they opened. We heard our names announced, and in unison, we stepped forward and started our entrance.

All eyes turned to us, and I scanned the crowd. I quickly found Amyra and Ivy standing near the bottom of the stairs on the right, and Ethan was not far away from them, standing with Lady Katelle and Lord Denenbaum. They appeared to have been talking to a man I didn't know. I suspected he was Prince Egan. On the left side, I noticed Spencer standing with his father. I recognized other faces from past travels. As we reached the top of the stairs, we paused, allowing for the room to bow and curtsy. I never could get used to seeing people defer to us in this way. Perhaps this was a custom that I could change. I'd rather people see me as their peer, not someone they ought to put on a pedestal to worship. We made our way down the stairs, and as we touched the bottom, the crowd finally rose out of their bows and curtsies.

Father and I stayed together as he steered us towards two gentlemen I didn't recognize. As Father introduced them, they bowed with synchronized precision, smiles poised just enough to suggest charm without sincerity. The only one I made a note of was Prince Frederick. The sight of him made me pause—his sharp cheekbones catching the light, his crisp posture exuding confidence that felt disarmingly earned. But, not in the flashy way of younger nobles eager for attention, his attractiveness came from a deliberate, polished manner that caught the eye without trying.

His sandy blond hair was neatly combed back, not a strand out of place, and the warm lighting of the ballroom brought out subtle gold tones in it. He had high cheekbones, a clean jawline, and a mouth always poised between charm and calcula-tion. It gave him an air of quiet authority. But it was his pale blue eyes, steady and assessing beneath straight brows, that truly caught me. They didn't flinch or fawn the way so many others had tonight. His gaze didn't waver, just held mine with a quiet steadiness, like he'd already played out every move in a game I hadn't realized I was playing.

We exchanged the usual pleasantries until Frederick, with a small, knowing smile, asked me to dance. I glanced at Father. He gave me a brief nod. Not permission, that wasn't needed any more, this was acknowledgement of our shifting roles. I no longer needed his leave, and that small freedom felt more satisfying than I expected.

Frederick offered his arm, and I accepted, letting him lead me toward the dance floor. We continued our small talk as we moved, his words light and well-chosen, slipping in a story about a mischievous nephew that drew a genuine smile from me. But as the music swelled around us, I felt his gaze sharpen, studying me not with the idle interest of a man seeking favor, but like a strategist reading a map.

"Princess Lyla," he said at last, his tone dipping into something quieter, more intentional, "I fear I'm boring you with stories of my family. My aim was to put you at ease, but you are not a woman easily disarmed."

I tilted my head slightly, intrigued despite myself.

"You're guarded — rightly so," he continued. "I imagine it's no simple thing to weigh a lifetime of partnership from an evening of dances. If I may ask something a touch bold?"

He paused, waiting for my nod of permission. His restraint was deliberate. He was drawing me in, and I found I didn't mind it.

"I've heard you are as intelligent as you are formidable. I doubt you'd step into an event like this without a strategy. Surely you already have names in mind, perhaps even a quiet ranking. Do you?"

His question didn't surprise me, but it impressed me. He understood the game. He understood *me*. I inclined my head, letting my silence invite more.

"If it isn't too bold, I'd like to know, is there a chance? Or should I just enjoy this visit to your kingdom for what it is, and look forward to strengthening our relations in other ways?"

A thrill buzzed low in my chest, unexpected and unwelcome. He certainly knew how to pull my attention and intrigue me enough to keep him around. Even if he hadn't made my original shortlist, his stories, his tact, and his respect for me stood above the rest. Lord Luther's support still gave me pause, but this man was playing a very different game.

I realized I'd let the silence stretch a beat too long. "Yes, sorry, I had planned to seek you out this evening, and you are indeed on my short list. I've heard good things and wanted to learn more about you."

His eyes crinkled at the edges, the corners of his mouth tugging upward with quiet amusement. "Then I am glad I did not squander this moment. I won't take too much of your time, but know this — if this dance were our last moment tonight, I would leave it content. Knowing you spared me a thought and shared your lovely smile with me — it would be enough."

The band swelled into the first notes of a new waltz. He gave a slight tilt of his head, his timing impeccable. "I'll take the end of this song as my cue to release you back to your court. May I have the honor of bringing you a drink before you move on?"

I nodded, warmth rising to my cheeks as he bowed low, pressing a light kiss to my hand before he stepped away. My gaze followed him, lingering longer than I meant it to.

There was something about him — something I hadn't expected. Clever, certainly. Calculated, yes. But beneath all that polished charm and diplomacy, there was a quiet fire, a man who knew exactly how dangerous the game was and played it anyway. I wasn't sure yet if that made him a threat or an ally.

Perhaps both.

Either way, I found myself wondering what it would feel like to stand beside him — not as adversaries, not even as allies, but as equals.

As I looked away from him, my eyes landed on Ethan, who was leading the man I saw earlier towards me. I looked beyond them, noticing Katelle and Lord Denenbaum watch them until another guest took their attention from us. I took a breath to clear my mind from Prince Frederick, and smiled as Ethan and the man reached me. Ethan spoke first. "Princess Lyla, you look stunning tonight! You must be pleased with Eliza's creation. She really outdid herself this time."

I smiled at the compliment. He might have seen me earlier, but he certainly knew how to play up the charisma at these events. "Yes, she really has. I'm forever indebted to her for this look."

I glanced down at my dress, admiring a specific orchid in her detailed embroidery once more. As I raised my head, Prince Frederick returned with my glass. He reached for my hand, and said, "Your Highness, as I promised."

I took the glass of wine from him, and he turned to Ethan and the man, saying, "Gentlemen, I apologize, I shall not interrupt or monopolize our fair Princess's time," and then turned to leave.

I stared after him, wondering how much of his kindness was real, and how much was an act to charm. I hadn't met many men who were truly kind for the sake of kindness, but it was still hard to know which way any person could lean. That Lord Luther chose him gave me appreciable pause, but his actions tonight spoke more in line with my values. How much is an act, and how much is genuine?

I brought my attention back to Ethan and the man, just as he spoke again, "Lyla, please, let me introduce you to Prince Egan."

The Prince bowed before me. "Princess Lyla, it is entirely my pleasure to make your acquaintance."

His stiffness in speech revealed his nerves. One downside to coming from a kingdom like his, where your court isolates itself and protects their activities, must be this awkward lack of confidence. I noticed Ethan offer a small nudge, which seemed to signal him to rise from his bow. Before I could mask my emotions with a sip from my drink, a hint of a smile escaped, despite my best efforts. I decided at this moment to play nice and help him guide the conversation.

"The pleasure is all mine, Prince Egan. Ethan has told me so much about you! I have heard that you enjoy a good theatrical performance?"

"Yes, m'Lady. Er," he coughed, realizing the faux pas in addressing me as a lady rather than a princess. I smiled again.

"Yes, Princess. The theater always helps me to feel so alive. I get lost in the magic of the costumes and the incredible talent of the actors. If I may ask, have you ever heard of the playwright Fennah Urvana? Her work always transports me."

With that, the conversation took off. This man may not have formal training with meeting other noble dignitaries, but it quickly became clear that when you get him to talking about his interests, he becomes alive and animated. He genuinely seemed like a good choice for my political worries. We could teach him the formalities and how to exude confidence. I needed to assess his existing views on core issues of faith and society to predict how easily he could be influenced. Ethan seemed to have relaxed about him as well, and after several minutes of us discussing our favorite plays and playwrights, the band prepared to start a new song, and Ethan picked the right moment to interject. "Lyla, isn't this one of your favorite dances? Egan, are you familiar with this one?"

Egan's brows knitted together, and his gaze flickered with momentary disorientation, reflecting what must have been his train of thought sputtering to a stop. He quickly recovered and held out his arm. "Princess Lyla, would you take this dance with me?"

I grinned while offering a quick curtsy and accept his arm. "Prince Egan, I would be delighted." Ethan winked at us and accepted my glass as Egan lead me to the floor. The crowd parted a bit to offer us space to dance.

His moves fared much better than his social skills, and we easily navigated the song. I questioned him on the last play he had talked about, allowing the conversation to resume. While I knew I should have been discussing more about his beliefs to understand the man more, choosing him for the trials was a foregone conclusion, so I enjoyed the break in serious discussions. I reasoned I had plenty of time to understand him later, and perhaps staying on these easy topics will make it easier to get his genuine beliefs and values later.

After the song concluded, I shuffled through a few other suitors. We went through the same basic formula: I paused for a song to have a drink of water or wine; a suitor approached and talked with me for a few minutes while we waited for the next dance to begin, and we took a turn through the dance floor.

I was hoping to find Spencer much earlier in the night, so that I could formally talk with him, but he evaded me until nearly the end of the night. The crowd had thinned some, with many of the older men and women, as well as most of the married couples, retiring. Some eligible maidens from my court still mingled with the suitors, though most suitors kept a respectful distance, likely worried about how dancing or deep conversation with these women might be perceived. I felt for them, waiting to see who my cast offs might be. Taking a rare break from the long line of men wishing to impress me, I briefly considered whether we could organize a less formal evening in a week or two to allow these women a better chance at interacting with those I didn't choose. This was when Spencer finally found me, as I retrieved a fresh glass of water from a waiter.

"Princess Lyla, how lovely to see you this evening. Your dress is just as stunning now as it was when you entered the room. Have you enjoyed the festivities?"

Why did his voice melt my insides? It felt like I was hearing a velvety purr, rather than the voice of the boy I grew up with. My stomach fluttered, a faint fizz of heat rising under my skin as I turned toward the sound. I tried to mask my face, to hide the smile I have when I see him, but from the smile his face reflected, I knew I had failed.

"Prince Spencer, thank you for the compliment. I shall let my seamstress know of her immense successes."

I watched his eyes trail down my body, and suddenly I became very aware of the heat within me that his gaze was causing. I quickly sipped from my glass to try futilely to cool myself down. I tightened my grip on the glass, fingers slipping against the condensation. His gaze lingered, and my breath caught before I could steady it.

How was I losing control like this? My mind drifted to the other times I felt this way, the evenings with Amyra that I would never forget. I remembered the soft look of her pale blue eyes as she had leaned in to give me my first kiss. My mind jumped to the sweet taste of honeyed raspberries between her lips, how silky her black hair felt as it tangled in my hands –

"Lyla? You're lost in thought, care to share what's stolen your attention from me?"

Spencer was grinning. Could he read my mind? Oh no, I've heard of folklore, where people used to read your thoughts. Surely, it couldn't be possible? I felt my cheeks redden with embarrassment.

He laughed. "I suspect I shouldn't ask that question among so many people. But I am dying to know. Was it about me?"

Heat crept up my neck. I dropped my gaze to the floor, searching for a way out, a distraction—anything but his knowing smile. I searched the crowd for Ivy. Amyra normally would have been a brilliant choice to save me too, but not after those thoughts. I wished it could be different, that I didn't have to ignore what she and I had. I can't let those feelings affect me anymore. A king, not a queen, is what I needed. Shit, I had been silent for too long. Now it's awkward. I glanced over to him to gauge how upset he was with my silence and found him staring straight through to my soul. He must have thought I was thinking about him some more. Men always thought that way.

He caught my gaze, giving me a knowing smirk. "Princess, I know I promised you a dance, but would you do me the honor of joining me outside for some fresh air?"

He may have wanted to tease, but at least he was being kind about who was around when he did. I took a deep breath and accepted his arm, allowing him to guide me to the open doors. We stepped outside, where I took a deep breath. I could feel my skin returning to its normal pale tone, and after a few more breaths, I felt composed again.

He allowed me a couple of beats of peace before talking again. "Lyla, you have been stunning all night long. I watched as you smiled and laughed with all these men, making what looked to be a genuine connection with each. However, your body language never communicated desire, lust, or any need for the men romantically."

Could he really read me that well already? Was I that obvious? I decided in that moment that I needed to hire someone to help me hide my intentions better.

Spencer continued, "Would you share with me what is your plan? Is one evening, ten minutes at most, with any man, enough to make a choice that will impact your personal life this deeply?"

I smile. He probably wanted to ask this last night, but Ivy didn't give him that opportunity. I decided to offer him some of the truth. He deserved that much after all the years we spent playing as children.

"You are still so observant, just as you were when we were kids. Tonight could never be enough for me to feel comfortable choosing a king. It doesn't feel fair to the kingdom to make a choice that carries decades of impact based on a few minutes with each person. It gave me the opportunity to meet and narrow down the choices. In the morning, I intend to inform the Council that I have selected three men to get to know more closely through a courtship. If I have luck on my side, they will not force me to choose only one."

I knew he wanted to know if he was on that list. I didn't intend to give him the satisfaction of knowing. My smile returned, knowing this was a bit of a tease I could return.

"Ah, so a list of three men? Do you know who those men will be?"

"I do." I smirked at him. He probably knew he was one of them. We may not have seen each other in years, but that didn't mean that we hadn't known each other. He was Ethan's best friend, after all.

"And you're keeping it a secret?"

"I am." I turned away from him to lean on the railing, using my elbows to support myself. He copied my movement.

"Even from me?"

I glanced at him and saw him making an adorable pout face. I giggled, turning away. "Yes, even from you. I can't play favorites just because you've had the luck of getting to know me when I was younger."

"Such a fair and wise decision, my Queen."

"It's still Princess, and you know that." I turned back, and my wrist brushed against his hand. I glanced down and felt a chill run through me. Why did he do this to me?

"You may be a princess to everyone else, but for as long as you allow me to court you, you'll be my Queen."

My eyes darted to his, and we held each other's gazes for a moment too long. We were so close to each other. I became acutely aware that we were alone on this terrace, and I considered leaning closer, seeking a forbidden kiss. Catching us would create a major scandal. I considered it anyway. And just as I started to move, he broke eye contact and straightened himself, ruffling his hand through his hair.

He cleared his throat before holding his elbow out. "We should return before too many notice our absence."

I nodded, inhaling deeply, as we returned inside. I told myself I was relieved. Still, my chest ached as if a string had been pulled too tight and left to quiver in silence. The disappointment was the most perplexing of emotions. I would have to deal with that later. I needed to return to the ball and complete my duties.

Once inside, he guided me to near the dance floor. Many more people had left during our time outside, and it had become clear that the evening was ending. I breathed a sigh of relief. Ivy approached us with a big grin on her face. As soon as she was close enough that no one else could hear, she asked, "Sneaking off, are we?"

I shushed her, and Spencer grinned. "Please don't worry, I have protected our Princess's innocence with all I am."

My face turned red again. "I won't be able to trust you two together, will I?"

Ivy laughed, "I wouldn't!"

She shared a devious look with Spencer.

"OK, well, Princess, this night is ending, and it appears that your chaperone is here to escort you safely to your chambers. May I help you with anything before you retire for the night?"

I grinned at his sudden formality. It almost felt sarcastic from him, but I also understood that he was performing, showing me he was prepared for the role. "No, but I am thankful for the time you spent with me this evening. As we spoke before, there will be a formal announcement in the morning."

Spencer bowed before leaving. Ivy and I turned to leave, and I realized that this evening went much better than I expected. I had found each of the men I intended to choose in the morning, and after meeting them, I could feel comfortable opening my heart and perhaps even my kingdom to them.

CHAPTER 8

In the morning, Amyra and Ivy met with me to have breakfast. Immediately after breakfast, I had to meet with Father and Ethan to discuss the ball; afterward, we would present our decision to the Council just before lunch. Amyra and Ivy not only wanted to have all the details on the men and how it all went, but hopefully they could help me process some emotions that came up. Just imagining a wedding veil over my head made my stomach churn. The thought of yielding my body—my will—to a man? I'd sooner carve my name into a gravestone than take his in marriage. I would rather die with the world believing me a virgin queen than to be expected to submit to a husband.

Ivy and Amyra filled the room with small talk while the courtiers work on the surrounding room. They shared how their evenings went, some of the silly mistakes that the single ladies made while watching the suitors, and how some suitors acted once they inferred they wouldn't have a chance. Some other potential courtships may have started last night, despite my concerns.

Once they cleared the room, the conversation immediately shifted. It was time to discuss the decision. Ivy started first. "OK, so Lyla, tell me, do you still think that Egan, Frederick, and Spencer are the right choices?"

"Yes, most certainly. Frederick seems to be genuinely kind and respectful. I still have my guard up, because I can't see Lord Luther sponsoring such a man, but he would make a good choice if that's the best option politically. Egan was charming in the bumbling idiot way, but we share some interests. Keeping him close might ease his nervousness from last night. Though far from kingly, a relationship could strengthen our trade and knowledge of their kingdom. I suspect I will have to tell him early that he is unlikely to win, because I don't think anyone has ever denied him anything before. I will have to feel out his emotional grasp before I make that decision. And Spencer is Spencer. He deserves that spot."

I avoided looking at Amyra when I mention his name. It was one thing for me to have to take a king, but I worry how she would feel if it's Spencer. She knew the history he had with my family, and it might have felt like a true betrayal. Good Gods, I really hated that. It was the last thing I wanted to be doing.

Ivy must have noticed the tension on my face. "Do you still believe this is the best plan? Are you sure you don't want to get out of taking a husband?"

My eyes locked with hers, burning. "I wish I could," I said, the words escaping like a cracked dam. I clenched my jaw to keep the rest from spilling out.

I let out a deep sigh. "Truly and really, I wish I could. I understand the need for two rulers. We don't have one god to show the way and thus we cannot have one person leading us there. But no one has ever told me why it must be a king and a queen."

I could feel my face getting hot with anger. I loathed this. Noticing Amyra's tearful gaze, I realized we were thinking the same thing. If I could be free to be me, if she could be free to be herself, there would be no question about who we would be.

"I'm so sorry. If you ever need to change our situation, or to head to your estate, please know, I will completely understand. I will miss you tremendously, but I never want to ask you to endure more."

"Never. Lyla, I'm here. I'm going to always stay here. I'll be by your side until they force us apart." Amyra grabbed my hands and leaned in to kiss my cheek. I smiled at her through the tears.

My chest tightened with every breath. I pressed my palms to my eyes, willing the tears away, and forced myself to count. Inhale. One, two. Exhale. One, two. I needed to calm down the emotions and to control my thoughts. I had little time before going to Father's office, so I needed to compose myself. Rising, I went to the bathing chambers to freshen my face. Ivy brought up one of the earlier topics, helping Amyra refocus her thoughts, too.

As I came back into the sitting room, Amyra stood up and moved to me, reaching for my hands. "You will always be my love, and I will never begrudge you for fulfilling your duties to the kingdom. Your commitment to Elthas is part of why I love you so much."

Ivy stood up with her but chose not to close the distance between us. "Lyla, we will both support you until the last of our days. Your rule will bring about a lot of changes, and we will always be here at your side to help you find the right balance."

I didn't know what I had done to deserve such noble women by my side, but I realized they spoke true. "Thank you, both of you. I don't deserve either of you, but I am forever thankful that you are my closest friends. I love you both, in such different ways, and I hope to be half the ruler you think I will be. At least then I know I will have provided well for Elthas."

Amyra's hand in mine. Ivy's steady voice. Their presence was a balm. Whatever gods I'd pleased, I silently begged them to let me keep this.

Amyra reached for me and offered a hug. We could never get enough of these embraces. Already, my thoughts twisted with the image of stolen glances, of all the words we wouldn't be able to say anymore. Once I took a husband, it would become so important to not allow him any hint of what may have been in the past. A sharp ache curled in my chest, like something splintering just beneath my ribs. I could barely breathe from the weight of what we were losing.

I broke our hold and took a deep breath. "I need to go see Father and Ethan. Will you come to the announcement? If I find a way out of this, I want you both there to witness it."

Amyra smiled. "We wouldn't miss it for anything. I hope you find the decision that brings you peace, even if it means having a husband. I know we were never truly destined to be together."

Oh Amyra, how could we be destined for anyone but each other? Why would the gods curse us with such love for each other when we couldn't really have it? Fate was so cruel.

I ARRIVED at Father's office before Ethan. A grin tugged at my lips. Of course he was late—just like every history lesson, every sword practice, every meeting where Mother waited, tapping her fingers in irritation. I reminisced through the times that our governess or Mother would scold him for losing track of time.

Father and I chit chatted some about the evening while waiting, but eventually, Father's patience grew thin, so we got into the details of this upcoming meeting. I finally briefed him on the plan for the trials.

"OK, so the plan you have is to select three men. And which three are they?" I briefly repeated their names. His eyebrow raised with Spencer's name. "The Vondalon Prince? Wasn't he Ethan's closest friend as a child? Are you sure?"

I nodded. "Yes. I know we have good relations with Vondalon already, but honestly, Spencer is the only suitor that I'm already willing to trust with the kingdom. If they force me to choose just one man, it will be him, but the Council likely knows that. I suspect that since Lord Luther and Lord Denenbaum each have a choice among the three, they will entertain this second stage, hoping one of the other suitors ends up the option instead."

Father smiled. "This is good planning. But is there actually a chance for the other men? Or are you stringing them along with this game for a different motive?"

I kept my expression composed, suppressing the range of

emotions I had over being forced into this choice. I hoped to convince them to let me take Amyra as my wife if I couldn't find a way out of the marriage altogether. But I was not ready to admit that, not even a little.

"They have a chance, yes. Prince Frederick was surprisingly charming, but I didn't spend nearly enough time with him to discern if it was a mask hiding something else, or if that's his true nature. Prince Egan was a bit more of a bumbling fool, but we genuinely share some interests, and there may be potential for teaching him etiquette and polishing him. Both could be great contenders, and I hope that if they don't marry me, they are wise enough to take the companionship we build as a sign of diplomacy and allow us to find other ways to improve relations with their kingdoms."

Father's brow arched, lips twitching like he'd tasted something sour but didn't want to say it out loud. I did intentionally avoid answering the question about motives, but hopefully he didn't catch that. Ethan knocked on the door, and Father called out to give him permission to enter. I exhaled slowly through my nose. Let that be the end of it.

Ethan quickly entered, quickly poured himself a glass of rum from the side table and then sat down. "Good morning, everyone! I hope you had a splendid morning."

He looks around with the same boyish charm he always had when he was late for lessons. I shook my head, a smile tugging at my lips. Some things never changed.

"Ethan, you need to be more mindful of your day and not keep people waiting. It's poor form and can cause your sister a lot of grief if she relies on you through her rule."

Father was most definitely not used to this, and his frustration with his lateness showed it. I already knew better than to plan for Ethan to show up to anything on time if it started before lunch. I probably would have told him this meeting started an hour earlier than it did if I had scheduled it. Ethan wasn't one to manage his time well, but it was easy enough to manage him.

"Yes, sir." Thankfully, Ethan had the intelligence to know

when to sass at Father and when not to, and this was a moment for the latter.

"Lyla, are you ready? Have you had the chance to decide if this plan will work?"

I nodded. "Yes, I think this will. If the Council objects, I will let them know Spencer will be the choice if they must force my hand, but that I would prefer time to learn and compare him to Prince Egan and Prince Frederick, so that I could make the best choice for the future of the kingdom. While I don't think they'll dislike Spencer, I think they would prefer one of their suitors, so it should benefit us. I can't imagine that anyone could argue effectively against a plan that puts the needs of the kingdom ahead of my personal desires, after all."

Ethan grinned. "You certainly learned how to play this game well. I hope it works. Well then, is there anything else we need to discuss before the Council meeting in twenty minutes?" He glances at Father. I'm so glad he took this lead and steered the conversation well past Father's question from earlier. Father nods, and Ethan stands. "It's been a pleasure, and I'm glad we all know the plan going into this meeting. I'm going to find some food before it starts."

I released a short laugh as I shook my head. "I'm so glad to see you're in better spirits today. It's refreshing."

Ethan turned and bowed as he approached the door. "I live to serve, my Queen." He winked at me as he turned to open the door.

"Just a moment, you two," Father called out while moving to stand at his desk. We both paused, turning to him. "There was one other important news to bring to the attention of both of you, but one that for now, we need to keep from the Council."

He motioned to us to sit back down, and we both sat on the sofa near the desk. Father offered me a small handkerchief before he spoke again. "The physician has confirmed with me that your mother's death was not from natural causes. He is still investigating what has happened, but he finds no evidence of any disease that would take her at her age. The only suspicion he has to work from is that unexplainable char mark on your mother's shoulder. I confirmed with him I saw nothing the evening before she...."

His voice wavered, and tears threatened to wash along his cheeks. After clearing his throat and blinking a couple of times, he continued. "Well, anyway, I must advise you to suspect all those who surround you, especially you, Lyla. Anyone wishing to gain the throne could have made that move."

Ethan reached for my hand, and I stared ahead, numbly. he warmth of his grin vanished from the room. Even the morning light seemed to dull. My throat tightened.

We sat in silence, taking in this information. A few moments pass before Ethan broke the silence, "Are there any leading suspicions about anyone?"

"Two of the Councilmen have been disagreeing with Mother on positions as of late. They seem to resent that she has authority over them. They wish to further a power imbalance that favors men."

Without naming names, I immediately knew who he was speaking of. And my heart dropped, as those two councilors were sponsoring my choices. I finally broke my stare to turn towards Father, to find him observing me. He softly added, "I don't think you should change course. Perhaps the councilors' sponsorship of those princes was politically motivated, but that doesn't guarantee the princes will pursue the councilors' ambitions. But I want you to have all the information you could as you make this decision."

It was too late for me to change my mind, anyway. The meeting was here, and I really didn't see anyone else of any caliber last night. I pushed up from the sofa, turning to Father, "I'll stop by my room quickly for some water, and I will meet you in front of the Council chambers in ten minutes."

I was determined, despite my reservations.

CHAPTER 9

I met Ethan and Father waiting outside the Council chambers. As I glanced in the mirror in this hallway, I noticed the weight on my shoulders had slowly started to feel familiar. I adjusted my stance in the mirror, and for the first time, the reflection looked like it belonged here. I had already changed so much since Mother died. The first time we stood here, I was so nervous about these men, and worried about how they would trample on me. Now, just a few short weeks later, I already felt confident in my ability to navigate them, at least with Father's input. As I examined myself in the mirror, I smiled, confident that I would once again get my way.

The doors opened, and we were announced to the Council. Their chatter died down, and they watched as I walked in, with Father and Ethan behind me. This was not a typical meeting, so I imagined they hadn't had a chance to really get deep into conversations before inviting us in. We took our respective seats, and Lord Luther called to start the meeting.

He immediately turned to me and coldly asked, "Princess Lyla, your event was last night. I believe you owe us your king's name."

His gaze pinned me like a spear, rigid and cold, daring me to defy him.

I smiled at him, offering the courtesy he attempted to deny

me. I briefly allowed my thoughts to wonder towards whether he was the reason my Mother was gone, before I stood and addressed everyone. "Good morning, Councilors. Thank you for prioritizing this special session despite your busy schedules. I have a decision after last night. I must admit, the evening was quite intense. Trying to meet all the suitors presented to me was a delicate and daunting process, but I was able to meet with each and evaluate them. However, I must admit, I find the idea of choosing a king, someone who would influence the future of our kingdom for decades to come, after just one or two songs with each of these men, to be unfair." I paused, as many of them murmured. I glanced at Lady Mallard and noted that she was hiding a smile. She came from a province that preferred to see two women ruling, as they thought that a matriarchal realm would fall more in line with the will of the Gods. My throat tightened at the thought—how easily I could have leaned into her vision of rulership, with Amyra at my side, but unfortunately, that wasn't something the Council at large would agree to.

I returned her smile before continuing. "I know. You want to have a name today. I can confidently tell you I have narrowed my choices down to three. If you would so allow, I'd like to run a tournament of challenges on these men. I feel that through the process of competing amongst each other, I will get a better grasp on their strengths. In the process of preparing for and executing these trials, I can also take time with each of them to understand them at a deeper level, and build a strong trust in them, that they will hold the values and needs of our kingdom at the same level of high regard that Father and Mother had shown me is necessary for ethical, fair governance. Would the Council allow for such an endeavor?"

As I expected, there were a lot of questions. I allowed them to shout over each other in a chaotic manner for a few minutes. Once it seemed like they would listen again, I cleared my throat. "I appreciate the enthusiasm over this proposal, truly. Unfortunately, I'm not able to understand the concerns present when you ask all your questions at the same time."

I smiled with my pause, allowing the Councilors a moment with their embarrassment, and glanced to my left. With a tone filled with honey, I asked, "Lord Luther, would you like to go first?"

His eyes shot daggers for just a split second, then his face returned to neutrality. I had gotten under his skin with this decision. The flicker in his expression said it all; this wasn't the move he'd planned for. While I didn't want to view the Council as my enemy, I didn't let my posture falter. Any hint of weakness and he'd seize it. I had to stay a step ahead—this was my only chance to bend the rules in my favor.

"Yes, Princess Lyla, I suppose first I would like to know who would be your choice if we insist you can only name one person?"

Exactly the move Father and I expected.

"Prince Spencer of Vondalon is currently my first choice. It is a slightly biased choice because of my time spent in Vondalon years ago. I know and trust him the most of all the suitors present last night. However, I think that the other two men have significant potential. I just don't know them well enough to know their intentions at this stage. I'd like to get to know them in a variety of situations so that I can understand who they are and feel more confident in my choice for the Kingdom's future."

Lord Luther scowled. He didn't seem to want to approve this plan, but it was hard to argue against such a reasoning. "And who are the other two men?"

"Prince Egan of Scoria Bay and Prince Frederick of Crystalford. They each held my attention in curious ways and showed unique elements of leadership. I would like to explore them further over the next few months."

His mouth twitched downward, and his eyes dropped to the table. The silence stretched just long enough for me to savor it. Since his choice was on the list, he would be remiss to stand against this. Also, since he was a leader among the more conservative council members, his vote would influence the others. Lord Denenbaum had suggested the other suitor. While we still didn't understand the choice, I knew that Lord Denenbaum represented the moderate group in the Council, so that meant their vote would be to support this, and with those six men voting in favor of this plan, it was as good as done.

"Any further questions?" I glanced down at the table on each side. I didn't expect any.

Lady Mallard cleared her throat. "I have one, Princess, if you will allow."

I didn't expect her to have questions and struggled to keep my face neutral as I nodded towards her, allowing her to continue to speak.

"While I support this proposal, and find it to be wise in this process of choosing a king, I must ask, how will we pay for this tournament? Will there be spectators at this event? How will we know how these men perform throughout the events?"

Internally, I felt giddy at learning that she supported my plan, but I kept my voice calm and measured.

"Thank you, Lady Mallard. These questions are very important. I must admit, budget planning is not something that I am strong with. I'd like to have the opportunity to work with Father, Ethan, and the accountants to come up with a plan for this. Including spectators would be vital to cover some portion of costs; their tourism dollars would benefit our city's vendors."

Lady Mallard smiled. "You will be a wise ruler, Princess. May your era bring prosperity and peace."

As I returned her smile, Father stood up and cleared his throat. "Council, I think it is time to call for a vote. Lord Luther, are you ready?"

Lord Luther nodded and led the voting process. The quick vote showed the Tournament was approved. My stomach turned, a knot tightening with every approving nod. One step closer to choosing a husband, and one step farther from living authentically. I blinked rapidly, fighting back tears. My fingers curled into fists in my lap, nails pressing crescent moons into my skin. Strength was expected of me—but I didn't know if I had enough left.

CHAPTER 10

As soon as I could, I murmured an excuse and slipped away, the weight of unshed tears pressing at the back of my throat like a dam threatening to break. I had little time before we presented this information to the dining hall, where most of our guests gathered to take their lunch. There couldn't be red eyes or a trembling voice when I stepped into that hall. Queens don't cry before a crowd.

Into a side room I dodged, closing the door and leaning against it. Ivy and Amyra would be great right now to help me through this moment. But they were both waiting in the dining hall for me, so I just needed to find my strength again.

I allowed a few, mostly quiet sobs to escape, and then pushed off the door in search of the mirror in this room. As I finally looked around, I realized I had just entered one of our guest suites and it was occupied. Before I could recognize the person who was staring at me, I hid my face with my handkerchief and started apologizing. "Oh goodness, I'm so sorry. I didn't mean to intrude. I wasn't even sure what room this was. Please forgive me."

"Lyla, it's ok, I don't mind. I'm bewildered and concerned for you, but I am not offended by your presence." His voice was familiar. I lowered my handkerchief just enough to see it was Spencer. Oh gods, of all the people! He was going to want to know why I was crying. I watched him share a disarming smile. Why did that make me want to tell him? I couldn't tell him, could I?

"Spencer, goodness, I truly am sorry. I will get out of your room."

I tried to turn and walk away before he asked—

"Lyla, you can stay, I promise. Stay until your tears are dry. Use my sink to freshen your face even. And you don't even have to share why you are crying. Every future queen deserves to keep her secrets."

Oh, this man. He was too kind. His kindness could be dangerous if trusted too deeply. I gave a stiff nod, blotting at my cheeks with the corner of my handkerchief, pretending my fingers didn't shake. He rested his hand on the small of my back and showed me to a seat.

"We have a few minutes before the announcement happens. Please sit here, if you'd like."

I followed his lead, but words caught in my throat. Thoughts tumbled over one another like stones in a flood— sharp, heavy, impossible to grasp. I couldn't have him knowing that Amyra was my love. What if I chose him as a king and he turned around and banished her? I couldn't live with that. I needed to protect her, to keep her with me for as long as she would stay.

I glanced at him, watching him pour a glass of water. He placed it in front of me, and I sipped from it. As soon as the glass left my lips, my mouth found itself again.

"I just never wanted to marry, and now the decision is official and I'm one step closer to a marriage and I don't know if I have the strength to do this."

Damnit! My words had run ahead of my caution. I turned sharply, cheeks burning as if the air itself had caught fire around me. He was probably already criticizing me, already planning ways to subjugate me, to use this weakness as a sign that I didn't know what was best for the kingdom.

I slowly turned back to see how much judgment he showed.

The panic must have reflected in my eyes, as his eyes softened from surprise to compassion.

"Lyla, my sweet friend, you have always been strong, and your strength has only multiplied since you were last in Vondalon. If I could see anyone negotiating a marriage to allow oneself the freedoms they crave, it would be you. I know that the suitors you have chosen would honor your strength and courage as much as you honor them by trusting them enough to consider them to rule by your side in your own kingdom."

"You would?" The question again left my lips before I could stop it. His eyes reflected a glimmer of satisfaction for just a moment.

"Should you select me as one of your suitors, I would be most honored to provide you with anything you need to feel free within our union. I want your happiness to be authentic in private and public."

His words gave me so much hope. Maybe he really could offer me a way to make this work. Could I trust him? Was he really that different from every man in Elthas?

"Is that your fear, Lyla? That you will not be happy when married?"

I nodded, not trusting my lips to keep my secrets.

"I don't pretend that I know what makes you happy. Whatever it might be, I want you to know, your happiness will be my primary goal. Of course, I also would want to learn the role of being a king in Elthas, because I want to make sure that your rule is everything you hoped it would be. My goal is your happiness."

My eyes allowed one of the many tears clouding my vision to slip down my cheek. He noticed and leaned in to wipe it away. Our faces were so close. No chaperone around.

His emerald eyes gazed into mine, and I swear I could see his soul. There was a depth in his eyes that made me ache—a steady warmth that reached somewhere I hadn't let anyone touch in a long time. He leaned forward, and our lips touched, hesitantly. His hand, lingering by the side of my face, pushed into the hair next to my ear, and he deepened the kiss. I felt myself close my eyes and return his passion, surprised, allowing him to lead. I never would have imagined this to feel so good, to ignite the same flame that Amyra and I so enjoyed fanning.

Guilt hit at the thought of her, and I pulled away. His hand remained longer, caressing my chin then down my neck, sending a shiver down my back. His smile dropped; he must have noticed the guilt on my face. "Lyla, did you not enjoy that?"

"Oh no, I did. I'm pleasantly surprised at how much I did. I think I need to get ready for this announcement, though."

I rose with a shaky breath, cheeks flushed, but the knot in my chest had loosened. The tears, at least, had been driven away. I moved to the bathing room to freshen up quickly and returned to the anteroom.

"Spencer?"

"Yes, Lyla?"

"I don't think this needs to be said, but I must have the highest of caution here. Please, not a word of what just happened?"

Spencer smiled. "Your happiness is my only goal. I will protect your reputation with all I have until my dying breath."

I nodded my head, a smile escaping. Frederick and Egan would have a very hard time competing against Spencer. I couldn't wait to share with Ivy and Amyra. Perhaps Spencer wasn't the escape from duty, but the shelter within it.

CHAPTER 11

S pencer hesitated in the doorway, his brows drawn in concern, until I gave him a nod firm enough to send him on. Only then did he offer a parting smile and slip into the hall. I took my time checking my appearance once more before leaving, to ensure that no one saw us leaving the same room.

By the time I made it to the dining room, the hall was packed beyond capacity. I made my way to the raised platform containing the dais, as people shuffled to make room for me to walk through. At the dais, I joined Father, noting Ivy and Amyra standing nearby. A neat line of suitors stood like chess pieces before the dais, each one watching me with a blend of hope and calculation. As I stepped up on the platform, the room quieted, and all bowed to show respect. I raised my hand as I had seen my parents do countless times, and the rustle of movement followed as the room rose in silence.

"Gentlemen, thank you for joining me here today. I appreciate the efforts each of you have made to travel to Elthas, and I appreciate the warmth and conversation each of you brought. The evening was most enjoyable, and I treasure the moments we shared. While I know many expect to learn who the King will be, I must inform everyone that we will not have that announcement today."

I paused, allowing the crowd a moment to process, and waited for the chatter to subside before I spoke again.

"Instead, I have narrowed my choice to three suitors. If they would honor me, I invite you to stay here in Elthas to allow me to get to know each of you. During this period, we will have a series of trials to help determine suitability. By the winter solstice, I will announce the one I will marry. Before I reveal the names, I must ask, is this something that the gentlemen will do?"

I looked down the line of suitors, paying close attention to Egan, Spencer, and Frederick, and all nodded or offered an affirmative answer, with various levels of confidence on their faces. I met each nod with a measured smile, letting my gaze linger just long enough to offer approval without revealing too much.

"Thank you, gentlemen. I invite the following suitors to join us for this competition: Prince Egan, Prince Frederick, and Prince Spencer."

I paused with each name, making eye contact with each man. They offered a small bow to accompany their grins of success. After announcing their names, I allowed a few moments of chatter before raising my hand. The crowd quieted down once more.

"For the rest of you, I enjoyed our time together last night, however brief it may have been. I invite you to stay for as long as you wish. You are always welcome in my court. I look forward to future meetings with you and your kingdoms as we strengthen our relationships in other ways."

With this last statement, I sat down in my chair at the table on this platform. I wanted to allow time for some of these men to visit before I returned to my room. Ivy and Amyra sat with me, and we each received a plate of food. We made small talk, aware that many could hear us, and that others might interrupt us at any time. After I had eaten quite a bit of my meal, some of the rejected suitors visited briefly to pay respects and inform me of their intent to leave in the next few days. I confirmed to others that there would be planned entertainment while waiting for the competition to start, in response to their questions. My event planners would work quite a bit the rest of this summer and fall to keep up with these plans.

Eventually, all three of the chosen princes approached at once. I wasn't sure if they had been talking prior to approaching, but I found the choice for all three to approach at the same time curious.

Frederick spoke first. "Princess Lyla, we are truly honored to have the privilege of participating in this, uh, event. But we were hoping to learn more about what the plan is, so that we may prepare. Could you elaborate on what this will be?"

A reasonable question, but unfortunately one I wasn't quite ready to answer. I nodded, "Yes, gentlemen. Thank you for accepting this invitation. I hope primarily to spend these next few months getting to know you on a more personal level. This morning, my council didn't approve my idea until I added the element of a competition to make it more appealing. This afternoon, I plan to meet with our event planners to complete the details. I would love for all of you to join me for dinner this evening, and I can explain more about the trials. I also want to make sure your accommodations are comfortable, so once we understand who is leaving this week, we will extend you offers to move into some of the larger chambers as well. If you are comfortable with your current situation, please don't feel you must change rooms."

Spencer's nod caught my attention. So that's why this morning had gone sideways—he hadn't even been placed in his usual rooms. I'd have to fix that. I wondered why he hadn't gotten that room to begin with.

"I will host dinner in my private dining hall this evening. Someone will assist you to the hall. I expect I will host us in there many evenings, at least to start, if that's ok with all of you. It allows us for more privacy in conversation than this room could offer us."

They glanced around, noting the amount of people still in this great room.

"Thank you, Princess Lyla. Your generosity knows no

bounds." Egan is certainly more polished now. I wonder if drinking accented some of his bumbling and nervousness. "I must wonder, though, are we going to have opportunities for more intimate conversations and outings as well? Chaperoned, of course, but time spent without these other, likely fine, gentlemen?"

"Yes, of course, Prince Egan. I'd like to arrange for plans for each of us to get to know one another on many levels. I look forward to it, even."

Egan and Frederick nodded, satisfied with the conversation. Spencer remained quiet, his gaze unreadable. Just as the others turned, I let the silence hang for a moment, an invitation left unanswered. I spoke before the silence dragged too long. "Again, gentlemen, I appreciate you accommodating me through these unusual circumstances, but I think the reward of getting to know each other at a more personal level will pay off. If you excuse me, I do have to prepare for my afternoon meetings."

I stood to leave, and Ivy and Amyra rose as well. The three princes stood up and bowed. Spencer finally spoke up. "Princess Lyla, the honor is all ours, I assure you. Would you like an escort of three back to your chambers?"

The thought of all six of us parading through the halls together nearly made me laugh. Half the court would whisper, and the other half would listen. I gently shook my head no.

"Thank you for the offer, but I believe we will be capable of finding our way safely. I look forward to seeing you this evening."

I hoped all three understood I meant all of them, but my eyes stayed on Spencer only as I spoke. I partly wanted to arrange more private time with him, though the idea equally horrified and thrilled me.

Ivy, Amyra, and I made it back to my chambers, and as soon as the door closed, I could almost hear all of us shedding our proverbial masks. My fingers found Amyra's without thought, as instinctive as breath. Her touch steadied something deep in me—something fraying fast.

Ivy, as always, was the first to speak. "The Councilors and the King and even Ethan made it in with plenty of time. So why were you late?"

A smile tugged at my lips. Ivy had such a knack for knowing where the juicy story was.

"I worried I was too close to losing my composure after the meeting with the Council, so I had ducked into a room to gather myself. I thought it was empty but..."

I trailed off. I needed to figure out how much of this I wanted to share with them, and especially with Amyra. It was one thing to know this relationship was inevitable. Another entirely to realize it had already begun.

"But what? Who was in the room with you? Oh goodness, what happened? Are you ok?"

"I'm fine! Nothing untoward happened... much, anyway. It turned out to be Spencer's room. Someone must have given him a small leftover room upon his arrival, not his regular one. I need to find out who's in his normal room and get that changed. It won't do for the long term for him."

"Excuse me, you were alone in a room with Spencer and you're just going on about how you're going to switch rooms for him?" Ivy's golden eyes sparkled with excitement.

I felt Amyra's hand squeeze mine. I glanced at her and noticed she's using the hand language we used to use all the time to talk in public spaces. She was telling me it was ok to share it all. I offered a little smile of gratitude to her as I told them about the kiss. I told them all about how it started because I was so upset at how this entire process could force an end to what Amyra and I have, especially if whomever I ended up choosing found out and felt jealous. How I just wanted a moment alone to work through those emotions threatening to overtake my poise before I had to perform for that crowd. Then I found out it was Spencer's room, and he was there, and how I wanted to tell him about all these fears but couldn't trust him. In the moments of deciding whether I could trust him, we instead kissed. I could tell that Ivy wanted to push more details on that kiss, but held back for Amyra's sake. Amyra's fingers squeezed mine, a familiar, silent vow passing between us. She would be ok. I hated that I had to put her through this.

"There's one more detail. Just before the kiss, he promised me he would put my happiness as his focus, as my husband. That he wants me to feel free if we were to be married." I looked at Amyra and really saw her.

"I think I genuinely believe him. I think he would protect us. I know you two don't know him like I do. But I don't want to confide in him until I know you are comfortable, too."

I faltered. Some part of me waited for a word, a sign, anything that meant we'd be safe to hope.

Amyra placed her other hand on mine, raising my hand to her face. She planted a gentle kiss on my knuckles while staring at me. In her pale blue eyes, I saw every stolen glance, every whispered promise we'd ever shared. I saw hope, and I knew that hope. I also hoped for a future where we could be ourselves. Maybe not fully in public, but at least we could carve out our moments, and she didn't have to worry about being sent away permanently. Finally, she spoke. "He is Ethan's friend, right? Is Ethan able to speak to his trustworthiness, too? Could he help you decide?"

Amyra raised a question I hadn't considered, and it sat heavy in the quiet between us. Ethan didn't know about us—at least, not for certain—but he had hinted. Maybe it was time to test the waters. "I can invite him to my chambers this evening, after dinner. We could ask him tonight."

Amyra smiled. "I suspect he will tell us what you already know. I think that if you were to choose a husband based on how he would allow you to live happily and freely, to love freely, Spencer would be the only choice."

Ivy let out a delighted squeal, springing to her feet with a twirl that sent her skirts flying. "Did we just pick the future king?"

Amyra and I laughed at her excitement.

"I wouldn't say that yet, Ivy! I must consider the impact the other two men might have on our kingdom. Both in making the choice to have them, and in making the choice to shun them. I couldn't make an informed choice until I know what they may do with that decision."

Ivy giggled.

"Lyla, we know you'll choose Spencer. It's ok, we can pretend like you will deliberate hard to balance this out. Maybe we can enjoy a bit of sport." Ivy shared with an eyebrow wiggle.

Amyra squeezed my hand, showing me her silent love and support again. I returned the gesture, locking eyes with her for a moment.

"Speaking of sport, I must get to my meeting with the event planners. We need to come up with a competition now, and I have no idea where to start." I stood up, smoothing my dress out. "I will see you two at dinner. Hopefully, I'll have a plan for the competition."

CHAPTER 12

The meeting with the event planners proved as fruitful as I had hoped. We decided on a multi-event competition. The first event was intended to prove strength and combat training. This one was mostly for sport, as a king would rarely find themselves in hand-to-hand combat, but it would be useful in a tie breaking situation. The second challenge would be a primarily mental one, where Father and I intended to devise a scenario to resolve through diplomacy, so that we could see how they would approach issues that would commonly come up. I decided that the last would be a three-way team challenge, with each prince leading the team through an obstacle course. The planners were to work with our military training unit to design an obstacle course, and the military leadership would choose teams from one of the military companies currently training nearby. After getting to know their team and working out their strengths, the princes would then work with that team to retrieve an object on the obstacle course. The first team to complete the obstacle course and retrieve the correct object would win. The first and final events would have the public invited along to watch, but the diplomatic event is more for evaluation among the Council and me, so we decided to not do it publicly.

Satisfied with this plan, we drafted up what we would need,

a rough timeline, and I sent requests to the Council and to father. We scheduled the first event for seven weeks' time, to coincide with the Autumnal Equinox. This gave the princes time to coordinate retrieving any equipment they may prefer from back home and allowed me time to get to know them personally. At any point, I reserved the right to call an end to the Tournament and declare a winner. Truthfully, knowing how that last competition would boost our economy, since my people were in love with a quest to win the heart of a fair maiden, I didn't foresee myself calling it unless something drastic occurred.

With the event planning underway, I returned to my wing to attend dinner with the others. I couldn't quiet the restless flutter in my stomach as I slipped into a pale pink dress. This was mother's favorite when she played matchmaker. Tonight felt different. She had always loved me in this dress when she was trying to introduce me to a suitor, so it felt fitting to choose it.

When I arrived, I was last to join, despite being early for the scheduled time for dinner. It appeared I wasn't the only one eager for this evening. Since this wasn't a formal event, there was no announcement of my arrival, for which I was grateful. Spencer noticed me first and stood so he could provide a proper bow.

"Princess Lyla, we have all been awaiting you. I am glad you are also early!"

The others hastily stood. This room had a round table with seven places set. Only one was unoccupied, left for me. Amyra had taken my right-hand seat, with Ivy next to her, and Ethan occupied my left-hand seat. Spencer chose a seat next to Ethan, with Egan next to him, and Frederick between Egan and Ivy. As I recalled the comments Ivy made about Frederick's physique, I mused on how this pairing was an interesting choice.

As I sat down, the waiter brought the wine to the table. My fingers tightened around the stem of my wine glass, the hum of conversation fading as doubt curled in my gut. As I sat down, I glanced around the table, grateful to find the others still deep in conversation. I realized they were talking about one play Egan had brought up the night before. I sat back, grateful to not be the center of attention, observing the interaction, hoping to find my confidence. Egan seemed quite confident in this setting. Perhaps his nerves last night were because of the high stakes of the evening. I couldn't fault him there.

Frederick was also not taking part in the conversation, so I glanced over to him to see if I could figure out why. I caught him studying me. His gaze lingered, unreadable. Was he sizing me up like a rival, or something else entirely? The conversation lulled, giving me an opportunity to direct it at him.

"Frederick, you have been quiet here. I know Egan and I could go on for days and days about theater, but what about you? What hobbies do you have?"

He smiled, gently swirled his wine glass, watching the red liquid dance.

"I'm afraid my interests of late tend to bore mixed company. I have been learning the art of preparing hide after a hunt. Recently, I made leather from a buck."

He watched me intently, gauging how I took this shift in discussion. Of all things, he chose tanning hide? A deliberate shift, calculated maybe, but I leaned in anyway.

"That's utterly fascinating. Most in a position like ours would leave such a craft to the men who sell these things at the market. What sparked your interest?"

The look that flashed through his eyes seemed to hold surprise. He must have thought I wouldn't have taken the bait. He managed his expression as he sipped from his wine before replying. "The elders in Crystalford have been speaking at length about a shift in climate that will change how we trade. I started learning to understand what my people will need. I have since found the art in the craft to be beneficial to my mind. It allows me the ability to mull over important decisions in a way I hadn't experienced before. Some of my best diplomacy has been after I have tanned a hide."

"That is truly lovely to hear. If you would like to have these supplies here during this time, please just ask and we will work with our tradespeople to bring the supplies you need and find a work area. I want to ensure you — all of you — are comfortable here."

Spencer jumped in. "Princess Lyla, we do truly appreciate your hospitality. I must ask, do we have the luxury of learning more about what's coming up next?"

I nodded, "Yes, of course! I could confirm three events today, designed to test your strength and fighting skills directly, your ability to lead a team, and your diplomacy and problem-solving skills. We will start on the Autumnal Equinox to allow you time to get any equipment you'd like shipped here. The first event will be the strength test. After that test is complete, we will start preparation for the other two tests. The diplomacy test, a more intimate affair, will be second. The third test, a war game, will involve you leading a team, practicing to learn their strengths and weaknesses, so that you can compete to capture and deliver an object to me at the throne."

The men each nodded once, then shifted their gazes to each other, sizing one another up. I looked at Ivy, and saw her biting her lip, and knew she was looking forward to the show. I shifted my gaze to Amyra and met her longing gaze. Her cheeks flushed, though she didn't break eye contact. She never does when I catch her in these moments. I looked away towards Ethan, who seemed to watch the men too, sizing up their reactions.

Frederick spoke first. "Three events, and three suitors. What happens if it's a three-way tie at the end?"

"If that somehow comes to be, I will speak with my council to review each of the events, and I will select someone."

Egan spoke up this time. "Will you share your reasoning for selecting who wins each event?"

I nodded. "Yes, I intend to be as transparent as possible. I hope that if you don't win, you will still be willing to work closely with me over the years and help bring our kingdoms together, so I intend to treat you as fairly as I can. I selected each of you because I have a personal connection with you, that I believe could develop into a strong relationship; however, this tournament will help me confirm you are also a good choice to lead Elthas alongside me."

Egan flinched, almost imperceptibly. For a moment, his eyes narrowed, and lips curled in a smear of disgust, before his face relaxed.

Spencer cleared his throat, interrupting my confusion about Egan's reaction. "Suppose one of us sweeps you off your feet before the last event?"

Heat crept up my neck; he was getting bold. That teasing glint in his eye would earn a quiet conversation later—preferably without witnesses.

"You won't. Because I am not deciding for just who will share my bed, but also who will help me rule my kingdom. I need to evaluate you on more than your charisma, to ensure that I don't bring ruin to my people out of my lust."

Ivy clapped, her eyes alight with approval. She was always good at building me up when she thought I gave an especially firm statement. I was glad that one hit for her, even if her clapping caught me off guard. Looking at Amyra, I saw it worked for her too. I checked briefly with Spencer and noticed his emerald eyes twinkling and his dimple betraying his smile. While observing their reactions, I saw the doors open; waiters brought dinner to the table and others refreshed the wine glasses.

Ethan cleared his throat first, commenting on the food. Ethan's presence steadied the room. If anyone could coax out their truths over a glass of wine and a well-placed jab, it was him. His insight would prove invaluable, especially if he could orchestrate some "just the boys" time to get them to talk about things that they wouldn't dare bring up in front of women, or the one they hope to wed.

Our discussion during dinner focused on what we were eating, sliced roasted duck with a mixture of vegetables in a honey sweet glaze. Frederick talked a bit about how their greatest minds were working on finding ways to better insulate greenhouses to help with colder, longer winters. I must admit, I was curious about why his people believed the climate would shift. I tried to ask questions related to this, but he dodged them while giving me a look of concern, as if to ask me to not push more. I made a note to plan some chaperoned time with him so I could see if he was more forthcoming when there weren't so many people around.

The evening continued mostly the same, with the princes sharing their interests and hobbies, and conversation danced along those topics. Frederick revealed he was a skilled hunter, preferring a bow, while Egan was quite the musician, able to play masterpieces on a piano and a guitar. Spencer's hobbies were not new to me, but I enjoyed hearing about his mastery in crafting rum that tasted like some of the delectable fruits grown in his country. He also shared some of his stories in learning metalworking to craft his own jewelry and weaponry. Their hobbies painted them like portraits—Frederick with his hunter's stillness, Egan's music still echoing behind his smile, Spencer as polished as the blade he'd forge.

CHAPTER 13

Towards the end of the evening, Ethan stood and excused himself. He invited the princes to join him for a tour of the training grounds so that they could decide what they may need sent from their homes. He tempted Egan and Frederick into following him out the door as they talked about the various tools and equipment they wanted to use for training. Spencer acted like he intended to follow them, but lingered back just long enough that he was the only prince remaining. Ivy and Amyra were still present as well, of course, and were about to follow me back to my chambers to prepare for sleep.

"Lyla, I didn't want to let the day end without offering my gratitude for selecting me as one of your three."

Spencer's eyes locked onto mine, the rest of the room fading in his periphery like we were the only two left.

"I meant what I told you earlier. I will do everything I can to ensure you are happy. I know many Kings have created rules in the past about which Ladies can serve their Queens or how they can serve, but I need to you to know, I wouldn't dare tell you which of your friends can stay with you, ever."

He reached for and took my hand with his to hold. My heartbeat roared in my ears, a drumbeat of panic beneath my ribs. I drew a shallow breath and steeled my face, desperate for a mask he couldn't see through.

"Thank you, Spencer, but I must admit, I don't understand why you're bringing up that specifically."

Of course I knew. Heat bloomed at the base of my neck, and my stomach twisted into knots. Was it that obvious? Did my castle have those rumors spread? Was Amyra's safety in danger? I knew what Luther and Denenbaum would do if they feared inappropriate relations would happen within castle walls. I didn't dare look at Amyra and give us away, but I did glance at Ivy. Ivy sat poised, hands folded neatly, but her knee bounced beneath the table, a quiet metronome of nerves I knew all too well.

"Please don't fret, any of you. No one speaks; no walls have told any secrets. I have my own secrets, and they tell me far more about people than others could know. Lyla, I want your happiness, and I've wanted to offer that to you for a long, long time. If your happiness is elsewhere, I will protect it as my own." His eyes left mine to look at Amyra. His gaze led me to her, visibly worried. I reached for her hand, clutching it to assure her she was mine and that I would protect her. I let go before anyone could enter the dining room and catch the gesture and turned back to Spencer.

"I will have your head if this gets out. I will have everyone's head. Tell me how you know this. I will spend the rest of my life worried about what else you know if you don't share."

He sucked in a deep breath, his eyes widened with a flicker of disbelief. On his exhale, his features returned to neutral. His mouth parted slightly, like he'd been struck mid-sentence. That same look—surprise turning to strategy—was becoming familiar between us.

"I understand the risk this request poses, especially with how late in the evening it is, but I cannot say this here. Can we return to your chamber, and I will be happy to share more freely?" He asked cautiously.

I glanced at Ivy and Amyra, who provided their nods that

they were okay with this. I nodded and then stood up. "Let's go. I suspect we have a lot to talk about."

I allowed Amyra to lead us back, placing myself between her and Spencer, who walked behind me. Ivy rounded off the end, and stopped to whisper to one courtier, who nodded and then left the room. With how well she always anticipated my fears, I hoped she was sending for Ethan to join us. Ethan didn't know about Amyra and me yet, but I knew that if he was aware, he would protect her fiercely, too. I had kept him ignorant to help him if rumors ever occurred. One of us needed to be clean of such a scandal. Luther would want to prevent the coronation if he knew and would want to prevent Ethan from taking the crown if he thought my brother supported my transgression. I needed to protect him and our kingdom from the power vacuum it would have caused.

We reached my chambers, and thankfully, no one was in the hallway to see Spencer entering the sitting room. At least, the chances of gossip spreading by the morning were low.

Once the door was closed, Spencer and I sat at my table. I settled into my normal chair at the head of the table, and he sat next to me. Amyra immediately moved to my other side and positioned her chair slightly behind me to remove my hair pins. Ivy sat on Spencer's other side, which I appreciated as a defensive move. What she intended to do, I did not know, but the sentiment was nice. I wanted to trust Spencer, but we had evaded notice of our relationship since I returned from Vondalon. Amyra and I had even cooled things lately, knowing the extra eyes were watching me after Mother's death, and I didn't want her to be at risk.

Spencer started talking before I could ask questions. "Lyla, I deeply apologize. My vagueness seems to have caused far more concern than it assuaged. I want to explain this by asking you, do you remember the stories that my mama used to share with us at dinner when you and Ethan spent time in Vondalon?"

I wasn't sure which story he was referencing, but nodded anyway. A knock sounded on the door, already interrupting this. I bit the inside of my cheek and smoothed the edge of my skirt, forcing a neutral expression as footsteps approached the door. I supposed part of the benefit of the chambers set aside for the king and queen was the extra effort it took to get through the layers of security.

Spencer paused for the interruption while Ivy rose to get it, since she was closest to the door. She said nothing, just opened the door to verify who it was before inviting them in. Ethan entered, and Ivy closed the door. My irritation quickly disappeared when I realized he was here at Ivy's request as I suspected earlier.

"Ethan, I'm so glad you came here. Before we start this story, Spencer, if you don't mind, I'd like to have a moment with Ethan."

Spencer moved to vacate the space.

"No, no, you can stay here. Ethan, can you join me in my bedroom?"

Ethan and I headed to the next room, and I closed the door.

"We have an issue at hand, and I need to tell you before Spencer talks. After you left with the others, he insinuated he knows a secret of mine. You should also know this because I don't know how he found out, and this could be devastating. I could get exiled if this secret comes out." I looked down at my hands as I rambled, wringing them to soothe my worries.

Ethan clasped my hands, holding them still while brushing a thumb across my knuckles. He was using Mother's old trick to help steady me. I smiled in appreciation and took a deep breath.

"Lyla, it's okay. Whatever it is, we will get through it. Remember, Spencer is a good friend and has been for years."

I nodded. "Okay, okay, yes, that's true."

I inhaled once more, calming my nerves.

"Spencer indicated he knows that I have an attraction to Amyra. More than- I have, uh. I am... we are-" I keep stuttering over my words, afraid to voice them.

"Oh, my sweet, sweet sister. I suspected this for a long while. She's a great friend, but you two sort of suck at hiding your emotions for each other. Most don't pay attention, but I have. I've always watched to see who else picks up on it, and no one of importance does. Mother did well with surrounding us with the right people, hiring the right people that will protect such a secret to their graves."

My throat tightened. Calm had fled long before this moment—now all I could do was hold on to the edge of Ethan's words like a lifeline. "Ethan! What if Luther or the other councilors figure out? They'd stop at nothing to stop the coronation."

"Luther doesn't know. You're right that he would do everything to ruin you over the idea, but he knows nothing. I've been watching, and only one Councilor seems to have noticed anything, and that's Lady Mallard."

"Oh, that's not good. I can't have any of the Council questioning that. I need to fix that."

"What you need to do is find out what Spencer is about to share. Then tomorrow afternoon, after processing the information, we can figure out what to do."

I nodded, and he gave my hands a squeeze.

"Yes, yes, that's a good idea. Thank you, Ethan."

He smiled and hugged me. "I've got your back. You will get your crown, and you will lead our people, and we both will make sure that you are the last monarch to worry about this."

I pulled away from the hug, returning his smile. "Thank you. Truly, just thank you. I hope we can."

He reached for the door, and we returned to the sitting room. I settled into my seat again, and Ethan sat down next to Amyra. She stood up to continue working on my hair. I suppressed a smile as a brief thought fluttered by, imagining what my hair must have looked like while Ethan walked me off that cliff of panic.

"OK, Spencer, just before Ethan arrived, you said your mother's stories related to your promise of happiness to me?"

He cleared his throat. "Yes. I'm so sorry for creating panic. It wasn't intentional. I just was trying to tell you about this, and I just picked the worst way. Uh, anyway, so those stories and fables about how people could sense things that others couldn't? The magic that our land used to have, and how different people could use it in different ways?"

"Yes, of course, but I don't understand how that applies to how you've heard these rumors."

"I didn't hear any rumors. I have poked and prodded for them, to be sure, but there is not a single rumor about this. Your courtiers, if they are aware, are invested in keeping outsiders in the dark." Spencer's assurances echoed Ethan's from earlier, and I felt calmer.

"Noted. I'm glad that no one is spreading unfounded stories."

"Unfounded?" Spencer raised his eyebrow. I averted my eyes.

"Anyway, those fables are real. Mama shared them with me, and with us, because she has a sense that allows her to see things others can't. I have that same sense. When I look at people, I see an aura about you, it's like a haze that speaks to me inside my mind. Your haze has changed since you left Vondalon. When we were there, it was earthy, almost smoky, and I could see flames when you had heightened emotions. I must admit, seeing those flames spark was part of why I would tease you so much." He smiled at the memory.

My face twisted in confusion. I looked at Ethan and he was also confused, and so was Ivy. Amyra was behind me, but I didn't have to see her to know she was just as lost as us.

"Sorry, you're still confused. The story Mama always told about the Gods blessing the change makers. It's real. Mama doesn't have a powerful ability; she isn't sure what she sees. Although she sees the haze, her view is less detailed than mine. She also only sees it for certain people. I was the only one she saw it with for the longest time. She says I have a greenish fog around me. She also saw it with you, too. From you: Earthen, brown tones were what she saw. She told me she told us stories about the Gods blessing change makers because she could see our hazes and that meant we are the change makers, and she knew we had to prepare us for that. I see more than her. Everyone has their own shades of colors and textures, and it's much stronger. I can sense emotions and there's something else I've started noticing that I just don't know exactly. I also can sense when souls connect and know one another. And I see that here. It's not anything that anyone told me. When I first saw you, your haze had changed. It flowed more like water than it did when you were in Vondalon, but I didn't know why. I see today that your haze is influenced by Amyra now. Amyra is an ice-blue mountain stream, and you are a fiery, earthy soil, and the two of you are meant to work together to create something new and good."

Amyra's hand landed on my shoulder, and she squeezed it, using our hand language. I extended my hand up and across my chest to hold hers and squeeze back. I turned my head to look up at her and she looked down, smiling, with a tear threatening to leave her eye.

Spencer continued. "It's love, isn't it? You two love each other?"

"We do." Amyra's voice was resolute, proud to declare it.

Spencer nodded, his shoulders easing as if he'd just confirmed something he'd dared only to guess. The flicker of relief in his eyes made me wonder how often he'd risked saying it aloud.

"I don't know about Frederick, but you can't trust Egan with that information. His haze is smoky, the type of smoke that burns in destruction. He acts smooth as butter, but he has something evil about him. His haze has a discomforting feel."

My thoughts went back to how Lord Denenbaum pushed hard for Egan to be my choice. The mark on Mother's shoulder crossed my mind too, though I couldn't understand how the two could connect.

"Anyway, Lyla, I just wanted to let you know I'm on your side. Any way you need me. Mama thinks we are meant to change the world together. I don't know how we'll do that, but I know you've always desired a better life and resented the limitations placed upon you because you are a woman. Let me help you open those barriers. You and Amyra, I will happily take the settee every night to allow the two of you all the privacy you need or want. We can figure out heirs when you're ready, if you ever are. I just wanted to offer my services, to shield you and give you the freedom to live your truth in any way you want."

My emotions spilled over, tears flowing silently. I could feel his genuine compassion for me. I leaned in and hugged Spencer. "You're a great friend, truly."

After a few minutes, I pulled away to turn to the rest of the people in this room. I had made up my mind. "Ok, let's say we throw this tournament and make sure Spencer wins. How can we do that? The diplomacy event is simple. I can share our notes once Father and I get that sorted. But how do we stack the deck for at least one of the other events to make this a straight-forward choice?"

"Capture the flag was one of our favorite strategy games as kids. I think we can work with the team you get assigned to plan the best strategy and get a sabotage or two in place on the other flags. The crowd will love it, and you will surely win. Leave it to us." Ethan stated, making eye contact with Spencer. They nodded their heads simultaneously.

"Ok then. And I will use this time to get to know the other two, and to figure out what Egan's end goal might be."

Spencer shook his head. "I don't like you being with Egan. Can you try to avoid that?"

A warm flutter stirred in my stomach, unexpected and confusing, like the faint brush of wings against skin. I paused for a moment, recalling the butterflies from when he first arrived. Was that just excitement because he was my ally? Could it be more?

"I can't, especially not if we plan to meet up on our own, too. I need a chaperone. Maybe Ethan can be that chaperone? You understand the risks and can prepare for them."

Ethan nodded. "Yes, that will work. I can chaperone you for all three men. Katelle might be upset at the lack of time we have, but her father brought Egan here. Until we figure out why Spencer senses evil around him, I'm uncertain I want to spend much time with her and her family, anyway."

Ethan's eyes met mine, darker now, shadowed by quiet grief. I tipped my head in acknowledgment, a silent promise passing between us, before turning my attention to Spencer. "And can you help us by telling us more about these hazes you see around people?"

"Of course, I'll need some help with learning who is who, but anything I can do to help, I'm yours."

"OK, I can't continually meet with you more than the others, but let's see if we can get Ivy to you. Wait, no. Ivy, you're my lady. That could cause rumors." I didn't want to ask Amyra, but I was out of people.

Amyra knew, thankfully, and she squeezed my shoulder. "Please, Lyla, let me. I'll help Spencer learn who these people are, and I can even carry messages between the two of you so that you don't need to risk so much."

"Amyra, I really appreciate that. I know it's a lot—"

"Please, Lyla, don't worry. We need to get through this tournament, and then we can figure out whatever this changing the world business is, once we have Spencer and you as our king and queen."

She smiled as she entwined both my hands in hers.

"This is the way for our future. I can feel it. I know this is the way."

Ethan stood up, stretched, and tucked his chair into the table. "Okay, I think it's time to call it a night. I'm meeting the princes tomorrow morning for the tour, so I need to be well-rested."

Spencer followed the cue and stood up as well. "Thank you, all of you, for listening and not judging."

CHAPTER 14

Once the men left, Ivy and Amyra helped me finish preparing for bed. And I couldn't help myself, after such a wild two days, so I asked Amyra to stay with me tonight. She answered with an affectionate grin that hinted towards her intentions.

As soon as Ivy retreated to her room, Amyra closed the distance between us like a tide coming home. I headed to the bath while she drew the water, and I wiped away the remnants of court makeup, the mask I wore for the world.

Spencer's words echoed in my mind. Our hazes, he'd said, were a blue mountain stream and earthy soil. The imagery reminded me of our retreat in the Frosted Forests. The scent of pine, the weight of snowflakes on fur-lined cloaks, the way Amyra's fingers had found mine by the fire, those were the moments I felt most like myself.

Amyra came over to help me out of the bathtub. The moment she drew close, that familiar scent wrapped around me, warm apple cider by a winter hearth. It made my shoulders relax, my body remember. That was Amyra, through and through—comforting and dangerous all at once.

As I steadied myself and dried my body, she positioned herself behind me, wrapping her hands around my waist, and kissed my neck softly. Her palm slid over my breast, the touch firm and familiar—like she was reminding us both this had always been hers. I leaned into her touches, feeling my chest push out while my head fell to the side, giving her more room to tease. In the mirror, I watched her eyes flutter closed as her hand roamed. She looked reverent, like she was worshiping a goddess rather than her lover. The other hand slowly worked its way down, though never reaching the destination I hoped for. She pushed her thigh between my legs to brace me, while she used her teeth to trace hints of what she would do if she didn't have to worry about leaving a mark. A tingle trailed down my spine, heat pooled deep inside.

Every brush of her mouth made time stretch, a slow, aching kind of torture I never wanted to end. When she finally pulled back, her hand still claimed my breast. A pinch and tug turned me toward her, and the grin she gave me was possessive mischief.

"My queen," she murmured low and steady, "I may be yours to rule out there, but in here, when it's just the two of us, know that you are mine to rule."

The way she said it didn't make me feel owned. It made me feel *chosen*. I kissed her like I needed her to believe she was chosen, too. Hunger laced the contact, the kind that lives in your lungs, in the blood, in the ache between rib and heart.

She pulled her mouth away, just to trail her kisses down my neck to my shoulders. The touch of her lips reached my breasts and sent shock waves through my body. When she reached my nipples, the flick of her tongue pulled a moan straight from my gut. I fisted her hair, holding her there. One hand braced us against the tub while the other slid between my legs, letting her thumb find her favorite spot and sinking her fingers inside me. Her thumb circled with unbearable precision, her fingers sinking inside. I could feel her purr when she found how slick I was for her.

She stood abruptly, her hand still nestled between my legs. "Come, my queen, let's find your bed and make sure you sleep well."

She winked, her fingers still inside me, then guided me backward in stumbling steps until my knees hit the bed. She then removed her hand, licking her fingers as I sat down.

"Mmm," she hummed, eyes half-lidded. "Honey from my princess, the best kind."

I pulled her onto the bed, letting her straddle my thigh. Our lips met again, and I tasted myself on her, a sweet, tangy flavor that mingled with the raspberry notes of her kiss. When she slid her fingers back inside me, I shattered. My hips rolled up against her, chasing every throb, my moans turning ragged. Her thumb was a compass, guiding me toward the kind of pleasure that felt like flying and drowning at once.

As I gasped her name, she offered her fingers to my lips.

"Taste what you do to me," she whispered, touching my lower lip.

She groaned, a low sound that curled heat low in my belly. I obeyed without thinking, savoring the way her breath hitched with the movements of my tongue.

Her mouth followed, replacing her hand with her tongue, devouring me slowly, deliberately. She didn't pause until I was begging. Only then did she stop, rising from my legs with a smile on her face.

"Please let me return the favor," I pleaded, breathless. I rolled her beneath me. I needed her breath hitching, her thighs shaking, her voice breaking the way she had broken mine.

I pressed my knee between her thighs as I twisted her nipple between my fingers, and kissed her. I could taste myself on her lips, mixed with her honeyed raspberry kisses and the faintest trace of cider still clinging to her skin. I replaced my fingers on her nipples with my teeth, moving my hand lower. I rubbed her just slowly enough to drive her crazy as I bit her, giving her exactly what she craved. Just when it seemed like she couldn't take it anymore, I pulled away, shifting to bury my lips into her neck, biting and sucking with just enough pressure to avoid leaving marks.

When she came, I felt it as if it had happened inside me, too. I immediately dove between her legs to lick up her sweet mess, using my teeth the way she used her thumb. I worshipped her with teeth and tongue. My fingers moved inside her in the rhythm I knew by heart, coaxing her toward a second, then a third release.

Only then did I relent, sitting up as I devoured her taste from my fingers as she whined, "No fair, you can't just keep going."

She pulled me down for a kiss and then flipped me around to be under her.

We collapsed at last, breath stuttering between us, limbs still entwined, our skin damp with effort and warmth. Her name lingered on my tongue, already aching with the weight of all the times I wouldn't be allowed to say it.

CHAPTER 15

The next few days turned into a whirlwind of information gathering. Father and I spent time together planning the second challenge in the tournament. I collaborated with the event planners on the logistics of the two public tournaments. We planned the first tournament for the military's training field. The planners agreed to construct bleachers and create a ring for the men to display their fighting skills. The military's commandant spoke with me, and we agreed that a timed combat would work best to show skills while minimizing injury. He had also set up a team to devise a way to challenge the princes fairly with his men. The military was also loaning use of their tactical field, which contained their obstacle courses for trainings. The space had a variety of walls, hills, small buildings, and trenches, making it the perfect place to navigate the 'capture the flag' challenge.

Once we sorted out the logistics of the event, we arranged a schedule for the princes to work with their teams in the mornings and early afternoons, and then to join me for either tea or dinner, or both. I created a schedule with Ethan where I could see each prince and still be able to dine with all of them together. By the time dinner came around, I found myself lingering at the mirror, smoothing my gown one extra time. I wasn't sure if I was dressing for strategy or something... more.

While I could tell that the princes were struggling to control their jealousy towards each other as time passed, they still had great camaraderie with each other, and it was entertaining to see them interact. Ivy and Amyra joined our dinners, allowing Ethan to spend these evenings with Katelle, since Ivy and Amyra prevented me from being alone with the men.

It was at one of these group dinners, a week before the first event, where the princes started to show off their temperaments. While Ivy always took the seat to my left and Amyra always took the seat to my right, the three of them seemed to prefer to rotate so that they would take turns sitting across from me each evening. On this evening, Spencer was across from me, Frederick had chosen the seat next to Ivy, and Egan was next to Amyra.

At first, it was all harmless chatter—teasing about mistakes made, playful bragging about their small wins. But under it all, a current pulled tight, waiting for someone to trip. Frederick shared a story about the three of them running through a warmup together when Egan had stumbled.

"It was so funny," Frederick giggled through his words. "You should have seen how his foot twisted over the other, and then his arms just flailed as he fell."

Egan's lip curled, nostrils flaring, and then—*bang*. His fist cracked against the table like a war drum, cutting off Frederick mid-laugh. "I thought I told you to not bring this up this evening, Frederick."

My back stiffened. The laughter died in my throat, trapped beneath the knot twisting behind my ribs. Spencer's jaw tightened, eyes narrowing as his left arm shifted ever toward his side. I didn't see any weapons on him, so he must have a hidden blade there. Amyra stiffened beside me, her breath hitching, while Ivy's fingers curled against her skirts, both pressing closer, as if my presence alone could shield them from Egan's outburst. Frederick's giggles stopped and his face fell into shock.

"Whoa, whoa, Eeg, it doesn't have to be that serious." Frederick tried to soothe the tension in the air.

"No, *Fred*, it does. I'm so sick of you and Spencer showing me up during training. Then you bring it to dinner. Why would you do that? I *don't* need to be embarrassed like that." He rose his voice and slammed his hand on the table again, standing up with the last words like he intended to escalate.

Frederick and Spencer also jumped up, ready to square off with him. Egan's jaw clenched; his eyes darkened.

I didn't need Spencer's gift of seeing the haze around a person to know that a storm was brewing. I signaled the safety gesture to a waiter standing off to the side, and she nodded and ducked through the doorway to the kitchen. We would have a handful of guards at the doors in just a few minutes, waiting for my command unless things escalated. We just needed to keep things calm long enough for that security to be useful.

I stood up and motioned for Ivy and Amyra to stand and move behind me. I took a deep breath, then tapped into my training. "OK, Egan, let's take a moment here. Can you look at me?"

I waited for him to look at me, and I smiled at him.

"Thank you. I know we have had some stressful few weeks, haven't we?"

Egan nodded before ranting unintelligibly. His gaze shifted, and he seemed like he's no longer focused on any of us. He turned from me, pacing while keeping behind Spencer and Frederick. He moved back and forth several times, all the while muttering, like he was talking to himself. I wasn't sure how to get his attention again, or what was upsetting him this much.

I watched in my peripherals as Ivy and Amyra inched closer to me. Amyra's fingers gripped my arm in silent promise. Ivy's palm steadied my spine. No words were needed; we had rehearsed this kind of protection in glances and whispers since girlhood.

My training was just in de-escalation and diplomacy. Many arguments about politics often resulted in outbursts, and knowing how to diffuse the situation without violence could help to make a hard deal go through. I steadied my breath, forcing my face into neutrality. Let him believe what he needed to. Let him think he still had a chance.

Unfortunately, Frederick didn't know about my skills, so didn't know to let me try to diffuse this. After several revolutions, when Egan's back was to him, Frederick moved to tackle him. The two rolled on the floor into the wall. Egan shouted some type of Gods awful, inhuman sound, and a strange light seemed to flash, but Frederick got the upper hand and pinned him to the floor. As they crashed into the wall, several guards rushed in. They positioned themselves between the tousling men and the rest of us, pushing Spencer towards me.

"Stand down! It's ok. Egan just had a moment, but he's fine. We are fine. Right, Egan?"

I tried my best to avoid a diplomatic catastrophe. The last thing we needed was for Lord Denenbaum to write to the king of Scoria Bay about how we have jailed his son.

Egan nodded while muttering, and Frederick allowed him to stand up.

"Thank you, gentlemen, for responding. I think we are going to wrap things up with no fuss." I nod at the guards, who didn't seem to think it was over. One stayed in the room, posted at the same kitchen door the waiter had used earlier. The rest exited through the kitchen.

Egan was standing at this point and shook himself as if to loosen up from the scuffle.

"Thank you, Princess Lyla. I apologize. I'm not sure what happened there."

He held his hand out to Frederick, as if to shake. "Are we alright here, Fred?"

Egan's eyes didn't quite meet mine. The apology was shaped right, but hollow in the middle. Something was off. I eyed Spencer, who was gazing at him with a strange look, too.

Frederick nodded in response to Egan. He seemed to think all was well.

"I think that's enough excitement for tonight, at least for me. Gentlemen, I hope you have a restful evening. We will take our leave now."

Spencer and I locked eyes for a moment, communicating without sharing a word. I turned to leave, knowing Ivy and

Amyra would be right behind me. The guard at the kitchen door followed us out of the room, leaving the three princes to figure the rest out.

I heard some mumbling as the guard closed the door to the room. I hoped Spencer was smart enough to stick around to gather more information to help us understand what happened.

ABOUT THIRTY MINUTES after we got back to my chambers, a knock sounded. My shoulders sagged before I even registered the sound. The knock landed like a lifeline. Ivy got up to check, confirming it was Spencer. "Come in, Spencer. We have been waiting for you."

Spencer entered, waiting for the door to close before speaking. "I'm so sorry for taking this long. As soon as you left, they started really talking, and it felt important to be there. That was... that was something tonight."

Ivy and Amyra nodded at him, too tired and confused to voice agreement. I couldn't wait for him to start. I had to get answers. "Spencer, what did you see? What did his haze thing do? Do they change in situations like this?"

Spencer nodded as he settled into his seat. "Your emotions affect how the haze moves around you. Calm emotions slow it down, intense ones cause swirls, like how you see dust pick up and swirl about when the wind is agitated. Each feeling has their own movement too; intense love and intense hatred move differently and impact the haze differently. I can't always tell emotions. Really, most of the time I can't, but intense emotions are the exception."

I nodded, wanting him to continue, but Ivy interrupted, "So when you said Lyla's had changed, you were seeing the love she has for Amyra?"

"Yes, that was the change. I couldn't place the emotion at first, but I could see it was there. I'm still trying to understand how this all works, so sometimes I'm not sure what I'm seeing. And tonight is one of those nights. It was more than anger. It almost looked like storm clouds charging up off the coast with the way his haze swirled and moved around him. But then, when he started pacing, just before Frederick tackled him, something shifted. The haze lost its stormy gray churn and took on something else entirely. It glittered, like light reflecting off raindrops, but it wasn't light, it was... I don't know what it was. It was like a black void was trying to glitter into existence. I don't know what that means."

None of us spoke. Even Amyra's fingers, so often in motion, stilled against her lap, clenched tight. I stared through a random spot on the table in front of me, trying to process it. The only thing that revealed to me was that we needed to find someone who knew what was happening. We couldn't put the puzzle pieces together, but maybe we could get more information.

"Spencer, do you know how you got this gift? We need to find someone who could help us understand what you're seeing. Surely, you and your mama aren't the only ones that have this."

Spencer shook his head. "Mama only mentioned that the Gods gave us this gift. She said..."

He paused, deep in thought, trying to recall her words. As I watched him think, I noticed his green eyes seemed to swirl, almost like the haze he talked about. The color seemed to glitter and shift, like I was watching a ribbon of sparkles dance through a potion in the sunlight.

"She said she learned how to understand hers from the Oracles of the Gelid. I know nothing about them. Have you heard of them?"

The name sounded familiar, but I hadn't heard it in a long while. I lean back in my chair, trying to recall what I knew. "Mother talked of them a couple of times in our history lessons. I think... I think it was long ago in Elthian history. They had some influence at one point. Let me do some research. I can also check with our last census. We record religious sects, so I can see if there are any left in the country."

Amyra leaned forward. "What do we do in the meantime? Do we trust Egan? First his weird aura, then this outburst. I don't think I want to be in a room with him without protection."

Before I could respond, Spencer opened his jacket flap. "I always have at least one dagger or sword on me. Whatever I can conceal. Knowing Frederick, he will arm himself as well, if he hasn't yet."

"I will make sure our dinners always have a blatant guard in the room as well. I appreciate that you two may be armed, but I want someone else to be alert and ready as well. He can earn back the privilege of foregoing a guard with time." I added.

"He will not like the extra babysitter, I don't think." Ivy's eyes were wide, imagining the possibilities.

I shook my head. "I don't care. He's betrayed my trust. I can't risk our safety for his ego. He can quit and go home if he wants. I might even pause all interactions with him until the first event if he struggles with this."

Spencer stood. "I'm glad things didn't get out of control tonight, ladies. May you all have restful sleep. I must retire for the evening; our training starts early."

I nodded. "Thank you, Spencer, for all your help. I can't say it enough. I will try to get more information about the Oracles of the Gelid and share notes with you. Will you come by tomorrow evening with Ethan?"

Spencer nodded. "I'll visit every evening you ask me to, my Queen."

I blushed at his flirting, glancing to Amyra, who had amusement dancing across her face.

He left the room. Ivy smirked as she poured herself tea, not bothering to look at me. "So, you and Spencer... that stare could light a fire, you know."

I stretched my arms overhead with an exaggerated yawn. "Then let's hope no one strikes a match. The last thing I need is another fire to put out."

CHAPTER 16

Sleep eluded me, every rustle of wind outside my window a fresh reminder of what we didn't know. Eventually, I gave in to restlessness and lit a lamp, dragging out old lesson books from beneath a dusty shelf. I found one that mentioned that the Oracles of the Gelid had a large temple in the Frosted Forests, and it said that they were keepers of magical secrets. Since Lady Mallard was from this region, if anyone knew the truth tucked between those snow-laced trees, it would be her. I needed to be cautious. I couldn't risk exposing Spencer, but we also needed help.

That morning, I reached her office just as she was approaching. Perfect timing.

"Princess Lyla! What a delightful surprise to see you in this area of the castle." She provided a warm smile for me and held open her door. "I was just about to take tea; would you like to join me?"

Lady Mallard may have only been a few years older than me, yet there was something timeless in the way she moved. The world around her seemed to slow just enough to listen when she passed. Her golden eyes shimmered like sunlight caught in amber. She wore a high-collared blouse tucked into a deep green walking skirt, both finely embroidered with mountain flora reflecting her home in the Frosted Forests. A fitted waistcoat in dove gray gave her the elegance of a noblewoman, but the braided ribbon in her dark, loosely pinned hair whispered of older traditions. She looked every inch the learned lady of court, but the air around her hummed faintly, like a forgotten spell waiting to be spoken.

"Thank you, Lady Mallard. You are most gracious. If you don't mind, I'd love to join you."

"Certainly. Right this way, the kettle should be ready shortly."

She showed me to a sitting area in her office. The room featured hundreds of books lining the walls and a desk positioned in front of a window overlooking the horse pasture. In the far distance, the permanently snowcapped mountains of her province rose to meet the sky.

She poured two cups of tea and brought over some tea cakes with the cups. I took a cup and sipped from it.

"While I most certainly adore this visit, I have to say I'm a bit surprised. Your parents rarely sought an audience with councilors on a whim. Is there something I could help you with?"

"My deepest apologies on the intrusion, Lady Mallard." I started.

"Oh, please, call me Juniper. I understand and appreciate formalities, but I prefer you use my first name."

Her smile softened as she folded her hands over her lap— not court-polished but easy, familiar. An invitation. Juniper had been a councilor for only three years, replacing the aging councilor from her area at that time. She was the youngest councilor, at just 27 years old, not too much older than me.

"OK, Juniper it is. Thank you. You may call me Lyla." I returned her smile. In a different life, I wondered if we would be fast friends. The formality of court had held such a relationship at bay so far, but maybe with my coronation and our working relationship, it could change.

She nodded her head, accepting our friendship, but remained silent to allow me to continue.

"I am here to seek information and perhaps find some answers. Are you familiar with the Oracles of the Gelid?"

Her eyes widened for a moment, before her expression settled into a pleasant neutrality. "Why do you ask?"

"In my preparations for ascending the throne, I've been revisiting some old history lessons, and their story intrigued me. I hoped maybe you had more information on them since their temple is in your province."

The lie slipped so easily off my tongue. My throat tightened a heartbeat later, guilt knocking politely at the door. I couldn't trust her with too much information just yet. I liked her, but I didn't know what she might do with what Spencer could see.

"They are a relic of our history books. I think I have some texts on them, if that may help you with your curiosity?" She moved to a nearby bookshelf and started looking for the books she intended to offer me.

"It most certainly can. I'm curious. Do you know if they still practice? Is the temple still used?" I watched her body language. Her face wasn't visible, but she paused mid-reach, fingers hovering just above a leather spine. It seemed this had struck a nerve.

"They might, I'm not sure." She pulled out two books and turned around. "I think these might help you with some of your questions."

I looked at the books she handed me. They were both old tomes focusing on the first few hundred years of Elthas, not the information I was seeking.

"Thank you. This could do it." The words felt hollow as I flipped through brittle pages, barely skimming the surface of what I needed. It seemed to be a dead end. Maybe there wasn't a way to reach out to the Oracles. Maybe they weren't there anymore, but there had to be someone who's familiar with this and knew, since Spencer's mother met them, so how could I find them?

Juniper stared at me, even as I looked through the appendix for the information I hoped to find. "This isn't what you hoped for, is it?"

I shook my head. My hand tightened around the tea cup. I couldn't give her everything, but I had to give her something, just enough to earn the next breadcrumb.

"I recall a tutor once sharing a story with me about the Oracles and how they could help some people with their choices in life. It might be foolish, but I was hoping to get some guidance."

I mentally crossed my fingers, hoping that inspired curiosity if not trust.

"Ah, I see." She offered a smile as she sat back down, picking up her tea. "Worried about which man to choose?"

"In a way. I want to make sure I build a solid foundation so that my time ruling Elthas brings about prosperity and good fortune."

"A wise and noble desire, one that many heirs before you worried about as well. Surely, your tutors and your parents have offered guidance on these worries?" She stared at me expectantly.

"They have, and their wisdom is invaluable, but there is one topic no one has brought up before, and it's become pressing. The Oracles of the Gelid seem to be the best place to seek to help with this."

She placed her cup down. "People shunned and exiled the Oracles because of their insistence that magic would return. We all know and have been taught that magic only existed until the Last Great War and faded away because of how detrimental it was to not just people, but all of nature. Your topic wouldn't have to do with this, would it?"

I tried my best to keep the panic from showing on my face. We hadn't outright said it, but Spencer's gift for seeing these hazes seemed to be one type of magic that the Oracles of the Gelid tried to preach about.

"Lyla, it's fortunate that only I am your audience. We will have to teach you how to control your facial expressions better so that you won't be so easy to read during council meetings."

My face flamed. I dropped my gaze, studying the swirl of tea as if the leaves might hide me.

"Please, Juniper, I need to keep this contained. Are you able to help me? Or do you know how I may meet with the Oracles of the Gelid without drawing attention to it?"

I looked her in the eyes and allowed my fear to show through, hoping that the honesty of emotions helped to encourage her to choose to help.

"I can offer you what information I know, but I'm afraid that we need to either leave within a few days to visit or wait until spring. Visiting them during the late fall or winter is deadly. The weather and mountains are too treacherous for most."

"I will hope that you can offer the information needed, then. We do not have the luxury to leave now, and I should like to have this resolved before the spring."

"What information are you seeking?"

I sucked in a deep breath. "Have you ever heard of someone seeing hazes around a person, like a cloud that reflects their energy and emotions?"

I studied her face. She didn't speak immediately; I could tell she was deciding how much to share. After what felt like an entire lifetime passed, I started debating if I should leave. Finally, she answered.

"You are right; the Oracles of the Gelid are best positioned to help with this issue. It's not you, though, is it?"

I looked down. "It's not, but I promised I wouldn't share who it is. Their mother had a similar gift and told them only enough to know that talking to people about it is not wise." I hoped she didn't press me on who it was.

"Their mother is wise. May I ask, why did they share with you, then?"

"They were worried about me. Someone else has a weird, disconcerting haze. The omen they felt from the haze recently seemed to intensify rapidly, and we realized we needed to know more about what they were seeing."

"Well, I can tell you this much. What you have shared so far tells me that your friend likely needs to spend time with our Oracles. Are they able to leave in the next week?"

I blinked, stunned. The walls of the room felt suddenly

closer, my breath catching as the implications settled like frost along my spine.

I shook my head, my shoulders sagging in disappointment. Spencer needed to be here for this tournament. "Is that the only hope of learning more about this haze?"

Juniper thought for a bit. "Let me propose this. I will write to the Oracles to send someone here and send the message off today. I sense this situation will grow if we don't get their help. In the meantime, can your friend come meet with me? I can begin with the unshared history."

"What history have people not shared?"

"Oh, my sweet Princess, history favors the throne, not the truth—and the Oracles of the Gelid lost their claim to both. There is much for you to learn. When can you let me know if this friend can meet with me?"

"I will have your answer tomorrow. Thank you, Juniper." I stood to leave.

"My dear Princess, if my suspicions ring true, it will be me who owes you all the gratitude."

She bowed to me. "I will tell only the Oracles of this, and I recommend you keep this secret limited as well, especially in discussions outside this room. The walls have ears, and your friend can't afford to have the gift known in this castle."

"Yes, of course. I will see you tomorrow."

CHAPTER 17

That evening, it was Frederick's turn to dine with me and Ethan. Rather than my dining room, which felt a little awkward to use today, I chose a dinner outside on the balcony. The breeze tugged gently at the tablecloth, and the soft glow of lanterns cast flickering halos on the stone. If anything could spark something more than polite silence from Frederick, perhaps it was this—moonlight instead of chandeliers, stars instead of court decorum. I could tell his small talk training was for large audiences, but one-on-one, I found him impossible to get to know. Each time I offered an opinion, he nodded as if rehearsed, repeating my phrasing like a mirror polished too clean. Even his laugh came half a second late, like he waited for permission.

Tonight, I longed a little for the dull pleasantries, and for a while it did reflect that. Around the halfway point, I gave him a question that he couldn't hide from.

"As I've gotten to know you, I realize that you are a very different person from Lord Luther. He is an experienced politician, and I've never known him to make a move that didn't have some level of benefit for himself. With how different you are from him in actions and beliefs, I am curious, why did he choose you?"

It was an interesting question. One that doesn't relay my

distaste for the councilor that sponsored his entry into the race and also needs Frederick to tell me something about himself without knowing how I'd stand on it.

He took another careful bite, chewing slower than necessary, eyes on the horizon beyond the balcony. Finally, he said, "I'm afraid the answer isn't as intriguing as you may have hoped. He's my mother's cousin, and I'm certain he just wanted to elevate the family's connection to the crown."

I nodded, that made sense, why Frederick was so kind and genuine, even a bit of a pushover, compared to Lord Luther's brash way of operating. "Did you grow up knowing him, or is this really the first time you've been around him?"

Frederick glanced towards Ethan, then me. "I hadn't met him before coming here for the ball. And, if I may confess, I find him to be an utter jerk. I'm so sorry, and I hope you don't hold his manners and beliefs against me."

Ethan and I laughed. "He never won any favor with my mother, and we certainly haven't been on the best terms either. Perhaps you'd be able to help me tame him."

The lines around his eyes softened, and his posture eased into the chair. His voice lost the stiffness it wore earlier, like he'd finally stopped waiting for a cue. I suspected that he was worried that I respected his distant cousin, and that was why he was so careful with sharing with me.

Once our plates were cleared, we sat back with an after-dinner drink and settled in for some more chatting. Or at least, I thought we had. Frederick cleared his throat and asked me if I would take some advice from him. I set my fork beside the plate, the clink against porcelain louder than expected. Something in Frederick's tone made the hair on my arms rise. I nodded as I dabbed my lips with my napkin.

"I appreciate you listening to me. I've been sitting on this since last night, unsure of what to make of it. Ultimately, I think the risk of sounding ridiculous outweighs the risk if my fear should come true." He paused, as if to consider how to share the next bit of information.

The name hadn't been spoken yet, but dread curled low in

my stomach. I could already hear Egan's voice, feel the tremor in the air from last night's outburst. I really needed to figure out why Lord Denenbaum brought this person to my home. I glanced at Ethan, and his face wore a look of irritated weariness.

Frederick started again. "When I tackled Egan to the ground, he made that weird sound, do you remember?"

I nodded.

"He also did something weird. Very strange. I don't know how else to explain it other than it felt like he struck me with lightning. I know that sounds impossible, and trust me, I wish it were. I have a char mark on my arm from where he was touching me, and I felt... whatever it was, enter my body."

He rolled up his sleeve to show the bright pink burn mark, zigzagging across his forearm.

"I don't know what to make of this, but I would be dismayed if he hurt you in the same way. I need to make sure you take all the precautions that are necessary, so sharing this seems like the best way for you to be prepared."

Ethan's skin had gone pale, lips pressed in a tight line as he stared at the jagged mark on Frederick's arm. My stomach turned in sympathy. Immediately, I knew we both were considering the mark on Mother. "Frederick, thank you."

I reached my hand out to his. "I certainly understand your confusion and concern. Thank you for sharing that with me. Have you seen the physician for this?"

Frederick shook his head no. "I'm afraid I haven't. I'm not sure what they could do. It only hurt in the moment; it's merely a mark now."

"Ok. I am afraid that these dinners may change, though I'm not sure in what way. I don't want you to think that it's punishment for you for sharing this. It will be purely to maintain a sense of fairness while I figure out how to maintain my security, considering this behavior."

Frederick nodded. "I understand. I will miss your company in the evenings, but I will always want your safety ahead of my pleasure."

"I certainly appreciate that, and the courage it took to share something that would sound outlandish if one wasn't there to witness the scuffle. Thank you."

He stood, tucked his chair into the table, and then moved behind my chair to help me stand. I took his hand, and he leaned in to kiss it. "If I may be so bold as to request a kiss goodnight?"

Ethan cleared his throat. "I don't think that's a wise idea."

I bit back a smile, appreciative of Ethan speaking up before I had to reject him.

"Oh—oh yes, yes, of course. My deepest apologies. I did not mean to be disrespectful."

"Thank you. I received no disrespect. However, I must unfortunately end our evening. I have an early meeting in the morning." I tried to give Frederick a simple escape, which he took.

Frederick bowed and left. "I look forward to the next time we have this opportunity, and I truly hope it's not too long."

I offered him a smile as he left. As soon as the doors closed, I turned to Ethan.

"Ready for the next meeting?" I smiled wryly.

Ethan held his elbow out and replied, "When you are."

With that, we walked to my chambers to meet with Spencer, Ivy, and Amyra.

We were the last to arrive at my chambers. Laughter drifted from the sitting room. Spencer leaned forward with a grin, Ivy gesturing mid-story, Amyra curled on the armrest beside her. My breath caught. If this was the life waiting for me, maybe I could stop running from it.

As Ethan and I sat down, Spencer wasted no time, asking as soon as the door closed, "Have you found anything useful to understand what I saw last night?"

Spencer's hand hovered near his knee, fingers twitching once before curling into a fist. His eyes didn't stray from mine, too alert, like he was bracing for bad news wrapped as hope. Frederick had said nothing happened today, but after observing this, I wasn't sure I believed him.

"Yes, and no."

I prepared myself a cup of tea before sitting down. I cradled the cup between my palms longer than necessary, letting the steam kiss my cheeks while I stalled for the courage to speak.

"Lady Mallard was apprehensive at first. I had to disclose the hazes that you see. I tried to imply it was me seeing them, but she immediately knew I was covering for someone else. She said the Oracles of the Gelid would be the ones to help, but their temple is deep within the mountains of her region. At first, she said we would have to leave within the week to get their wisdom, or wait until the snow melts, because their temple becomes inaccessible during the winter. When I said that wouldn't be possible, she offered to ask for one to come here to help if they can. She also said they would help only on the condition that she meets with both of us to share what she can while waiting for their response."

The crease between Spencer's brows loosened. He let out a breath he probably hadn't realized he was holding. "I didn't think we would find answers so easily."

"Will you be able to join me in a meeting with her tomorrow after lunch?"

"Yes, I can, and I hope we find answers."

Ethan shifted in his seat, knuckles tapping once against the armrest before his throat cleared—a subtle signal that the tone of the evening was about to change. "We have more complications, Spencer, and I believe you all need to know this to be better prepared."

Ivy threw her head back with a groan, flopping a hand dramatically over her eyes. "Why is everything getting so weird now? I just wanted to see desirable men tussle before we started picking napkin colors."

I offered a small smile before sharing. "Unfortunately, Frederick shared more about, uh, the incident last night. He mentioned that apparently when Egan made the weird sound, he also, somehow, struck him with lightning. I saw the char mark; it matched exactly the pattern you'd see on a tree after lightning has struck it."

Ivy and Amyra both gasped, bringing their hands to their mouths. Spencer didn't flinch. His gaze dropped to the floor, unfocused, like he was replaying something in his head on a loop. One finger tapped a silent rhythm against his thigh.

Seemingly before he realized he was talking, Spencer shared. "He was different today. Withdrawn, going through the motions but not actually engaged. He didn't talk to us today either. His haze was different too. It still has the glittering black void that his powerful emotions caused, like he is just barely in control right now."

My tongue pressed to the roof of my mouth as I hesitated, tasting ash and uncertainty. The words needed to be right—measured. "I think we need help to answer all the questions this news carries. I don't know the right way forward with the information we have. What if he's not in control of this? What if going forward with this first challenge in the tournament is far more dangerous for the other men, and maybe even the spectators, because of his determination to win my hand in marriage?"

I looked around the room. Ivy's hand dropped from her mouth to her chest. Amyra didn't blink, like she was afraid the moment would break if she did. Ethan's lips moved slightly—no words, just shapes of thoughts too large to speak.

These weren't questions to answer tonight. These weren't questions any of us could answer, I didn't think.

"I think we need to talk to Lady Mallard about this. Hopefully, she can help us understand what we are facing."

I looked around, waiting for one of them to come up with a better idea. When no one did, I posed my other worry, "When do we bring in Father?"

More quiet looks reflected to me from around the table. After a few minutes contemplating the dangerousness of this situation, I shoved back my chair, the scrape sharp in the quiet. If no one else could voice a path forward, I would carve one myself.

"OK then, here's what we are going to do. Spencer and I will meet with Lady Mallard. We will put all our cards out for her. She's been with the Council for a few years, so maybe she knows more about Lord Denenbaum and can help us figure out how he brought Egan here to begin with. We'll also discuss with her about talking to Father. Since she is trying to bring a member of a supposedly extinct religious order to the castle to help Spencer, she should have some say in what he knows. Ethan, in the meantime, find out more about why Lord Denenbaum is connected to Egan."

Ethan nodded. "I can try, but it'll mean spending more time with Katelle, so I'll have less time for these dinners."

"Good. My next suggestion was to cancel these dinners and time alone with Egan, and honestly, Frederick too. I don't trust either one. I know Frederick hasn't technically done anything, but until I understand what is happening, I don't want to be around anyone I don't need to be."

I looked around the table once more, waiting for objections or anything, really. No one said anything.

"OK then. I suppose its time to call it a night. Let's meet back tomorrow evening with updates."

CHAPTER 18

Spencer and I met in front of Juniper's office. The skin beneath my eyes ached with fatigue, and each blink felt slower than the last. My body dragged behind me, a quiet protest after another night spent chasing sleep that refused to come. If I had my choice, I'd have tried to stay in my room with Amyra all day. Once upon a time, not that long ago, I would have been able to do that. There was a time when curling into Amyra's arms beneath the thick quilts of my bed could hush the world into silence. Now, even that sanctuary felt distant —too fragile to hold back what was coming. Of all the things I needed to do, at least spending time with Spencer had quickly become one of the better ways to spend an afternoon.

I knocked on her door and heard a "Come in!" from the room behind it. I glanced at Spencer, and he shrugged at me, so I opened the door to enter. Juniper rose from her desk, brushing ink-smudged fingers against her dress as she eyed the clutter of parchment like it had personally offended her.

"Come in." She repeated. "I am glad to see you today. Shall we have tea again?"

She had a pleasant tone and was moving towards her kettle to start tea, but the whole time she was staring at Spencer as if she was evaluating him.

"Yes, thank you. This is Prince Spencer of Vondalon. Spencer, this is Lady Juniper Mallard."

I approached the seat I had yesterday and suggested to Spencer to take one next to me.

"Prince Spencer, I'm pleased to finally make your acquaintance. Lyla, he looks to be the friend you mentioned yesterday. Is that right?" Juniper placed a cup in front of each of us and then turned to pour her own cup.

"He is, yes." I drew out my words a bit, making the suspicion in my tone palpable when I answered. As I sipped from my cup, I glanced at Spencer, watching him shift uncomfortably in his seat, seeming to mirror my own concerns.

"You can call me Spencer. I don't really like being addressed with my title unless it's necessary." He offered to break the tension we all seemed to have.

Juniper smiled at him. "Thank you, Spencer. I prefer to be called Juniper. You appear to have this gift of sight, though it's quite unusual that it chose you. Lyla said it was a haze that you see around people. Is that right?"

Spencer nodded. "Yes, I do. Why is it unusual?"

"And what does my haze look like?" She ignored his answer.

pencer's gaze swept her form, pausing as if translating colors only he could see, his brow furrowing like a man deciphering a half-remembered dream. "Your haze is a light blueish gray color. It reminds me of the first snowfall over an evergreen forest."

She nodded. "Good, yes, that is how my haze should appear. Do you actually see the forest, or what gives you that impression?"

Spencer shook his head. "I don't see an actual forest; it's just a swirl of colors in vague shapes that evoke that kind of memory for me."

"And has this perception improved? How old are you now?"

"Yes, ma'am, it has been getting stronger in the last few years. I'm 25. Why do you ask?"

"Over the last 5 years, would you say?"

Spencer's eyebrows came together as he answered, "Yes, yes, around that time is when it started giving me more details."

"OK, right on time then." She took a sip of her tea.

"I'm sorry, on time for what?" Spencer glanced at me; we were both cautious about how she wasn't really revealing much. Hopefully, this would change soon.

"I'll get to that in a moment. How much do you know about the hazes that you see?"

"Not much. My mama has a similar gift, but she sees it only on certain people. As far as I know, she's only seen it on me and on Lyla. She tried to get information when she saw mine and found out that her gift was telling her we were going to be change-makers, but she didn't really learn much more, at least that she's told me. I see it on everyone, so surely, it's not that I am seeing change-makers, but I don't know what it means. I have learned that they move and react to emotions, so I have been trying to understand that to help me predict how people will behave, but that's about the extent of my understanding."

Juniper's eyes softened, the corners of her mouth twitching in approval as she gave a single, measured nod. "I can clarify some information here. This type of gift usually goes to women, which makes your powerful skill interesting. I just received word before you two arrived that the Oracles of the Gelid will send down three acolytes to guide you two this winter and teach you about what this means, and hopefully help you prepare. Spencer, you're one of the competing princes, yes?"

He nodded. Juniper turned to me, grabbed my hand, and demanded, "You must choose this man. The other two may be fine, gentlemen, but Spencer is by your side. He will guide you through what is coming, and you need his sight."

Her voice cut sharp through the room, leaving the air taut and my heartbeat stumbling. I blinked, spine stiffening as if she'd physically struck me with her certainty,

"I'm sorry. Can you explain more? What's so important about choosing him? Why are the Oracles also coming to guide me? He's the one with this gift, not me. And how did you already get word back from the Oracles? It was just yesterday that you sent your letter, wasn't it? ' I glanced at Spencer, and I could have sworn I saw the emerald color in his eyes swirl with glitter again.

"Oh goodness, I just realized how this all must seem. They taught you two the wrong history."

She released me, standing stood up and moving to her desk to grab two books along with a plain satchel. "We don't have time to read through these books, so I'm going to advise you two to read them on your own time. But these documents hold the genuine history of the Oracles of the Gelid, a history that would scandalize Elthian and Vondalonian historians were it to come to light. You must protect this information. There are many lives that would end if these books get into the wrong hands. The Oracles are the last remaining religious order that communicate directly with the Gods, and this realm does not want to hear their Word."

Spencer and I each reached out for a book, and Juniper placed the satchel on the table between us. The books appeared old but had no titles or markings on the covers. Elthas had many religious groups that all claimed to hear from the Gods. Because their beliefs always conveniently supported whichever side of the current political issue they favored, I never paid much attention. I had never been much into any religious system, as I had seen none that impart more wisdom than the others.

"Thank you, Juniper. What can you share with us?"

Juniper wasted no time sharing.

"The Oracles have guarded knowledge of a magic long believed erased from this world. According to them, this magic wasn't erased, but we were blocked from sensing or manipulating it because of the way we abused it. What official historians don't share is that long ago, before the Last Great War, we had full access to magic. Men and women could use it freely, and they mostly did. Unfortunately, some people's greed led them to use magic destructively to gain more power than they deserved. They became rulers in many of the old countries, or they worked with the current rulers to corrupt them, and they created many inequities. The world became dangerous, and many smaller wars waged on in attempts to stop this greed. Eventually, The Last Great War came, and nearly erased humans from the lands using weapons that caused death and destruction on a scale we can't imagine today. The Gods attempted to intervene to stop this greed and the tragedy of their destruction, but humans fought back."

"Eventually, of course, the Gods win, because humans can never win against the Gods, and our punishment resulted in the Gods stripping magic from us. They provided a pathway for magic to be restored, one that would allow people to prove that they have developed systems to encourage altruistic use of magic, to prevent the destruction and power struggles that had plagued us. The Gods provided a prophecy. I can't quote it exactly, but they told us that when we have proven that people are ready to have magic restored, they will provide one last test for us and restore magic if we succeed. The Oracles have maintained the texts that wrote this prophecy and have been the ones that tried to guide us back to that."

She paused here, to allow us to take this all in. My childhood bedtime stories, once harmless tales of glowing forests and whispering winds, suddenly felt more like warnings disguised in lullabies.

"OK, so if the Oracles want to restore magic, why have the previous leaders in Elthas shunned them to the mountains?" I knew the members of the Council and most of our past rulers had been power hungry. I couldn't understand why they would have tried to avoid this power.

"Restoring magic requires acknowledging that men and women are equals in all ways. Men are not yet ready to give that up, and with this many years since we have lost magic, they choose to live without magic rather than acknowledge that the Gods' version of equality is far more giving than what we have present. Their individual power is more important to them than the collective."

"How many men on the Council are aware of these prophecies? What about Father?" My mind swirls with the implications of what she shares. Yet, it all makes so much sense. I wondered if Mother had been working towards equality for this very goal.

"All Councilors are educated on the prophecies. Whether they believe them is an entirely different story. Your parents were as well, and so were the leaders in your government, Spencer. The past generations have smeared the reputation of the Oracles and create religious confusions with all the other sects they have started. They did their jobs so well that most who learn of the prophecy think it's nothing more than a fairy tale. The King was especially resistant to these ideas."

"How do we know this prophecy is true? What makes it more right than any other religious sect?"

"Do you mean besides the fact that Spencer has a magical gift?" Juniper replied with a half smile, and I blushed. Of course, that helped to confirm it.

"Lyla, how else would you describe what happened to Frederick?"

With Spencer's words, realization hit. That would have been magic, too. This prophecy could be real. This history could be true. *Does this mean that something magical killed Mother?*

Juniper frowned. "What happened?"

I recounted the details from our dinner to her, and as I did, her face drained of color. "Who did you tell? Who all knows? Where is Egan now?"

"We didn't tell anyone else, and neither did Frederick. Only those in the room know—so that would include my ladies. Oh, and Ethan. He wasn't there, but he has been helping us plan for how to deal with it since then."

"Egan should be training with his team for the third challenge right now, out in the field." Spencer added.

Juniper stood up and moved with a swiftness that I have never seen before. She instructed us to stay put as she reached a door and went through. A few moments later, four of her courtiers rushed through the room from that door, and she followed, closing it tightly. The courtiers all left the room without a word of acknowledgement for us. Juniper went to the windows and looked toward the military's training field, even though she couldn't possibly see it from here.

"Which Councilor sponsored that man?" She asked, irritation seeping into her tone.

"Uh, Lord Denenbaum. Can you fill me in? What's happening?"

"Denenbaum? Isn't that the father of Ethan's girlfriend?" In her urgency, Juniper completely ignored my question.

A cold knot coiled in my gut, twisting tighter with each breath. My fingers curled into my skirts, knuckles whitening under the pressure. Spencer reached over and grabbed my hand to offer soothing support. "Ye- yes..." I stuttered.

"Gods damnit. Where is he?"

"I'm not sure at this moment, but I planned to meet with him this evening."

"I'll find him."

She went back through that door, and a moment later, two more people came through and scurried out through the castle.

"Spencer, tell me everything about his haze before, during, and after this incident. How did he act yesterday and today?"

Spencer recounted the details while Juniper wrote notes furiously. As soon as she finished writing, she blew furiously on the ink to make it dry faster before folding the paper shut and sealing it with her wax imprint. Juniper whispered words I didn't recognize, her voice a rustling breeze over ancient syllables. As her hands sliced a pattern in the air, the parchment shimmered—and vanished with a pulse of light that left the hairs on my arms standing upright.

"That went to the Oracles, didn't it? Is that how you got your response, too?"

It was probably an easy guess, but I needed to confirm.

Juniper nodded. "There has been an entire generation of people born with magic. We have been coming into it for the last ten years. We are the first in many generations to access magic like people used to."

"What was in the letter? What's going on?" I asked.

Juniper stood up, looked out at the training field again. After a moment, she took a deep breath and slowly exhaled.

"There is a lot to teach you before you can understand the extent of what's happening. To put it shortly, Egan's lightning strike shouldn't be possible. There is only one history book that mentions this type of power, and it was inside of such an intense story of a battle that it came across as fiction even with what we understand to be true. The Oracles saved it for centuries. So many assumed that it was reality, but we do not know where that kind of power comes from. All we can guess is that it's not from the same source of power that we have. I sent out people who can secure him if he shows other signs of that power, and without understanding how Denenbaum's connection to it, I sent for Ethan to join us here. I don't think it's wise for him to be around such a danger for now, not while he's next in line for the throne, after you."

"We need to tell Father, and the Guards."

"When Ethan gets here, we will get him caught up and decide if you should present to your father. He has been one that insisted the stories about magic were little more than fairy tales and has shut down discussions with me about this topic."

"Could you send for Amyra and Ivy? They are my ladies and will be my closest advisors once I take the throne, and I'd like for them to be caught up as well. They're both likely in my room."

Juniper nodded and then disappeared into the other room to send for them. Two more people headed out, and Juniper returned.

A letter shimmered onto Juniper's desk. She opened it and read the reply. "The Oracles are sending several higher priestesses to assess the situation. They will be here in two days' time."

"Could I learn how to do shimmery disappearing objects thing?" Spencer gestured to where the letter had arrived.

"No, it doesn't seem possible, at least from the records we have. Magic, as we understand it, is tied to eye color. Your eye color is green, the color of spirits. The hazes you see are the souls of the people. I have golden eyes, which give me the power of air. One skill I've developed has been the ability to send items through the air."

"Will I develop magic? That happens around twenty, right? That's why you knew Spencer having it manifest five years ago was on time?"

"That is why, but I don't know if you will. We haven't found a reason some have it and some don't. If you do, it'll likely be soon."

"What would mine be?"

"Your brown eyes would give you access to earth magic. You'd be able to cultivate plants, speed growth in the garden, perhaps loosen soil to make preparing the land easier. Some of the strongest have been able to use the surrounding land to build small structures and furniture."

"Oh, that's rather anticlimactic." I sighed.

Spencer snorted, and Juniper tsked at me. "Princess, you can mitigate and maybe even prevent famine and other agricultural disasters. You can help build or rebuild a war-torn district. That's an important talent for a ruler of a country this large."

I blushed. "Well, when you put it that way…"

A knock sounded at the door. Juniper rushed towards it, pulling it open slightly to check to see who was there. She then pulled the door all the way open, welcoming in Ethan. She allowed one of her courtiers to enter and then quietly asked the other to perform another task before closing the door. The first courtier went back to the room they were in, leaving us alone in this room.

"Prince Ethan, thank you so much for joining me on such an immediate notice. I apologize for interrupting your afternoon."

Ethan smiled, "It's my pleasure, Lady Mallard. I knew Princess Lyla was meeting with you this afternoon, so I assumed it was connected to the meeting."

Juniper nodded. "Yes, yes, it is. Please, you can call me Juniper. I suspect we are about to spend a lot of time together. Lady Ivy and Lady Amyra are on their way as well, and when they arrive, we will get everyone caught up on the situation we have on our hands. In the meantime, can I interest you in tea?"

Before the words fully left her mouth, Juniper was already gliding toward the hearth, the kettle clinking softly as if it, too, had been summoned by her will. She had a way of disarming you when you first entered the room. I made a mental note to study more of her techniques and to ask her to help me learn these methods.

Ethan nodded as he joined us at the table. Thankfully, this table seats eight people, so we are realistically ready to accommodate any small committee here. I suppose this would be the first meeting of the magic minders. I smile at the little nickname.

We made small talk while waiting for Ivy and Amyra to join us. They didn't take much longer, thankfully. Juniper offered them tea and her first name before we settled in. Juniper started off by recapping the information that she shared with us and making sure they were aware of the information we shared with her. Then she dived into the details.

"I believe that Egan's zap was evidence of something sinister. Lord Denenbaum has had a shift in energies in the last couple of years. While he claims to represent moderate policies, he increasingly adopts more conservative positions, echoing past criticisms against the Oracles of the Gelid. I don't know what has been going on, but I can't help but feel as if that is connected to the reason he sponsored Egan as a suitor. Can you tell me what you know of him?"

I shared information about the interests he's shared with me. I mentioned how he was socially awkward at the ball. Spencer shared about how he struggles to lead on the field training exercises, but he excels in individual workouts and sparring matches. We ended up agreeing that he's not likely to be a political mastermind, and that he may not be aware of what he is taking part in, whatever it might be.

"His skill in lightning is not one that we have seen in the texts that educate us about magic. I am aware of only one mention of this type of power, and it seemed to originate from something… otherworldly. The high priestesses will be here in two days to see if they can figure out what's happening, especially with his soul being so dark." Juniper finished.

Ethan interrupted. "Sorry, two days? Isn't the Frosted Forest a 5-day ride from here, plus a few more days through the mountains to reach the temple?"

Juniper nodded. "Air magic allows for its strongest users to move people through space. We call it winnowing. There aren't many of us that can winnow people, so it's not a common method of travel, but the Priestesses will tap into it when it's necessary. Those winnowing the group will need some rest when they arrive."

"Can you tell us more about this magic? How do other eye colors work?"

"Gold eyes are typically associated with air elements. They can control the air itself. The most useful aspect is winnowing objects, but it can also literally create wind. Green eyes have spirit magic. For most, seeing souls is the simplest manifestation. For stronger users, they can influence your actions too, through a type of connection they can foster with your soul. Blue eyes are water bearers. They can control water, and they also have a healing energy. Brown eyes are associated with the earth. They can impact agriculture and the soil itself. The strongest of these could carve the temple into the side of the mountain with their gifts. And the old texts have mentioned red eyes, though we have never seen them. These people could control fire. The texts mention that this also allows them to control emotions of people, and to amplify what others are feeling."

"Mother was always commenting that my eyes almost seemed red when I get excited. Is that possibly related?" The ability to control emotions seemed like a heavy burden, but I was curious about what I might do, all the same.

Juniper stared at me for what felt like an uncomfortable eternity, contemplating it. "I haven't read about anyone mixing gifts. Your eyes strike me as a true brown for now. I guess only time will tell."

"What about this lightning?" Amyra asked.

She had been sitting quietly, taking it all in. She appeared pensive, but the way she kept twirling a strand of her hair gave away her trepidation about the situation we found ourselves in.

Juniper took a deep breath. "That's what I need the Priestesses for. I only heard of that type of gift once, in what I thought was a fairy tale, where the wielder was portrayed as evil incarnate. It was very destructive in the tale and was a force that was harnessed and used to fight with the Gods. I thought it was simply an old tale used to explain to children why magic left the realm."

I stood up and walked to the window. "If you had to guess, what do you think it could be?"

Juniper sighed. "I couldn't say. The way you describe Egan tells me he's certainly not a leader of any type. I don't think he even knew he could use lightning like that prior to that scuffle. He's probably here, acting under the orders of another. I don't think we should trust Lord Denenbaum until we determine he isn't that person."

It was my turn to breathe deeply as I took in the gravity of the situation. "There's one more piece of information to share. Father had instructed Ethan and I to not share it with the Council, because he has suspicions."

Ethan stood and moved to the window to join me, knowing what was coming would bring up difficult emotions. My hands shook, almost imperceptibly, thinking about Mother. When he reached me, he touched my shoulder, providing a reassuring pat as I tried to compose myself.

I exhaled a deep breath before continuing. "The physician pointed out that Mother had a strange mark on her collarbone at the time of her death. He calls it a char mark. It looked suspiciously like Frederick's. I'm worried that the two might be connected, and learning about magic being... real, I guess, makes that seem more likely."

I turned around, nervous to see how the others react. So much fear and uncertainty showed on my friends' faces. Juniper hid the fears I'm sure she had, and after a beat, she nodded her head once resolutely.

"When the Priestesses get here, we can have them consult with the physician if they agree that it's related." Juniper stated quietly.

I nodded, "What about Father? You said he wouldn't listen before. Do you think he will now?"

Juniper paused for a moment to consider. "I think the best chance we have of getting him to listen would be if you talk to him about it. Your experiences here may be what he needs to change his mind."

Ethan and I exchanged a look.

"What if he doesn't? What if he tries to ignore this?" He asked me.

I sharply inhaled. "We can't follow suit. So, I suppose we would need to face this without his support."

"Without the King's support? Is that even possible?" Amyra asked. I didn't know the answer to the question, and it seemed no one else really does either.

Before we get lost down that train of thought, Juniper added. "I know you'll make the right choice."

"I think we make it so he can't ignore it." Ethan offered. "I think he's worked with the Council for decades, and likely can add context that we need."

I nodded. After waiting to see if anyone else wanted to weigh in, I turned back to Juniper. "Would you come with me to help me tell him about this magic? I'm not sure I could explain it properly."

She nodded. "Of course. I'm here to support you as the future queen of this country."

"OK, I already have an appointment with him in the morning. Could you come then?"

Spencer's jaw dropped. "You need to schedule an appointment to talk to your dad?"

"Not for family stuff, but we agreed to keep official business during appointment hours unless there's an emergency, just to be sure that we are respecting the difference between family and business." I assured him.

"On a related note, since we are all here, there doesn't have to be a meeting in my quarters this evening, but you're all welcome to come by anyway, Juniper included. It'll just be for this family, for fun."

I smiled as the rest started talking, trying to convince Juniper to join us. Once she relented, we ended the meeting. We were cautious about leaving, with Ethan and Spencer leaving together, and then Amyra, Ivy, and I left several minutes later. It might be paranoid, but this ensured that no one saw Spencer with me and reported back to Frederick, Egan, or the Denenbaums.

CHAPTER 19

The next morning, Juniper and I met at her office. She gathered a book and a few other items for my meeting with Father and we walked over. Despite the time we spent together last night in a social setting, we were tense this morning. I supposed that any time you walked in to meet with the King to tell him that there was potentially a disruptive plot occurring within your castle walls using fairytale ideas to undermine us, tension would exist.

We reached his office, and I knock. He called out to allow us permission to enter. Juniper followed behind me, and Father's eyebrows rose in shock at her sight. I started before he could express his surprise. "Hi Father, I know we had plans for this meeting, but I'm afraid we have to shift focus. Lady Mallard and I have something more pressing to discuss."

Father's face showed concern as he invited us in to sit at his conference table. He shuffled in a corner alcove before turning and offered his Vondalon rum to us, which I smiled and accepted. He only pulled this rum out for special guests, and I appreciated the sentiment he shared by doing so. Once we have our glasses, he sat.

"Please, let's get started. What's going on?"

I opened by sharing what had been happening with the princes. Father's eyes widened as anger spread across his face when I described the evening with Egan's lightning strike. He stood up, slamming his glass so hard on the table that I was shocked it didn't shatter. I placed a hand on his arm and asked him to hold off until Juniper explained what we thought was happening.

She then covered magic and the history, reaching the point where she explained that Egan's power was not what the Oracles of the Gelid were familiar with. She explained her concerns, and that the Oracles were set to arrive the next day to help with the situation.

We both paused after the explanation and gave him time to take it all in. He looked a bit stunned, staring off into space as he processed the information. After a few minutes, he rubbed his eyes with one hand, then turned to look at me. "Lyla, sweetheart, I am so sorry that all this has been happening. Are you ok? Do you feel comfortable with Egan remaining here? We can make him leave today, if that's what you wish."

I smiled, grateful for the offer. "Father, no, please. I don't want to ask him to leave currently. That doesn't seem wise to me. I think he's just a pawn in whatever is happening. I would like to take the time to figure out who he's working with, if we can. But Father?"

I pause, waiting for him to look at me, knowing I needed to say this but wishing I could leave it unsaid.

"I think he's connected to Mother's death."

Father stared at me for a moment. I realized he hadn't realized the incident with Frederick resulted in the same mark Mother had. I could tell that his thoughts were racing, trying to understand what all this means.

At long last, he stood, looking out the windows but not yet moving. He used all his authority in his voice as he decreed. "You will not be the one figuring this out. If he has killed, and if he's that volatile, I don't want you leading this charge. I will set people to trace his movements and screen his incoming and outgoing letters."

I nodded. "Thank you. I need to be involved though, as the next Queen. I'm also worried about Lord Denenbaum. He's the one who invited Egan here, and I don't know how he fits into all this."

"We will also monitor him. I will say I have seen nothing suspicious from him, but I have lost my faith in him as of this moment."

I breathed in a sigh of relief.

Father sat back down in his chair and reached for my hand. "Lyla, you are most important to me. You can always bring your concerns to me, and we will face them together. No matter who sits on that throne, I'm here for you first."

His eyes glistened as he offered a small smile.

"I don't want to lose you. Or Ethan. Losing your mom was more than enough for me."

"I know, Father. That never worried me. I am relieved, but I never doubted you."

"Let's talk about this tournament. Should we continue to host it, considering we don't know what Egan can do, or if others he may work with are here or can also do that?" Father looked to Juniper at his question.

"Your Majesty, I don't know the right answer for that. Cancelling now could cause more turmoil. However, there is a risk of death that wasn't previously accounted for, including whether Egan is working with others. I think that the Priestesses that will arrive soon will have better guidance to provide."

Father raised his eyebrow. "Are you not a Priestess too, Lady Mallard?"

Juniper blushed. "Yes, I am. The identities of the Priestesses remain closely guarded information."

"I have my ways of finding information no one wants to be known. I have known long before you arrived."

I looked between the two, shocked.

Juniper glanced at me, as if she had forgotten I was here for a moment. "Princess Lyla, please don't—"

"I would never. Your secret is secure."

I offered her a reassuring smile, which she returned. "We have five days until the first trial. I think waiting for the Priestesses to get here and then consulting with them will be the best option at this point?"

Father and Juniper nodded. "I have one question. If we cancel the tournament, which suitor would my daughter pick?"

I glanced away, towards the windows that overlook Mother's garden. Before I could talk myself out of it, I lead with my vulnerability. "If I had to make a choice at this moment, I would try to ask the Council to allow me to marry my girl-friend." I avoided looking at Father. I can't risk seeing whether he is disappointed.

"Oh, Lyla." His voice conveyed only compassion. I turned to look at him and saw tears in his eyes reflecting the tenderness his words held. "I would love to make that happen for you. For you, I would move the stars to make that happen, but the Council would remove both of us from the throne if we tried."

The tears in my eyes threatened to spill. I knew that answer. I looked to Juniper, who nodded sadly. Taking a deep breath, I continued my answer.

"Then I would choose Spencer. His magic let him see that my soul rests with hers. He said he would not stop our love. It's the closest I can get to her."

Father hugged me. "He's a good man. I hope he brings you all the happiness you deserve."

CHAPTER 20

The next day, the Priestesses arrived early in the morning. I could watch them enter the grounds from the balcony in my chambers. I found myself surprised to see them enter with a full traveling coach and horses. My thoughts trailed back to where Juniper said that they were winnowing everyone across the lands to speed up their travel. I supposed I had imagined them to be arriving without a normal travel ensemble, which was ludicrous. It would look absurd to arrive on foot after traveling such a distance. I chuckled at imagining the reactions to seeing people from across the country just walking up to our gates with no beasts or coaches or signs that they had been traveling long distances. How tiring it must be to carry all those wagons, the horses, and people across such a distance. I concluded these priestesses must be powerful to have achieved so much so quickly.

I watched Juniper open the carriage door and welcome five women while I sipped on my tea. I was too far away to hear what they were saying, but I could imagine the urgency they feel. As I tried to lip read from this distance and failed miserably, Ivy came out to the balcony. "There you are! I was about to send for the guard to look for you around the grounds."

I didn't normally take breakfast alone on my balcony, and

Ivy knew my habits better than me. She knew I would have been in my chambers, trying to avoid starting the day.

"Come, let's get ready. Juniper wants you in her office as soon as you can this morning. Spencer will be there, too." She picked up my dishes and started shooing me inside.

As I prepared for the day, I saw Amyra still sleeping. My heart broke all over again that I could never make her my Consort, though I still selfishly hoped she would always be at my side. As I watched her breathe peacefully, smiling through her dream, I decided in this moment that I would behead any king that came between me and her. I didn't think that Spencer would, but it's always good to have a solid backup plan. Maybe once the King was dead, the Council might allow me to take a wife and make her my queen.

"Hurry!" Ivy rushed me, snapping me out of my daydream. "You can come back to her later."

I checked my hair in my mirror to ensure that all pieces were in place and then opened the door. I came face to face with Spencer's fist, ready to knock. He froze, and I covered my mouth to hold in the laughter and not wake Amyra. I stepped out the door, Ivy right behind me as she closed the door.

"Nice timing, Spencer." I winked at him.

He blushed. "Ready to head down to the meeting?" He offered his arm to escort me.

"The other two are still out training, right?"

"Yes, of course. They left half an hour ago to meet with the Captain."

Once he had reassured me, I took his arm. I felt a spark of excitement run through me from my hand as soon as I touched him. I glanced up through my lashes, biting my lip to hold back my smile. He looked down at me like he felt it, too. He placed his other hand on mine, holding me on his arm. "This way, my Queen."

The way he called me his queen settled deep within me. I felt the same energy that I felt when Amyra was around, flirting with me. I didn't know what to make of it.

"Your soul is speaking some interesting things, Princess."

I could hear the smirk in his voice as he said that and blushed so hard. Biting my lip, I answered, "What is my soul telling you, Prince?"

"Many interesting things about what must be going on in that head of yours."

"Well, I guess you'll have to tell me what you can read in my mind after this."

"Your place or mine?"

I would have playfully smacked him for that, except that we rounded a corner and could see Juniper and her guests coming down the opposite side of the hallway. It seemed we were arriving at her office at the perfect time. We paused, allowing Juniper and her guests to enter her office first.

Juniper started pulling out her tea set, letting us know she needs to speak with the Priestesses privately before they meet with us. She invited us to make some tea for ourselves while we waited.

The Priestesses disappeared into that side room that all her courtiers were hiding in the other day. Spencer and I lost the flirty energy we'd shared in the hallways; a more nervous mood, reflecting the gravity of our upcoming discussion, replaced it. We each poured our own cups, and then swirled them, staring into the shifting liquid, waiting for the Priestesses to join us.

It didn't take long, thankfully. The six women filed out of the room briskly, and one took charge, speaking immediately.

"And you," she pointed at Spencer, her green eyes swirling with emotions, "you're the one with the sight?"

He nodded, almost afraid to speak. Her command of the space was intimidating, to say in the least.

"Tell me what you saw on that boy."

Spencer explained Egan's haze. They interrogated us about the altercation with Frederick, asked if Frederick knew anything about Spencer's gift, and everything else that they could think of about what we have seen or heard.

They asked me if I've had anything manifest. When I answered negatively, the one with eyes the color of chocolate looked me up and down and made a slight face of disapproval.

The leader told me I'll spend time with that priestess to see if there're any gifts preparing to manifest. I felt dread at the idea of spending time with someone who seemed to think lowly of me already.

"Why are you so certain that I'll also have magic?" I asked. The Priestesses all appeared to freeze, while the leader turned to Juniper.

"What does she know?" She asks Juniper.

"She doesn't. I didn't know how much to share." Juniper confessed.

I watched as the two seem to have a silent conversation.

Then the leader relented. "I'll teach you two this as well, though it's not high on the priority list. A prophecy reveals when the land's magic will return. It speaks of a gifted king and queen."

"I... wait, you're telling me that someone long ago saw that I'd marry Spencer?"

"Perhaps. If you're gifted. We'll have to test you. Have you ever gardened before?"

"No, I spent more time in the classroom as a child, preparing to lead a country. I mostly just admire the gardens."

With that, the brown-eyed priestess rolled her eyes, and the one in charge tsked at me. I felt small, inadequate.

"What about his mama seeing that we are both change makers? What does that mean?"

The Priestesses exchanged looks, and while it seemed wild to believe, they looked like they were talking within each other's minds again.

Finally, Juniper nodded and turned to me. "This is the prophecy. This paper cannot leave this room. You can read it here, but we don't have time in this meeting to explain what we understand it to mean. We must start understanding what threat Egan poses. Once we've dealt with that, we can focus on this."

She had reached into an inner pocket of her coat, though I see a slight shimmer suggesting she pulled something through with magic. She handed me a folded, aged paper with handwriting on it. I unfolded it and held it for Spencer and me to read together.

When the Queen of the realm binds her fate to a King who sees the depths of souls, she shall cause the land's heart to bleed flames into the sky and will herald a change in the realm itself.

When the earth trembles and rivers of fire reshape the ocean, the Gods will wake from their celestial sleep. Amidst the tumult and the awe-inspiring spectacle, they shall bring life into a new Goddess, born not of flesh but of magic, destined to weave balance into the very fabric of existence.

She will destroy the way of life, her steps resonating with power older than time itself. Through her touch, greed and envy will find their match, and the realms shall know an era of unparalleled enchantment.

Thus, the ancients foretold, their voices a whisper carried on the winds of destiny, for in the union of Queen and King lies not just the union of hearts, but the awakening of powers that shall reshape the world.

I stood up and moved towards the window as I contemplated the meaning. Spencer most certainly fit into this; I could tell why they accepted him. I couldn't see how I fit in. I didn't have magic within me, and even if I did, it would be magic to grow plants, not to cause fire and destruction. Sure, I had the luck of being born to the sitting king and queen, but they couldn't possibly be speaking of me, could they?

I took a deep breath. I needed to play through this game to understand what they were trying to tell me.

"Ok, so we need to find out how this magic works within me. How do we do that? Do we just go to the garden and try?"

The brown-eyed priestess scoffed. "Absolutely not. We know there is evil within these walls. We will go outside the walls to the temple to try."

My face twisted in confusion. "There are no Oracle temples in town. I've lived here all my life and haven't seen one."

Juniper smiled. "My sweet Princess, that's only because you weren't invited in."

I looked at Spencer, apprehensive. This plan was feeling quite dangerous. His eyes swirled, reflecting his fear. But what choice do we have? We were in too deep to back out now.

"OK, let's do this."

CHAPTER 21

Two of the priestesses departed the room with me. The others will spend time with Spencer to understand his command of his powers and to learn more about Egan. Before we left the castle grounds, they insisted on going to my chambers. I led the way. Once inside the chambers, they busied themselves in my wardrobe, pulling out a set of clothing that closely resembled their own.

"It's not what acolytes usually wear, but it'll do well enough." I heard one mumble.

Amyra was still sleeping in my chambers, but Ivy was not in sight. My eyes lingered on her, watching her breathe. One priestess caught my gaze, raising her eyebrow at me, but didn't ask questions. They hurried to change my clothes and restyle my hair. Once they were done, I looked more like an ordinary citizen than a princess. I supposed that would make it easier to navigate beyond the walls without any of the usual fanfare. They handed me a cloak long forgotten from the depths of my wardrobe.

"You'll need this to help cover your identity. No one can know you left the grounds today." Both looked over at my bed, at Amyra.

I nodded. As we left the room, I started down the hall to walk towards the main staircase. "No, this way."

The brown-eyed priestess tugged on my arm, and I followed them into a door that winded through to servant paths throughout the castle. How did they know the layout of this building this well? I had the feeling that I shouldn't ask questions until we reach our destination, so I added it to the growing list.

I followed the women through the hallways, long after losing track of where we were. Eventually, we climbed a staircase and approached a door to the outside. This door opened into an alleyway within the town outside the gates. I didn't know that this was possible, and yet these strangers just knew how to navigate around this place?

We walked through the streets, zigzagging down alleyways and along major thoroughfares. It felt like they were trying to shake off someone following us, but I couldn't see anyone behind us when I had the opportunities to look. I didn't dare drop the hood to look around more, just in case they were noticing something I couldn't. The weather at least made the hooded cloak make sense. A light drizzle fell, and many of the people we passed were wearing their own head coverings to shelter from the weather.

Eventually, we found our way to the city edge and into farmlands. We noticed the potent smell of manure, suggesting the livestock were well-fed and healthy. Other plots of land clearly used some of that manure for fertilizing. I had never walked this far from the walls guarding the castle before. The carriages we used would breeze through this space within minutes so that the smell never lingered. It took us much longer to trudge through on foot.

Eventually, we made it to a forested area. The stench dissipated as we dodged into the narrow entry of the thick woods, the priestesses easily locating the walking path. We could only walk single file through this area. Thick undergrowth hid the path, making it invisible unless you searched for it. I was stunned once more by how well these women knew my own lands. I wonder if they had grown up here, and if they had, what led them to the Oracles out in the foothills?

After what felt like an eternity of walking through this forest, we approached a clearing. Although we saw no buildings, several rounded stones formed a circle. Inside the circle of stones, nothing but dirt was present. Outside, the grass and undergrowth didn't start growing until a solid six or seven feet away from the circle. The ground looked well worn, like many dozens and dozens of feet have walked this area. The trees were another eight to ten feet from the start of the grassy area, providing a large clearing. Its simplicity truly made the space breathtaking.

"Where is the temple?" I whispered, in awe of what I could already see.

The brown-eyed priestess walked to the center of the circle as she explained, "The Oracles don't need a building to accomplish our goals. This space is for understanding our magic, which flows from the earth and returns to it after. We use this space to ground ourselves, become one with the nature that provides for us, and open our hearts to the source of our gifts."

The second priestess, whose eyes were pale blue, almost a perfect match to Amyra's, followed her. They sat on the ground, inside the circle of stones, closed their eyes, and started a chant. After a few moments, water rose from the ground, swirling around them like a ribbon. It flowed through and around them for a moment, then shifted and aimed for me. Before I could even react, the water swirled around me in the air, like a small stream suddenly formed around me, unable or unwilling to follow the laws of nature. I could feel it tugging, though it never touched. The water ribbon pulled me towards the priestesses and returned to the ground once I was standing next to them. Instead of just falling to the earth, the stream left the area we were in, flowing along the ground to make a small pool on the other side of the clearing.

The brown-eyed priestess wordlessly invited me to sit. I quietly mimic their position, touching each of my knees to one of theirs, like how they were touching each other. She started instructing me as soon as I was sitting, guiding me to a meditative state.

We spent hours trying to find different ways for me to use this magic I'm supposed to have. They had me sit, stand, lay down, and move in every way they could imagine. Every so often, we returned to meditation. Without these meditation breaks, I was certain I would have lost my mind. I couldn't seem to harness this magic to save my soul, let alone this world they thought I was going to save. I started to wonder if Spencer should be marrying a different queen-to-be.

During one of these attempts to move the soil, I gave up and sat down in frustration. I turned to the brown-eyed priestess, who I've learned was called Zoya, and just poured out all my questions. "What is wrong with Egan? How do you know my castle so well? What if I never show magic? Maybe I'm not this Queen of prophecy. What is 'a river of fire'?"

Both Priestesses giggled. Zoya turned to the blue-eyed woman, Lettie, and said, "You were right. She didn't make it to lunch."

Did they take bets on me? When did they even have time to do that? My skin burned with the anger I felt welling up inside me. Before I could go off on them, Zoya answered.

"The other priestesses know more about Egan. All I know is that he's an abomination and shouldn't be able to do what he did. As for your castle, the Oracles of the Gelid were once a critical part of the ruling of this kingdom. We keep substantial records, and it only took a bit of studying to get familiar with it. A river of fire is just that... rock melted and burning, flowing downhill like a river. As for if you'll show magic, well, you will. I can feel it inside you when you try. We just haven't figured out how to connect your will to it."

She smiled at me, smug that she could answer my concerns so easily.

I flushed with embarrassment. I focused on them to steer attention away from me. "How did you first use your powers?"

Lettie answered first. "I was cooking at home for my family, and the pot of water I was boiling bubbled over. I panicked about the fire being put out, and the surge of adrenaline allowed me to pull the water away from the pot until I could reach the pot and pull it off the flame."

Zoya paused a moment before answering. "I also accessed it in a moment of panic. There was a fire coming straight for our home, from a neighbor's building. I knew my baby sister was in the room closest to the fire and none of us could reach her before the flames did. I created a wall of dirt out of instinct, to keep the flames from licking the house."

Lettie's eyes lit up. "We need to make you panic. How can we do that?"

I groaned. "I don't want to feel panic. Surely there's another way. What if it's just any heightened emotion?"

Zoya smiled. "Should we bring your girlfriend out here with us? Maybe she can cause some heightened emotions."

Her eyebrow raised. I flushed with embarrassment again.

"I'm sure we can find something respectable to do that wouldn't risk my role as future Queen. The men on the Council would strip me of my titles and exile me if they knew of her."

"Ohhhhhh," Lettie groaned. "So that's why you're pretending to marry Spencer?"

"I haven't announced a betrothal to anyone."

Zoya rolled her eyes. "Are you telling me you don't intend to tell Elthas that Spencer is your choice?"

She pursed her lips; her expression reminded me of Mother's when she knew I was feeding her lies.

"I didn't say that. I just don't need people knowing what's going on right now. Egan is also a candidate, and I want to avoid fueling his anger with rumors that he won't be chosen."

"He truly scares you?" Lettie softly asked.

"I have seen angry men in my life, but something about that night, that sound he made, it wasn't human. I don't know what it was, but that wasn't human." Lost in thought about the evening, I stared into the distance.

When my thoughts returned to me, I noticed that both Zoya and Lettie were watching my face with concern in their eyes. I shook things off and then tried to refocus the discussion on magic. "OK, so what can I try to do to get this magic to connect with me?"

Zoya shook her head. "You were getting there. You need to talk to us more about Egan and that night. Tell us what you were worried about that night."

I stared at her, waiting for her to tell me she was kidding, anything.

When nothing came, I answered. "The room was so small. He was directly across from me at that table, and so many of my loved ones were there too. Amyra, Ivy, Spencer… I was so worried for all of them."

"OK, good, lean on those feelings. They're working. Tell us more."

Zoya forced me to recall several moments where my adrenaline spiked in fear, not just from that night, but from moments where Amyra and I nearly got caught, while learning how to sneak around, and even from my childhood. I focused so hard on my memories, with Zoya walking me through the emotions. The fear, the pain of losing Mother, the anger at not being allowed to live authentically were all used to feed whatever was in me.

Without warning, I felt my body shake with a force I had never felt before. My breath left me, and I felt frozen, completely unable to process what had just hit me. Then a whirlwind of dirt and plants and the stones surrounding us with rose and started swirling around us, lifting me up. I held completely still, not sure what to do, afraid to take in more than a small breath. The debris rose above the tallest trees and formed a swirling, rocky vortex around us, with me hovering about five feet in the air, locked into my sitting position. I looked down at Zoya, who was grinning.

"What are you doing?" I whispered.

"Princess, that's you." She had pure joy in her voice. "Let's get these back down. Take a deep breath and picture them slowly descending to the places they came from."

She walked me through calming down, and I watched the air around us clear and return to normal.

Once it was safe to move, Lettie and Zoya bowed deeply towards me. "You just did something that took me years to have the strength to do. You are our Queen. The Gods will wake when you call them."

I stared blankly for a moment, unable to process what Zoya just declared. "What do you mean?"

"You are naturally incredibly strong. With practice and training, you'll be able to move land in ways I've never seen before. It took me a year to move one rock the size of this." She held up a stone about the size of her hand. "We hoped for you to move a handful of dirt today, not create a tower of dirt visible from the sea. I was supposed to train you all winter, but truthfully, I'm not sure what I can offer for you."

I breathe deeply, taking the time to process this. With my hands in the earth, I sat on the ground. I could feel what must be the magic flowing through me. It was a soothing feeling, helping me to calm my thoughts as they race around. If Zoya was right and I was already this powerful, then maybe that prophecy really was about me. What did that mean for me?

"What we can do," Lettie started, "is head back to the others and see what they think should be done. While Zoya can't help you strengthen, there are methods to learn control, so at least we can cover that information this winter, and maybe the others know more about how we can help you harness strength."

She must have read my mind. I gave her a grateful smile and stood up. As I stood, dirt rose with me. I looked at Zoya in a bit of panic.

"Deep breaths, center yourself. It'll drop. When you ground with the earth like you just did, it basically combines to your will. It will move the way you will it, which this time was the way you needed to move." Zoya explained.

I listened, and as I took my third deep breath, the pebbles and soil dropped from the air.

"I have never been so glad to live in the castle before… wait, could I move the stones there too?"

Zoya shrugged. "Probably. Maybe not now, but I would imagine you could with time and practice." Mischief glinted in her eyes. "Makes it much easier to hide things… or people."

Our giggles echoed in space as we started back.

CHAPTER 22

That evening, Spencer snuck to my room to join Amyra and me for dinner. Ivy found reasons to not be there, conveniently. I was grateful for the opportunity to just be the three of us. I knew I could trust each of them with my life, and I hoped that they could learn the same for each other.

Dinner was mostly light conversation. We were all exhausted from the heaviness hitting us lately, and the conversation showed that. But once dinner wrapped up, I showed off a little with my newfound skill. In my bathing room, I had decorated with potted plants around my window to help provide some privacy. I grabbed one of the smaller pots and carried it to the sitting room.

I opened with, "Do you want to see something really wild?"

Amyra and Spencer nodded, curious to see how this would go. I sat the pot on the table and then stuck my fingers into the soil. I used the trick Zoya teased me with earlier and started thinking about the things I'd want to do with Amyra while I stared at the dirt. My thoughts shifted to kissing her soft, full lips, and how they always taste of raspberries and honey. I thought about how thrilling it is to hold her hair in my hand, tugging on it while I have my fingers buried inside of her, taking orgasms from her. I imagined what it tastes like to lick those orgasms out of her, tasting her honey dripping from her as I hold her thighs open for me.

The dirt rose. I willed it to flow like a ribbon around my wrist and then up through the air, like how Lettie played with water this morning. I watched as it swirled in the air, dancing towards Amyra. It flowed behind her head, then laced itself around her arm in a spiral. I heard her breath hitch, like it was tickling her arm as it made its way down. When it reached her wrist, I willed it to reach out for Spencer's arm, just a few inches from hers. I found it intriguing; my will seems to have taken on a life of its own. I watched the dark brown ribbons of soil flow around his arm, then dance along his cheek before wrapping behind his head to the other side of his neck, and then down his chest. Once it disappeared below the table edge, it seemed to beeline beneath the table back towards me, up my front and around my neck before finishing its circle around my body. All three of us had a ribbon snaked around us, tying us together. The poetic nature of the image doesn't escape me as the dirt ribbon breaks into three and then flows around each of us before returning to the pot.

Once the last of the dirt returned, I removed my hand from the pot and finally looked at them. "I have a new skill." I whispered, an excited smile on my face.

Amyra released a slightly louder squeal. "Lyla, this is so exciting! How does it work?"

She held nothing but pure joy in her eyes, and she reached for me. This woman was my biggest supporter in life, and it was moments like this that made me so grateful to have her by my side.

"I honestly don't know. I just feel it inside me, and when I connect with earth and then feel powerful emotions, I can make it move based on my will." As I shared that tidbit of information, I looked at Spencer and blushed. I basically just admitted that I teased him with my power. I didn't mean to, but apparently, I needed to learn how to influence my will before my subconscious steals the spotlight again. Marrying Spencer wasn't for love or lust or anything. It needed to be just for satisfying the Council and apparently satisfying this prophecy.

Spencer noticed my flushed cheeks and his eyes darkened. He knew what it took to make that show happen. But it was Amyra who asked, "What emotions did you just channel to do that?"

I looked at her with my cheeky grin and wiggled my eyebrow. "Are you sure you want me to answer that?"

Her cheeks flushed with a bright pink, but she nodded.

"I thought about how delicious you taste when I get to show you the stars."

Our first time together was under the stars, while traveling to Ashenwoods. Ever since, that's been our code for wanting each other when in mixed company.

Amyra whipped her head to look at Spencer. He clearly understood what I had just said. She turned back to me, shocked, but also... was that amusement in her eyes? She leaned forward, and before I could even understand what was happening, her lips were on mine, and I was tasting the honeyed raspberries I just imagined. My eyes closed, my skin tingled, and my core burned, aching for more. I reached up and pulled her closer, deepening into this kiss. The world disappeared around us, and I felt her hands on me, teasing my breasts. A fresh wave of fire rushed through me, ending between my legs. I moaned into her mouth and reached around her dress.

Spencer cleared his throat. Amyra broke her contact with me. I opened my eyes to see her entire face flushed with embarrassment. I took a few breaths to calm myself.

"Sorry to interrupt, ladies, but Lyla, you probably want to avoid such activities for a bit... the dirt flew out of the pot as you got into that."

Spencer nodded towards the potted plant that had shifted, sitting crookedly in the pot and the mess of dirt around the table.

I jumped up and started trying to straighten the plant and wipe the dirt into the pot from the table. "They didn't tell me that would happen! Ugh, thank you, Spencer."

His lips curved, and his eyes sparkled.

Amyra smoothed her skirt back down while delicately saying, "I suppose we can take this moment as an opportunity to talk about what the future will look like?"

Spencer nodded. "Yes, that's a good idea. I see the love you two have. Your traditions dictate that the King and Queen must share a bedroom, but I want to do whatever I can to allow you two the ability to nurture your love. I've never encountered a love like yours in all my travels. Your souls were clearly meant to intertwine."

"Are we? That prophecy says otherwise. The Queen of the realm binds her fate to a King who sees the depths of souls," I repeated from earlier.

Amyra looked confused. "Prophecy?"

"Oh, goodness, I didn't tell you yet." I filled her in on the prophecy we read earlier. I read it so many times this morning, then repeated it in my mind during the magic practice, that it's now committed to my memory.

After I caught her up, Amyra took a moment, staring at her hands in her lap, folded neatly, holding her emotions in. "*In the union of Queen and King lies not just the union of hearts,*" she repeats quietly. A shaky inhale lets her speak a bit louder. "That doesn't really leave much space for me, does it?"

I reached for her hands.

"It doesn't close you out completely, either. I don't know what will come for Spencer and me. Maybe our friendship is enough."

I looked at him and offered a smile, which he heartily returned. My gaze returned to her. "But I love you, and Spencer promises that you and I will have our space. I will make sure of it, even if I need to use my magic to move stones and make the chambers a bigger room to fit another bed."

Amyra looks up with amusement. "Could you even do that?"

I shrug, "The Priestess thinks I could. I lifted some enormous stones this morning, so it's possible. And more importantly, Spencer, she can share our chamber, right?"

Spencer nodded. "I will use a second bed. You are her love, Amyra. I would be just her king."

I felt a flutter within as he shared that. I didn't know what I did to deserve him, or why he was so committed to seeing me happy with someone other than him, but his commitment to Amyra and me flooded my heart with so much emotion.

Amyra's smile reappeared tentatively.

"I could just kiss you for that." She said. Then she leaned towards him, as if she had decided she would. She planted her lips squarely on his. Spencer's eyes widened, and he looked at me with confusion and shock.

I smiled at him. I was just as confused, but I didn't feel any pangs of jealousy. He accepted the smile as reassurance and closed his eyes to return her kiss. I watched as his hands tentatively rose to the back of her head, where my hand had been just a moment before. Her hand reached for his chest, almost the same way she had held mine. On him, she trailed it up and to his neck, then to the back of his head and through his hair. My heart swelled watching them enjoy each other's kiss. After a moment, they pulled apart.

"Uh, well, that was unexpected." Spencer said.

Amyra grinned. "I don't know why I did that. Please let me apologize. I just suddenly felt immense love for you, like I had known you for years and that you are mine."

She held her hands to her eyes and rubbed them, as if trying to rub that feeling away. "Lyla, I am so, so sorry." She turned to me and reached for my hands.

I offered her the same smile I gave Spencer before. "Amyra, love, no, please don't apologize. I only felt love watching that. I wish I could explain. It felt like it was meant to happen that way."

We exchanged looks with each other, not understanding what had just happened between us. Without warning, Amyra was back in my arms, kissing me again. We stood in unison this time, and we took our familiar dance to the settee nearby. We lost ourselves in each other. I ran my hand through her hair, and she lightly scratched my back with her nails.

146

This time, I remembered Spencer was in the room before I lost myself in her love. In my lusty haze, I held out my hand, inviting him to join us. He moved to sit behind me, unsure of what to do at first. I guided his hand to my breast, my fingers over his as I showed him how I liked to feel fingers on me, teasing my nipple. After a moment, I moved my other hand to Amyra's breast to tease her and broke our kiss to turn and kiss Spencer. The moment my lips touched his was electrifying. I felt an aching need for more. All I could hear is my blood pounding, and I felt my skirt rustling as Amyra expertly weaved her hand between my legs to swirl her thumb and tease me. I moaned into Spencer's mouth, feeling his free hand tangle itself in my hair as he passionately explored my mouth. Amyra tugged my cleave over my neckline, placing her mouth around my nipple, giving it the attention I've missed most from her. I felt my heart pulled to both.

Without warning, Spencer broke the kiss and pulled back.

"We shouldn't do this." he took a deep breath to calm himself.

Upon opening my eyes, I fixated on the bulge between his legs. I had never been this close to being with a man before, and never in my wildest dreams would I have imagined wanting to. I leaned into Amyra, half hugging her, feeling her breathing as hard as mine.

"I'm so sorry. We need to protect your purity." Spencer returned to the dining table.

I laughed. "My purity? Amyra and I have left that behind long ago."

Amyra touched my arm. "It's ok, Lyla. He's right. We need to be careful. You and I can't do the things he can, plus, remember how he saw how my soul changed yours? What if someone working with Egan can also see that kind of thing? And then they see his soul intermingled with yours? We need to be careful until we know who they are and what they can do."

I took a deep breath, and then another, grounding my emotions, bringing my back down from the heavens. She was right. He was right. We needed to tread carefully.

"You are right, both of you. Thank you. We need to play this smart, but that doesn't mean I don't want this. I can't explain why, but it feels right with both of you."

A smile slid across my face as my next thought formed. "At least we know one bed could do just fine."

CHAPTER 23

We had reached the day of the first event of the Tournament. I had never felt so much fear in my life. In the days leading up to this, the priestesses worked with Spencer and me to help us learn to harness and control our magic. While doing so, they used their own skills and one of them, with a gift to see into the future, saw a grim sight for this day. We talked with Father about this, but during that conversation, since we couldn't be sure what will happen, we kept the Tournament going.

They didn't let me see the men before the event started, so I couldn't give any last words of wisdom. I instead went to Juniper's office and worked my way into a panic about how today could go horribly wrong. Juniper called Father to her office, and we tried to talk to him. She trusted that my intuition was telling us what to do, and she needed us to hear it. We tried to argue with Father about canceling the event, but no luck. Father worried we would alert Lord Denenbaum or any others working with Egan, and that we would trigger some other disaster in trying to avert something happening during this event. As much as I hated that, he was right, and we couldn't take that risk.

Eventually, the time came to gather for this event. Over the last couple weeks, my event planners had coordinated constructing a dirt covered ring, with stadium style seating surrounding the ring. They also created a special raised seating area for Father, Ethan, and me to sit in, along with our assorted people.

They really sold the whole concept of this for tourism as well. Within our private area, they set aside space for a scribe and two assistants. Their purpose was to document all that Father and I did for the official record of the event to be preserved for generations. Two other journalists would be side by side with them, meant to share "officially nonofficial" reports throughout the kingdom, and in the kingdoms of the Princes.

Because of all the attention on us, Ivy and Amyra worked diligently with Eliza to style an outfit for me on this occasion. They placed me in a white dress, fitted to accent my breasts and waist, then flowing down to the ground. The dress had tiger lilies embroidered around the bust and used a matching pale orange gauze to cover my shoulders and upper arms. They styled my hair in a delicate, loosely gathered bun to keep the hair off my neck as I sat outside watching the event. They used orange amaryllis to decorate the clips holding the hair off my face, creating a faux crown of flowers.

But we made it perfectly on time. They had planned for me to be the last to arrive. I got there just as Father was walking out to the viewing box, so I was barely on time for my entrance. We planned to create a grand entrance for me, with trumpet fanfare and announcements. The men would be on the field, waiting for my arrival.

My fear felt palpable. I was grateful to be last to leave this private staging area, as it gave me a bit of time to hold hands with Amyra and Ivy, and I needed their support to keep my emotions in check. The last thing I needed was to accidentally raise the dirt of the arena with the heightened emotions I was feeling.

The signal for my entry sounded, and we started. I dropped their hands and shrugged my shoulders to shift into my commanding stance, schooled my face to portray a calm determination, and then we started up the stairs to the dais. As I reached the top of the stairs and stepped into the viewing box, the trumpets halted and the announcer began explaining the purpose of the tournament and the rules of this event.

We scheduled four timed rounds of fights for today. For the first three rounds, each of the Princes would face one of Elthas' best fighters the military has to offer. Our generals scored the fights on technical aspects, and I scored them based on my opinion of each round. We would combine the scores, and the two princes with the highest combined scores would face off in the final round to determine the winner, assuming both could fight a second round. If one could not fight, then the other would be the default winner.

I had explicitly instructed them to not make this a battle to the death. This was a show of strength and style, and to show that they can engage in hand-to-hand combat. Our Kings had not needed to fight in the field in many generations, not since the Last Great War. Father and I had hoped that this would be a subtle message to deter countries from seeing such a young set of rulers as people to trifle with, so that we could gain our footing without challenges to our seats.

Facing Egan's electrifying complications, I worried my instructions wouldn't matter. Going into this, I fully intended to score Ethan lowest. It might not be enough to keep him from the final round, but it was the best I could do. We decided that informing the Generals of the magical risks was not safe enough. We didn't know who to trust, and we couldn't let anyone report our distrust to the wrong people.

I arrived at my seat, center front of this box, and I'm relieved to see that Ivy and Amyra have seats positioned closely enough that I could reach for their hands. Strategic use of this was necessary. I slowly inhaled a few deep breaths, and after my third, I heard my cue from the announcer for my speech. I stepped forward, and welcomed the crowd and the Princes, and wished them the best of luck in their efforts today.

Despite my attempt to avoid Spencer's eyes, we made eye contact instantly. I felt a flutter deep within me, and my fears rose. I shoved it down, deep within, and finished my speech. Back in my seat, the other two princes and their opponents also returned to the shaded seating, leaving Spencer to face one of my men. I sent a prayer to the Gods that would listen, asking them to stop Egan from using his powers during his face off.

As Spencer and the soldier prepare to fight, one journalist called to me. "Do you have any hopes for one of these princes to prevail?"

I glanced over at them, seated just beyond Father, eagerly posed with pens in hand. They were all ready to record my words. I directed my gaze towards Father, who provided a small, almost imperceptible nod, and then I glance at Amyra, seated between Father and me. She simply watched me curiously, waiting to see what I would say. I turned my attention back to the journalist and offered, "It's much too early to have a true favorite, don't you think?"

Amyra's smirk was just within my peripheral vision, letting me know she thought the lie as amusing as I hoped she might. If we lived the way the conservatives in this country hoped for, then women weren't supposed to make playful banter or have quick wit. It might be small, but these quips were one way I fought against this idea that I was supposed to be this meek, submissive wife standing by my husband. I folded my hands firmly in my lap, wishing I could reach to Amyra and offer a love squeeze.

Trumpets sounded, indicating that the fighters had one minute until their battle started. I watched as they squared off with each other, waiting to go. I started practicing the meditation techniques that Zoya taught me the last few days, grateful that I had these available to me. The signal to start sounded, and I watched as Spencer and the soldier go at each other. For every attack the soldier made, Spencer deflected flawlessly before returning an offensive attack of his own. Most of his were also deflected, making this fight somewhat anticlimactic. I felt my lips turn up with each win that Spencer has until I hear the journalists whispering and glanced to see several of them frantically writing things down. My cheeks flushed. I'm not used to having my every thought analyzed in real time, and it was embarrassing. I took a breath, erased the smile from my face, and returned my attention to the sparring. Just in time, as Spencer missed defending against a sword coming at his midsection and finds himself shoved a couple feet from the force of the impact against his armor. I grimaced, thankful that they were dulled practice swords, but it would still leave a decent bruise. He caught himself repositioning to protect his side better and returned the attack. His opponent easily deflected him, then a second hit felled him. Two in a row? I could see the confusion on his face as well. Returning to my deep breaths, I try to keep a neutral face. I looked down at Egan and notice that something seems off with him. His face held a scowl, like he was concentrating too hard.

I reached for Ivy's hand to get her attention, and she leaned forward to allow me to whisper. I remembered how I heard the journalists muttering, and realized they were too close to feel comfortable even whispering, so I offered a slight nod towards Egan. She noted his weird stare and then glanced at me. I saw the question in her eyes and offered her a nod. She stood up, paused at Father for a moment to curtsy, as was custom, and then I heard her footsteps leave the box.

I returned my attention to Spencer. He seemed to be in a pattern now, alternating between successful deflection and painful blow. He was losing strength in his movements, and I could only hope that the time ended soon.

Ivy returned just as they sounded the bell to stop the match. I looked at her, but she shook her head with a subtle glance towards the journalists, telling me she couldn't share what she found out. I looked back at Egan and saw him grinning. Spencer just lost this round. Rating him high would be impossible. I was grateful the official scorekeeper would conceal the actual scores, preventing anyone else from knowing I still rated him first. I started hoping that Frederick does much better than Egan, to help make Egan's loss make more sense. Egan making it to the final round crossed my mind, but I immediately dismissed it. I couldn't think about that right now.

They helped Spencer to a doorway; he disappeared, and I knew he would head straight to the infirmary for a medical evaluation. I took a moment to scan the crowd and made eye contact with Juniper, sitting in a shaded seat. She nodded to me, looked to the doorway Spencer just went through, and then returned her gaze. Does she mean the Priestesses will help him? I try to ask her with my eyes about Egan. Could they know what he was doing? Did he do something? Juniper shook her head no, but I didn't understand why. Did she read my mind? I took a deep breath, trying to refocus so my emotions stay with me. Frederick had less than a minute before his round starts. I looked over at Egan again, and he looked smug. He must be doing something.

I felt helpless. My mind raced, going through so many scenarios. Could he have more than the ability to shock people? Did he have a magical ability to control how people move? Was that even something that could happen? Maybe he was getting in their minds. What if he could make the soldier hit harder than intended? Amyra's hand reached for mine. Her touch brought me back to my body, and I realized that the dirt in the box was dancing along the ground. I took a deep breath, and then another. I tightened my grasp around Amyra's hand, signaling a thank you to her. She replied with her hand squeeze for 'I love you.' I focused on my lips to hold back the smile that always came with that squeeze and squeezed 'I love you' back to her.

I turned my focus back to Frederick to watch his sparring. He was much better at this, thankfully. He deflected more blows and stayed strong the whole time. I watched Egan throughout the fight and realized he wasn't as focused as he was with Spencer. He likely thought that he had the win in the bag. I wondered if he picked Spencer for a personal reason. Could Egan and Frederick have already known that Spencer would be selected after this tournament?

Frederick's round ended, and he was the clear winner,

looking like he had just stepped into the ring while his opponent looked like he went through the ringer. Egan and his opponent prepared for their round. I stared into the arena, zoning out, almost dissociating. There would be a break of thirty minutes when Egan's round was done, and I was hoping to find any of the priestesses. I couldn't visit Spencer without being seen, but I hoped a priestess would give me information.

The signal to begin Egan's round trumpeted. I watched him intently. Just before his first move, he turned to my box and mimed removing a hat while bowing to me. He deliberately waited for the signal before doing this, even though he risked being hit for leaving his guard down. When he rose, he had a grin not just for me, but for everyone. After turning to the crowd, eating up their applause at his antics, he turned back to his opponent to start the fight.

The crowd stayed wild for it, while Ivy and Amyra squeezed each of my hands, a show of support and strength for me. I worked to keep my face as neutral as I can, but inside, my emotions were swirling and skidding around. I couldn't afford to lose control of my powers, but I was angry. That he pulled off that stunt had my blood boiling. His opponent shouldn't have allowed that to happen. Did that soldier allow that as a favor to allow Egan to flirt with the future queen, or was that a brazen statement designed to make me question Egan's military connections?

I watched as Egan has the perfect fight. He only allowed the soldier to hit him twice. Both times were barely a graze across his arm, almost like he was off by half an inch in their practiced movements. The soldier took a good beating and would be sore for days, maybe even a week.

They called the match and declared Egan the winner. Spencer was the only one to lose. I breathed deeply, then again, once more. I stood up, turning away from the journalists that surely wanted to read into my every micro expression, to just be confronted with a courtier, holding a paper and pen to write my choices down. Spencer was ranked first, then Frederick, then Egan. I didn't want to think about straying from the plan, even if the Generals had no way to score him high enough to make it.

After sealing the vote, Amyra and Ivy stood on either side while we made our way to my family's designated break space. As soon as I entered the room, I saw Father already there, and heard Ethan behind us, quickly closing the door behind him.

CHAPTER 24

"What the hell was that?"

I couldn't help myself. That was the first time Father had ever heard me curse. "How did he find out who he's paired with to throw that round so perfectly? And what did he do to get to Spencer's opponent?"

I started pacing the room. Father poured drinks for all of us. Amyra took my glass and waited until I slow down to offer it to me.

"I found Juniper, and she said she would investigate and make sure a priestess comes here to speak to us. Her initial guess is that someone was wielding magic of some type, but she wanted to confirm." Ivy offered.

"And that look he gave me once his match started. His opponent should have knocked him off his feet. I can't believe that. He's trying to become a crowd favorite so that the city turns on me when I don't choose him." I reached for my forehead, rubbing it in confusion and frustration.

"Lyla, please, if you're going to fret, at least keep your hands away from your hair. We don't have time to fix that." Amyra offered. "Could you sit and maybe drink some of this?"

I nodded and sat, taking the glass. I didn't want to drink anything and risk nausea, but the glass would give my hands a job to do to keep them from my hair.

A knock sounded, and Ethan checked. "Juniper, please, come in. We are hopeful you can shed some light."

I turned to her, but she had a grim look. I would not like what I'm about to hear.

"I can. Before I do, I need to check, Lyla. You are so new with your powers, we normally don't recommend such emotionally charged situations at this stage. Are you holding it together? One of my priestesses can help you with maintaining your control if you need it."

A moment of relief hit me, and I nodded gratefully. "I'll need that for this next round. If Egan gets into that ring, I don't care if it's Frederick or Spencer. I don't think I'll keep the panic down."

Juniper nodded, pulled out a small square of paper and a pen, wrote the request down, and the letter disappeared. I could never tire of seeing such an act. The novelty helped to cool my temper, too.

"Emberly will be here soon. Now, for what I found out. I got confirmation that he was using powers to throw Spencer's fight. Nothing happened in Egan's fight, and they also ignored Frederick's fight. But one priestess confirms that she sensed power surging the moment that Spencer started getting hit. We got a priestess in with him at the medical bay to help speed up with healing."

"Wait, some of you can heal?" Amyra wondered out loud.

Juniper looked amused. "Yes. If you gain powers, you could be a healer as well. It's part of mastering your connection with water."

Juniper turned her attention back to me. She moved a chair directly in front of me and sat so we were eye to eye. "Lyla, please, look at me."

I lifted my head to look into her eyes. She reached for my chin and held my head still while she moved around. "The natural light in this room is a bit too dark. Does anyone have light?"

Father carried a candle over and lit the wick.

She held it up to my face. "Your eyes, they're red," Juniper nearly whispered, mostly in awe.

"I told you that Mother told me that all the time. What does that matter?"

"Your eyes are swirling with red right now. They have been since Spencer's sparring. If I didn't know better, I'd have guessed that they were red, not brown." Amyra leaned in to look and nodded.

"What does that mean?" I suddenly felt very uncomfortable with everyone looking at me.

"Have you ever had an affinity for fire, or find yourself fascinated with fire?" Juniper dodged my question. I hated when she did that.

"I've found meditation is easier when staring into a fire, but doesn't everyone? Please tell me what's wrong. I can't take much more."

At that moment, a knock sounded on the door. Ethan checked again and allowed the Priestess to enter.

"Oh good, Emberly is here." Juniper said, letting go of my face and turning to her. "Her eyes turned red when she's upset."

Emberly takes a quick inhale, her eyes widening for a moment, before composing herself. I recognized her as the Priestess who seemed to make decisions at their arrival. The candlelight danced off the green sparkles of her eyes, and I realized she shared powers with Spencer. My heart skipped a beat, thinking about him.

"Princess, please do what you can to keep him out of your thoughts for the moment." Emberly gave me a knowing look.

My jaw dropped, and I gasped. "I, h- how did you know?"

Emberly looked at Juniper, who shrugs. She turned back to me. "Seeing souls is just the initial onset for those of us with green eyes. Those who harness the energy can read minds, and some can even control minds."

"Is that what Egan did? Did he control Spencer's mind? Or that soldier's?"

"We can't say. He shouldn't have that ability, but he

shouldn't have any abilities at all. He's an abomination, and we are working to understand what's happening." Emberly sighed.

"Now, please, let me work with you so that I can help you control your emotions. The last thing you need is to start a fire or throw rocks when you see Spencer again."

I nodded. "OK, what do I do to control these emotions?"

"You'll need to let me into your mind, and I will walk you through calming techniques in real time as you need them."

I nodded again, not sure how to start that, but accepting instruction all the same.

'*Can you hear me?*'

My eyes widened, and I responded verbally, "Yes."

'*OK, good. Can you respond mentally?*'

I thought the word '*yes.*'

Emberly nodded. "Good, we can communicate this way. I will connect only enough to read your emotions during the next round, and I will receive your thoughts only if you intend to send them, as you just did. So, you will have some thoughts held private still."

I took a deep breath. "How much longer do we have?"

"Just a few minutes," Father replied.

"OK, can we regroup after, in Father's office? Spencer included, if he's able to leave the medical bay. We need to get more information about what is going on with Egan's network."

Everyone nodded. Juniper added, "He's going to leave the bay now, so hopefully he's not squaring off against Egan if he makes it to the next round."

The signal to return to seats sounded. I sent everyone else out so that we could go through the planned grand entrance again.

CHAPTER 25

The event announcer proclaimed that Spencer and Egan were to square off for the final round. Emberly was deep in my thoughts immediately, coaching me through many breathing techniques. I was holding Amyra's hand so tightly that I worried I might just break it. They were reviewing rules of engagement again. I felt so overwhelmed and worried I couldn't handle any of this. I wished more than anything that I could watch in privacy.

'*Spencer will be ok. Breathe in, hold it, and then breathe out.*' Emberly tried to soothe me.

'*You can't guarantee on that. Egan is unpredictable and we don't know how much power he can control.*' I argue back.

'*Breathe in, hold your breath, breathe out. Focus on keeping your face neutral.*'

Amyra swirled her thumb around the back of my hand, trying to offer a bit of comfort as well.

'*We have plans in place to assist Spencer if or when Egan tries to use magic. Our healers gave him some tools to help guard against what he may do.*'

'*If I don't see it's working well, why can't I just create a wall to separate them?*' It made little sense. I could help, couldn't I?

I could feel Emberly's sigh in my mind. My lip twitched, almost showing a smile. '*We know he suspects you're able to move the earth. One of his goals is to turn your people against you, and he can do that if he convinces them you are a witch. You cannot move the earth during this, no matter how tempting it might be. He might not publicly accuse you, but it'll give them ammo.'*

My stomach twisted and a cold numbness spread through me. My heart pounded in my ears.

'Caution, Princess. Breathe in, hold it, breathe out. You will get all the information after this. Watch your future husband earn the privilege of marrying you.'

She was right. I needed to watch this fight. It had already started. Spencer was doing well, thankfully. Egan was also doing well, unfortunately. Breathe in, hold it, breathe out. Spencer twisted away from Egan's offensive swing and then launched his own. Egan blocked, then attacked again. Back and forth, back and forth, they kept trading off. At the current rate, they would've scored basically equally for this round. I was proud of Spencer; he was doing better than anyone could have expected or hoped for after that first round.

Then something shifted. Egan gained the upper hand. First, it was a glancing blow across Spencer's arm. Then Spencer missed a hit, and Egan landed one on his back before Spencer could even see it coming.

Within moments, Spencer was on his knees on the ground, his sword several feet away.

My breathing hitched. *'Calm, Princess. Juniper has it under control. Focus on your breathing. Breathe in, hold it, breathe out. Breathe in, hold it, breathe out.'*

Egan tried to go for the final blow. He raised his arms up, sword high in the air. The crowd's cheers were deafening.

Egan seemed to lose balance. His ankle bent awkwardly as he tried to regain control. As people watched, gasps filled the air, then silence fell. My own hands moved to my face, Ivy and Amyra's hands, trapped in my grip, followed somewhat awkwardly.

Spencer had only a moment to roll towards his sword, but that was all he needed to get it back in his hand.

A crack echoed through the hushed arena as Egan fell. His

foot didn't move with the rest of his body in that fall, and that crack was in his ankle.

Emberly popped back in. '*I told you she would make it happen.*' I was grateful for covering my mouth, as I couldn't help smirking at her words.

'*Tell her I said thank you a million times.*'

Spencer stood. He held his sword in one hand, ready to react defensively. "Egan, friend, concede and let me help you to your feet."

His voice was quiet from this distance. The crowd was so quiet that we could all hear it. A gentle applause started at his show of sportsmanship.

Egan snarled in reply. He reached for his sword, trying to get to his knees. Spencer looked at the timekeeper, then at me. He was unsure what to do.

I debated calling out to stop the match. There weren't any rules against it. Then I considered the reaction Egan might have if he thought I was being patronizing. '*Don't, Princess. Your fears about his reaction pale compared to his thoughts. Let the timekeeper do his job.*'

Breathe in, hold it, breathe out. He would get there. There couldn't be more than a few seconds left. Spencer could easily stay out of reach. And if Egan tried to walk, he could do further damage.

The signal sounded. The match ended before anyone landed another blow. I exhaled. The crowd cheered, but I technically had to declare the winner. Within a minute, the courtier from earlier brought me the note with the General's pick for winner. While I made the final decision, their input still mattered. I opened it, and didn't bother hiding my smile. Spencer won, as he deserved. He showed humility and kindness when it mattered.

I stood, and the arena hushes once more. Ready to announce the winner, I took two steps forward. I felt Father stepping into place behind me, silently offering his support for my answer.

"Today's event goes to Prince Spencer of Vondalon, for his bravery and his sportsmanship." I announced.

The crowd's energy mixes. Some in the crowd cheered excitedly for the results. Others clearly felt disappointed Egan didn't win. I kept my face neutral while I surveyed the crowds. No one stood out to me, but the energy felt wrong.

Father's hand touched my shoulder. "Come, it's time to leave."

I heard something about his tone too. He noticed that wrongness. I checked that Ivy and Amyra were following and hurried back towards the safety of the castle.

CHAPTER 26

We regrouped in Father's office as planned. It took several hours for Juniper and Spencer to arrive, the last of us. She looks almost haggard as she ushers him through the door. Once the door closed, Father opened his mouth to speak, but Juniper shushed him.

"Apologies, Your Majesty, but before we begin, I need to check my notes for something."

Father and I exchanged a look. We were confused. Instead of paper, Juniper pulled a bundle of twigs out of thin air and lit them. She started mumbling quietly and very quickly, too fast to hear or understand her. She walked the perimeter of the room, waving the burning sticks' smoke into various nooks and crannies as she mumbled. Juniper stopped in one area of the bookshelf, closest to the conference table we normally sat around to discuss things. The smoke was drawn sideways into a crack behind the books. Juniper repeated more unintelligible words quickly while fanning the smoke at the crack. Nothing seemed to change. She seemed to start this ritual over, still with no change. Turning to us, she stopped and held a finger to her mouth. She then sat her twigs down on the table and wrote a note.

This room has ears to hear. We need to move to my office to

discuss what we came to discuss, but we can't let on that we know the room has ears.

As each of us read the note, we nodded. Juniper made a loud ruckus with her papers, and then said, "My apologies again. It seems I've misplaced the notes for this. Can we reschedule for tomorrow?"

Father nodded. He's clearly thrown off his game by learning that someone was listening in. After a moment, he remembered he should speak. "Yes, of course. Today has been an eventful day. How about we just retire for the evening? I'll send a message in the morning where we can meet once I review my schedule."

Juniper smiled. He fake-canceled the meeting perfectly. "Thank you for your kindness, Your Majesty. I'll make myself available when you next have time."

We trickled out of his office, trying to avoid appearing as if we were in a rush. When Amyra, Ivy, and I left, I led us away from Juniper's office, towards my chambers. I figured if anyone has eyes on the doorway to Father's office as well, seeing us go in different directions may help to deflect concerns about our discovery.

A while later, we were all regrouped into Juniper's office.

"What do you mean by that room having ears? Wasn't that just a crack in the wall?" Ethan started.

Juniper shook her head. "It's designed to look that way, but it's a magical tool the Oracles have used for centuries to listen in. We didn't create that one, and it's immune to our closing spell."

"How do you know a past priestess did not create it?" Ivy asked.

"We keep detailed notes of all ears and close them when we are done with them. That one was relatively new; I've searched the room before." Juniper ducked her head towards Father.

"My apologies, Your Majesty. We had suspicions about a trade agreement. I had to protect my region."

Father nodded. "I am grateful for your actions, in the past and today."

He smiled at Juniper, which she returned.

"OK, so what do we know about Egan's group? We know for sure it's a group, right?" Spencer redirected.

I was momentarily surprised by how quickly Spencer healed. The blows he received during each round seemed so painful. I wondered how many bruises he still had, though he showed no signs of feeling discomfort.

"Yes," Juniper replied. "Egan is working with at least three others here. He's also sending off letters daily through traditional means, so we believe this is just a cell within the capital, and that there is more going on."

"Do we know what they want?" I knew I had asked this before, but I needed to continue asking it until the answer was obvious.

"They seem to work with a network that is against the return of the Gods. Ironically, they call themselves the Priests of Bel, a long-dead god who once lived among us. They share conservative views and apparently support the men who opposed the Gods in the Last Great War. Over the years, they had released many missives about how women need to be subjugated and subservient to their husbands, to worship their husbands as if he is a god walking this land."

"And Lord Denenbaum, not Lord Luther, sponsored him?" Father questioned.

I nodded. Juniper added, "Eric doesn't seem to share all their views, at least through his voting history, but he has financial ties to the Priests of Bel. We don't have any evidence yet that Eric and Egan are directly coordinating this together. It seems like the Belus priests has influenced him to sponsor Egan without knowing him well. We have an acolyte making friends with Katelle to gather more information on that aspect."

Ethan nodded at the mention of his fiancé.

"So, what do we know? And is any of this tied to Mother's death?"

Father's face tightened, though I wasn't sure if it was because I brought her up, or if it was because he knew the answer and that I wouldn't like it.

Juniper answered, "We have some circumstantial evidence that the Denenbaums played a role in her death. They have Ashenwoods acquaintances who have noted that they were bragging about Katelle becoming the next Queen in the months before Her Majesty's death."

Juniper paused, letting me take in that information. "Ethan and your father have been working with some of my network and the official guards towards confirming that. If they can, then we will strip the Denenbaums of their titles and lands."

"Wow, ok. Here I thought Luther was going to be the biggest pain." I inhaled deeply, absorbing all this information. "But why do the Belus priests care? Who are they?"

"They demand the entire realm obey their teachings and subjugate all women. Their overall plan is to infiltrate every monarchy, and to force the ruling families to conform to their beliefs and changes in rule, or face death." Juniper paused.

"But for here, it's worse. Since the Oracles of the Gelid originated here, and they believe we are their biggest threat since we can harness the magic of the Gods, they intend to kill you, Lyla. They won't offer you the choice to bend the knee. They think that Ethan will bend his knee after seeing his sister die. We know that Katelle also believes their teachings. We don't think she's involved in the plot against Lyla."

Spencer stood up indignantly, attempting to hide his wincing as he did. "No, if you know this to be true, why haven't they all been dealt with—murdered, exiled, or arrested?"

My heart leapt at his rush to defend me, even as it hurt him. He added, "I should have taken Egan out today."

Father moved towards Spencer. "Trust me, son, I would have already killed him if we could defend that choice."

I felt another flutter when Father referred to him as 'son,' followed by guilt over the knowledge that he would never accept Amyra like that. "We don't have quite enough tying Egan to this group. Some members are sitting in the dungeons now, but we are letting others roam free, strategically. We need to have firm proof of a neighboring kingdom's prince planning to kill the heir to our throne before we make such an accusation."

The tension in the room settled down as we lost ourselves in thought, processing this. I realized that some of the excitement came from my magic stirring up the dust and soil in Juniper's plants.

"Do they also know what the Priestesses suspect about me, Juniper?" I asked carefully. In trying to assess the threat that they posed to me, I needed to know if they also know the prophecy, but not everyone in this room did.

"With the amount of hatred we heard within Egan today, we fear they do."

I nodded and sat with my thoughts. My gaze drifted down to where my hands rested in my lap. I started softly rubbing my thumb around the back of my other hand, a mindless gesture while I considered what steps to take.

'*Lyla?*' This wasn't Emberly's voice; this voice is much too deep and tender.

Without raising my head much, I looked at Spencer. '*You learned too?*'

Spencer nodded, almost imperceptibly. '*I will protect you to the ends of the world until my dying breath. You are mine. We may not have taken any official oaths, but I will not let that stop me from treating you as my wife, my queen.*'

Tears welled up, threatening to spill. Amyra reached into my lap for my hand. She must have thought that the tears were because of the threat on my life. I made eye contact with Spencer. '*You are my king, my future husband. From here and now until the end.*'

I inhaled deeply to gain control of my emotions. "OK. I need to cancel the Tournament. We can use Egan's injury for justification. That should have caused a delay of at least a month anyway, and by then it will be too cold for an outdoor spectator event. I can't have Egan traipsing around my home, putting me and my loved ones in such danger. They already took my mother, and I will not allow them to take anyone else."

Father and Juniper both shook their head.

"We can't gather intel on him if we send him away. We need him here." Juniper said. "Your Father and the Guard just had this discussion yesterday, while you were at the Temple. Egan won't be leaving the capital."

My stomach twisted, and for a moment, I forgot to breathe. My heart pounded so hard that I could hear it in my ears and my vision darkened a bit.

Father added, "We have more guards stationed around your chambers, in main hallways and along servant hallways as well. Ethan, you're also under extra surveillance."

As he said it, I heard the pebbles and rocks land along with my anxiety calming.

"Can Amyra and Ivy also have them when they're not with me? And Spencer and Frederick need them, too. I know he only targeted Spencer today, but Frederick could also be in danger." I refused to allow anyone to be hurt because of me.

Father nodded. "Already bumped it up after the event today. Spencer will find extra bodies at his doorway, and Frederick should have already encountered his. We also sent two to Egan's room, with the order to follow him anywhere he goes. Instead of protecting him, they will gather information. They're from the intel battalion. He was told it's because of the Tournament bringing so many extra guests to the city, and that they're not supposed to leave him alone."

I nodded; it doesn't hurt to have an extra set of eyes on that man. Or two, in this case.

"The second challenge tests diplomacy. Do you think we could rework it to get intel from Egan? If the games must go on, maybe we could change them to help us."

"Clever woman," Spencer smiled.

Father nodded. "Indeed. We can, and we will. Lyla, I'll design it with my intel chief. He will have some good plans on how to get him to reveal information he doesn't realize he's sharing."

I nodded. I really wanted to cancel this tournament, but if we must go on, then I supposed it was time to use it to our advantage.

CHAPTER 27

Over the next couple of weeks, I met with Zoya to learn control of my powers. From time to time, Spencer and Emberly joined us for practice, which seemed to be the only way I could get time with Spencer. The extra guard duty made it impossible to find excuses to have dinner together without planning events that included Egan, but his new ability to speak into my mind helped to make the time apart not so hard.

I could find great control with my powers, and my neutral face became much harder to break as well. Spencer loved to test this by telling me some things he hopes to do to me one day while we are around others.

Fifteen days after the first event of the tournament, Father sent word that he wants to hold a meeting. He scheduled it for Juniper's office again, since they hadn't fixed the 'ears' in his office. We hadn't met since the day of that event, so I was both eager to find out what he wanted, and nervous about it. I knew it was ridiculous to hope, but I wanted it to be that he had enough to lock Egan in a dungeon so we could end this tournament.

I also hoped that this meeting would let us get away with a private dinner with Spencer again. My memories keep going back to that evening before the sparring event, and how much I wished we could have continued.

Amyra, Ivy, and I rushed to get to the meeting and ended up being the first to arrive. Juniper had invited Zoya and Emberly to be with us as well, and they arrived shortly after we did. While waiting for the others to come, Zoya and Emberly experimented with Amyra and Ivy to see if they might have magic as well. They had Amyra with a glass of water in front of her, trying to get a drop to lift. Ivy, with her gold eyes showing powers like Juniper, was trying to convince a piece of paper to move without touching or blowing at it. Mostly, the only thing they could do was giggle at the attempts.

After one giggle fest, Amyra and Ivy started taking deep breaths to calm down. I tried to help Amyra a bit. I leaned over and whispered into her ear. "You laugh now, but imagine what you'll be doing when I have my head between your legs, and my hands holding your hips down?"

Amyra blushed furiously. She tried to push me away. Zoya scolded her. "You need it if you want to be serious about figuring this out. Plus, it's more fun to watch. Now look at that glass and think about that rain drop."

I bit my lip as I leaned towards her ear again. "How many times do you think I can get you to scream my name? Last time was seven... do you think we could go for eight times tonight?"

Amyra squirmed, but her concentration stayed on the water.

"I really hate you right now." She said with a grin.

"Mmm, but that's never what you say when my fingers are deep inside and my tongue is where it belongs, is it?"

Ivy squealed. "You're doing it Amyra!"

I pulled away from her ear and looked at the glass. There were several drops of water floating above the rim, suspended in the air. I covertly placed my hand on her lap and rubbed her thigh over her dress. "That's my girl."

A knock on the door interrupted the moment. I pulled my hand off Amyra's leg, and she allowed the water to drop.

Juniper checked the door and opened it to welcome Spencer, Ethan, and Father.

I still had my smirk and Amyra was blushing wildly, as if anyone but her knew what I said. Spencer's voice entered my mind. '*I can imagine what you said to her. But why?*'

It was my turn to blush. I still was getting used to this mind talking. I replied, '*helping her find her water magic. She lifted a few drops just before you arrived.*'

'Good girl. Both of you. I can't wait to hear more about what you said. Or see what you promised.'

I looked at Spencer as he took his seat across the table from me. Father and Ethan had chosen the last two seats by me. He smirked, and I just knew that he enjoyed he could see how he tortured me.

Juniper cleared her throat, giving each of us a raised eyebrow. "Before we start on the big news, a small win to share. Amyra has found her magic. She can use water, and if she trains well, she will also be able to use healing magic. I am glad that we brought enough priestesses down the mountain for this winter."

As people congratulated her, I watched as she suddenly blushed before looking towards me with a tinge of guilt on her face. I looked at Spencer, and he has that knowing smirk, telling me he spoke in her mind too.

Father cleared his throat after a moment, and all three of us turned as red as raspberries with our embarrassment. He didn't seem to notice, thankfully. "We have some more information about Egan. We think his father, King of Scoria Bay, is involved with his plans, and is the one who ultimately planned the plot against our princess here. Imprisoning Egan without sufficient evidence risks alienating Scoria Bay's allies. Since one of those countries is Crystalford, Prince Frederick's home, we need to tread carefully to not create a second problem."

Crystalford imported a lot of our meats and cold weather supplies, and losing their support could deeply impact Juniper's province. I nodded in agreement. We still needed to justify this to the Council as well, which meant being able to outshout Lord Denenbaum in an argument.

"What more do we need?" Ethan asked.

"We need to tie him directly to a high-ranking Belus priest, as they are the ones that are more vocal about the desired assassination. Or we need to prove what's in the letters that we think are going to his father. Or we need to prove he's wielding magic at all. He's smart to use powers that aren't visible in public."

"Is there anything any of us can do to help gather that information?" Spencer asked. His dedication to stopping the plot overwhelmed me, bringing tears to my eyes.

Father sat and thought for a moment. "Emberly, Spencer, you can speak in minds, but are you able to read minds you don't speak into?"

Spencer shook his head no. "I haven't figured that part out yet."

Emberly didn't speak, but how she looked at Father and he looked back, I could tell they're having a mental conversation. As the rest of us sat awkwardly waiting, I wondered if this was how it feels for others when Spencer and I did this.

Father cleared his throat. "OK, thoughts aren't an arrestable offense, but this can be helpful. Now, it's our belief that Egan and the Priests of Bel know that magic is alive and well in this country, and that the Oracles of the Gelid are assisting our people with mastering its use. So, the test will incorporate that knowledge. It will be intense, and Spencer, all three of you, will take part together. It is unwinnable. We hope that Egan will lose control as he realizes he is losing, and that he will either reveal magic, or that he will say the quiet parts out loud."

"So, you don't think we can cancel this?" I hated how my hopes felt dashed.

Father shook his head. "Unfortunately, no, we need to trip him into sharing more than he has so far."

"Do we still plan for me to be present?" I really dreaded being in the same room with a man who was working to kill me, even if Spencer would be there as well.

Father nodded. "Since they announced that aspect, it must happen. However, we are taking many precautions to provide safety to all in the room. Emberly, I need to meet with you to navigate how we could use the priestesses to enhance that security."

I nodded, unhappy to share a room with Egan, but knowing there wasn't much of a choice.

"OK, so the show must go on. Is it still delayed because of Egan's ankle break?" Ethan asked.

"Not currently. Our healer evaluated him personally, and she believes that whatever magic he has is helping to mend it quickly. It's not as fast as what our healers can do, but he is healing faster than he should."

"Do we know where this magic is coming from?"

"Our Priestesses back home are still trying to find any historical documents about that, but we don't know. All our texts showed that magic was traditionally granted to create a level playing field. There is one ancient text that hints that individual gods could grant powers to mortals at will, but we have no signs that any gods are awake, so that doesn't seem to be the answer."

"What are signs that gods are awake? Could they be happening in Scoria Bay, but not here?" Amyra asked.

"There are many signs, but the biggest one is that when a slumbering God wakes, the earth shifts and creates a mountain to welcome them home. There haven't been any newly formed mountains."

"Could this God have been awake the whole time? Maybe that's why Scoria Bay is so secretive about what they do?" The question came out before I even understood what I was saying.

'*Astute guess, Princess.*' The voice was unfamiliar, not Emberly's or Spencer's. It echoed in a weird, unsettling way that others hadn't.

My eyes widened. I motioned for a pen and paper. As soon as Juniper handed them to me, I wrote, *A man just spoke to me in my mind: Astute guess, Princess.*

All eyes shot to Spencer. He held his hands up and shook his head. I wrote again, *I've never heard this voice.*

Juniper rushed to her desk and pulled out a fresh bundle of twigs, lighting them to search the room for ears.

'That's right, Princess. We haven't had the pleasure of meeting yet.' The voice shared again. 'Though you have certainly shared many other pleasures with me. You're quite the naughty little girl.' A grotesque laughter fills my mind.

And again, I wrote. 'And he's able to read what I'm writing.'

I laid the pen down. I didn't know who or what this was. Emberly snatched the paper and showed it to Juniper. They turned to me, and the fear between the three of us was so heavy.

"OK, well, I think that this meeting has gone well. I'll send a message when it's time to reconvene." Father said, standing. Everyone else nodded, getting up to leave quietly.

I remained almost frozen in place. The only place to get answers was with a priestess, so I was not about to leave yet. Spencer and Amyra stayed too. I wasn't sure if it was in solidarity and support for me, or if they had questions for the Priestesses too.

We spent an excruciating ten minutes of waiting, while Juniper checked the walls and Emberly disappeared into the next room. Once Juniper checked her other room, both returned and addressed me.

"Come, we have a place." Emberly said, with a tone that left me feeling incredibly nervous. Amyra and Spencer stood with me, each placing their hands on my shoulders, offering the most support they can. I followed Emberly through the doorway.

Emberly opened another doorway within that room. Calling it a door was generous. It seemed like a giant hole cut out of the wall and shifted to the side. Emberly gestured to me to follow her through the hole.

The smell in this passageway once we left the room was moist, slightly mildewy, like this space was rarely used. The cobwebs and fine layer of dirt on the floor further hinted at that fact.

We walked down a set of stairs, lit only by a torch that Emberly had picked up. As we came to a twist in the stairs, I looked up to see Juniper use her wind magic to pull the boulder closed and light up her own torch. I had a horrible feeling about this, but it's too late to back out now.

'*We got this, Lyla.*' Spencer's voice was such a comfort to hear inside my head. Not like that other one. That voice felt so violating.

We reached a chamber, mostly empty. The room seemed to be carved out of a cave, with a solid stone floor turning to stone walls slanting into a ceiling. The only thing in the room was a boxy stone in the middle, that seemed to serve as some type of table.

"Where are we?" I asked.

"Not yet," Emberly chided. She pointed to Juniper, who was rolling a thick stone disc to cover the doorway. The two of them then joined hands and chanted a spell. As they chanted, a glimmering wind swirled around the room up to the peak in the ceiling and then fell to the stone table.

Once the shimmering stopped, Juniper finally spoke. "This space was carved before the Great War and was used to facilitate conversations without mind intrusions. There are ways to block people from your mind, but it takes time to learn."

A sob escaped from me, before I even knew I was reacting. Amyra reached out to hug me, and Spencer held his hand on my back. After a moment, I gathered myself together. "Uh, thank you. His voice was so intrusive, I felt so violated."

Emberly nodded, a look of compassion and comfort crossing her face. "Can you describe what he sounded like? Any details?"

I recounted the words said, the echoey, surreal sound of the voice, the unease it created.

"If I ever find him, he's dead." Spencer clenched his fist and clenched his jaw.

"Easy, killer," Emberly teased. "The sounds she described are reminiscent of one person described in our books. If it is, then we might have just found the answers we have been searching for, and it's not good news."

Juniper spoke up. "Do you remember, when I told you I needed to call the Priestesses here for help, that I mentioned a fairy tale that fit Egan's powers, that evil incarnate wielded the power to fight the Gods?"

Spencer and I nodded, but Amyra looked confused. Juniper quickly provided the fairy tale with a bit more detail. "We teach this tale to explain to our children why magic left our realm. In it, a single entity, evil incarnate, walked this land and fought the Gods for full control of the land. The fairy tale says that the Gods banished him, sending him to an eternal prison, and removing all power from the land until people could again be trusted with it. We recite the story as if the entity is a person, but our researchers have found a potential source for the fairy tale. In that source, the entity is a lost God. The God of Death."

"We don't have a God of Death, though?" Spencer asked, confused.

Juniper smiled. "Not anymore. That used to be one of our gods. He led men in the Great War, to create inequalities in the realm, because inequalities mean more death. He was supposed to be sent to a prison he couldn't escape, to live out his punishment until the prophecy could be fulfilled."

"So, we are supposed to have eight gods and goddesses?" I asked.

Emberly shook her head. "No, nine. The prophecy foretells of the ninth Goddess coming to life."

"And you're telling me that the God of Death is talking to me in my mind?"

Juniper and Emberly exchanged a glance, then both nodded. "It might be. And if that's who it is, then we need to teach you how to block people from your mind, to protect yourself. As long as he can access your mind, you simply aren't safe. He can find you and send anyone he wants after you."

"Is he the one who wants me dead?" I was afraid of the answer. I didn't want to hear it said out loud. Why did I say that?

Spencer pulled me in for a hug. He must have heard my thoughts spiraling.

"Most likely."

"Shouldn't everyone in that meeting learn how to block him out of our minds?" Amyra asked. "I don't want him in mine." I reached over and pulled her into this hug Spencer started.

Emberly nodded. "Yes, I can work with all three of you to learn that. Spencer already has had some lessons, but he needs more. Spencer, I'll need your help too. Once you're able to do it, I'll need to use you to teach others. We test their skills by trying to penetrate. Unfortunately, you and I are the only two here that have that gift. It's too late in the season to bring more priestesses down."

I felt Spencer nod, his chin brushing the top of my head. "Yes, of course."

"We need to postpone the next tournament event until everyone that will be in the room can guard their minds. Egan will benefit from reading minds. He probably already knows what Father has planned, and that he's going to lose this tournament if Spencer is alive." My thoughts just ran straight out of my mouth without filtering.

"Maybe this is enough information that we can imprison Egan and cancel the tournament. Even if it starts a diplomatic nightmare, we need to consider the threat Egan poses if he can channel power through a God." Amyra offered.

The five of us stood in a semi-circle, mulling over her words.

Finally, I spoke. "I need to meet with Father, and the General of the Army, and prepare for this."

Everyone nodded. "Can we use this chamber, Juniper?" I ask.

"Princess, all my rooms are yours to use. I will ask the researchers at the Temple to see if they can find a warding spell for your personal chambers, so that you can feel safe there."

CHAPTER 28

I t took three agonizingly long days to get Father and the General to agree to the meeting. I asked Spencer to attend, and Juniper of course, but limited it to just the five of us. In that time, Juniper could use various objects to ward my chambers and Spencer's helping keep our minds free of this God of Death. Ivy and Amyra had taken to sleeping in my chambers for their own comforts as well. Emberly had given us some techniques that seem to work to guard our minds. I hadn't heard from Death, as I started calling him, but I didn't know if that's because it's working or if it's because he was letting me think it was working so he could continue to listen. I wasn't the only one worried about that, so Emberly had really been pushing hard on us to keep our guards up, even when in our warded rooms. She worked with Spencer and me all day until we were exhausted. It was already becoming second nature to protect my mind.

Spencer and I had arrived early for this meeting with Father and the General. Spencer challenged my mental defenses while we waited in Juniper's office. To the outside world, we probably looked like a couple of lovebirds. It felt a little surreal. Just a few months ago, I was positive that no man existed in the world that could be tolerable. Who could ever compare to my Amyra? The thought of losing her made me feel like I couldn't breathe. But something with Spencer caused me to drop my guard, and I couldn't be happier. I never imagined picking a husband who could recognize and respect that I loved Amyra first, and that I would always love her.

'*Aw, but will you love me too?*' Spencer's voice broke through. I grinned.

'*Guess you'll have to work hard and see what that gets you.*' I tease back.

'*I'll work hard all night long if I have to.*'

'*I bet you will.*' I bit my lower lip, looking up at him through my lashes.

A knock sounded, ending the flirting. I put my wall back up and then felt him tapping against it. He squeezed my hand, his way of praising me when he can't whisper into my mind.

Juniper opened the door and allowed Father and a General in. I realize that this man was a newer one I haven't met. I stood to greet them, with Spencer following suit. "Hello, good morning, Father and General…" I read his name tape and emphasize his unfamiliarity. "General Simms, it seems. I thought General Kellen would join us. No offense, Sir, we just had sensitive information and requested him specifically to manage that."

Father allowed one corner of his lips to curl, a nonverbal acknowledgement on his otherwise stoic face. I would bet anything that he had the same objection in his office.

"Yes, well, the General is busy this morning, and I'm available. He read me into the situation."

I raised my eyebrow at Juniper, just to catch her writing a note. She folded the paper and then turned to a bookshelf. When she turned back a moment later, the paper wasn't in her hands. If I didn't know that she waved it away, I would have assumed she shoved it between books. She positioned herself in front of her desk, and I knew she was both waiting for a reply and hiding the magic from this man. The priestesses hadn't vetted him.

"All the same, as the heir to the throne, I expect you and other leadership to check with me before making such unilateral decisions. Sometimes, other matters must yield to my meetings.

This is one of those times, but the timeliness of this issue is also a factor. Tell me, Sir, is the General in the castle at this moment, or has his pressing needs taken him off the grounds?"

I was hoping to buy time for Juniper to get the information she needed, all while feeling this man out and how he intended to treat me as his queen and his boss's boss.

He bowed. "My apologies, Your Highness. I will speak to the General about this request to ensure you approve deviations."

I nodded and glanced at Juniper. She was still waiting.

"Thank you, Sir. Can you tell me what the General informed you about for this meeting? I'll have to adjust how much information I present once I have a grasp on your knowledge."

'*God, it's hot to watch you make this man squirm. Guard up.*' I shot Spencer a glance, both of gratitude in his reminder, and slight embarrassment of his praise. He knew how to distract me with just a few words.

General Simms explained what he knew about Egan, but mentioned nothing about the Priests, our suspicions with the King of Scoria Bay, or show any familiarity with magic. He had positioned himself between Juniper and me, facing me, still standing. As he was explaining his knowledge, Juniper received her note, and after reading it, she gave me a nod.

"OK, very well. I'll have significantly more explaining to do, as he left off more information. Juniper, will you open the door for the meeting room?"

Father's smirk returned, along with a look of curiosity. No one had taken him to that room yet. I wasn't sure if Emberly or Spencer had been working with him about mind shielding.

Juniper nodded and invited us to her next room. General Simms took the lead, which gave him a full show of watching Juniper move the wall without touching it. His jaw dropped. "Uh, yeah, I didn't get those details. Can you…"

"Yes, we will. But first, if you will, follow me." I reached for a torch just as Juniper lights it and assumed the lead. Spencer was close behind me, never one to let me get far while we walked through these tunnels. Juniper took the rear so she could close the doors behind us.

Once we arrived in the room, I placed the torch in the holder and found my seat at the head of the table. Over the last couple of weeks, we had taken to making this cave room to be a bit more comfortable by bringing chairs, pillows, and even some blankets down to help protect against the damp chill. Juniper closed the room and then warded it. Once she completed her spell, I spoke again.

"A lot has happened in the last few days, since we last met, Father. I know this room isn't one that we are used to, but you'll understand why when I'm done. First, let me fill in the blanks for General Simms."

I explained magic to him. Well, I asked Juniper to explain it to him. She had a knack for sharing only the information needed. We also provided him with the other holes in the theory about who's backing Egan, and what magic he had used to be such a threat. Once he heard the magic, he rubbed his neck and said, "Oh, the precautions we're taking against that scrawny kid make more sense now."

Spencer didn't bother to stop his chuckle from escaping.

"And now we are to the last meeting Father attended. During that meeting, someone spoke to me in my mind, a voice I didn't recognize that deeply unsettled me. He didn't identify himself, and we ended the meeting immediately to avoid discussing things when we didn't know who this was and how he fit into the situation. After the meeting, Emberly and Juniper brought Spencer, Amyra, and me down here to talk. This room's design protects against mind reading, and we added a ward to keep information spoken here confidential. What we realized is that the voice I heard must have been the God of Death."

I paused, not sure why. Father used the pause. "Sorry, we don't have a God of Death? What do you mean?"

"We used to. He caused the Last Great War and was supposed to be banished. It seems as if that banishment has ended early, and we strongly believe he's behind the Priests of Bel and Egan."

Father had the deepest sigh. It was General Simms' reaction that felt the most unsettling. The color had drained from his face, his lips parting slightly, yet no words came. His fingers twitched at his side, then curled into a trembling fist, his gaze locked on the stone table as though it might rise and strike him down where he sat. Finally, he spoke. "Yes, the General should have been here. I will make sure he doesn't underestimate you again, Princess."

I nodded. I'm not sure what else to say to such a statement, but appreciate his acknowledgement.

"We are about to start a war, Lyla." Father said, and I agreed.

"I know. I think we are past the point of avoiding that."

And with that, we settled in and planned how to handle this plot to end my life.

CHAPTER 29

The day arrived to put the plan into place. As far as people know, this was to be the second tournament challenge. There were two schedules floating out there. One covered what the public knows, and the other was the plan to arrest Egan. After Egan's arrest, Father intended to address Lord Denenbaum as well, but he hadn't revealed his plans to me.

The day would begin with commencing the second event. My event planners recommended announcing the event's start time and, later, the results, although it wasn't intended for a public audience.

Ivy and Amyra helped me into my gown for the day. We had Eliza modify the gown to include hidden armor within the corset. It was incredibly uncomfortable, but I appreciated the extra layer of protection. The dress reflected the colors of the season, one of my favorites. The red and oranges of the leaves are always so vibrant this time of year. Eliza used a large red ruby at the center of the sweetheart neckline and scattered smaller red gems and glass beads across the rest of my neckline, which helped to draw the attention away from the rigidity of the rest of the bodice. Ivy gained a new tiara for me as well, featuring a red ruby at the center, with red and deep orange glass gems shaped into colorful fall leaves accenting it. I almost felt like I was wearing a crown of fire.

The plan was to use the announcement of the second event to commence to announce instead that Spencer was the winner and that we would be wed this spring. We expected Egan becoming enraged at the deviation in planning and the realization that he was not to be Elthas' King. We hoped he then could not control his powers, like the way he was at that dinner many weeks ago. At that point, we could easily arrest him. The Priestesses would be nearby, ready to contain most of his reaction, if needed. Amyra and I had been working to create walls with our ability to control water and earth, but we had made nothing that can stop a stick penetrating it, let alone something worth protecting. We had also been testing to see if I could connect to fire since my eyes turn red when I had heightened emotions. Unfortunately, we hadn't had luck on this avenue.

We also hoped that others might act out, not too many that we couldn't handle it, but enough to bring attention to Lord Denenbaum and any other conspirators. General Kellen had agreed to station many of his men among the crowd in plain clothes, supplementing the castle guard, in case fighting broke out.

I was nervous. Provoking Egan, and potentially a God of Death, was intimidating, but it was necessary to get this plot against me under control. I hoped that word of the spectacle would prevent Scoria Bay's allies from blindly siding with them, but I didn't think I would believe a report that includes magic if I wasn't a witness.

It was time to make this announcement. My stomach flopped, and I worried I might be sick. Ivy was standing behind me, staring at me in the mirror. "Are you ok, Lyla?"

I nodded. "I can't say I'm excited about this, but I am ready for this to be over."

Amyra and Ivy both nodded their agreements. "Let's go, my Love." Amyra holds her arm out, inviting me to grasp her elbow.

They planned to make this announcement at the grand

castle entry, an enormous staircase from the courtyard to the castle doors. This was the traditional place for major royal news, such as announcements of betrothals, births of new heirs, and so on. The stairs had three landings since they went so high. Father, Ethan, and I planned to stand at the highest point, and the princes would stand at the landing just below us, ten steps lower. We expected the Council and Priestesses to stand at the lowest landing, and we invited the crowd to stand around the courtyard, but not within ten feet of the bottom of the stairs.

People packed the place. My anxiety spun out of control. *'Breathe, baby girl. And guard your mind. But most importantly, breathe, we planned for this.'*

Relief flooded my emotions when I heard Spencer's voice. I searched for him and saw him standing right next to Frederick and Egan, positioned between them. I didn't know if I wanted to be mad at him for standing right next to Egan, or to be grateful that he positioned himself to keep Frederick away, since he was just as innocent as the rest of this crowd.

I joined Father on the platform, as planned. Ivy and Amyra stood to the side at the top of these stairs, along with the personal assistants for Father and Ethan. I looked through the crowd and found each of the Priestesses positioned as they promised. The Council looked unaware of the plan. I was supposed to seek their approval for this selection before telling the world, but we couldn't risk Lord Denenbaum or anyone else telling Egan in private. I knew that I'd have to answer to this decision later.

I looked around to take in the crowd. It seemed like the entire city showed up for this announcement, which surprised me. I didn't expect them to care about hearing something starting behind closed doors. I noticed the sky was blue, not a cloud to be seen, and it was clear enough to see the sea. Just before the horizon, you could barely make out the small islands that mark the beginning of Scoria Bay's territory gently sitting on the water.

Father's hand reached out to my shoulder, showing it was time to speak. We both stepped forward, on the edge of the landing, so that our voices could carry far enough to be heard by everyone. A trumpeter standing on the side provided the signal to calm down, and the crowd stilled.

"Thank you, everyone, for arriving this morning," I began. My stomach started doing its own somersaults, and I wondered if eating breakfast this morning was wise. "I am honored to have all of you here, to see through this tournament to select my betrothed, and to find you, the people of Elthas, a King worthy to lead you." I paused for the applause, waiting for it to die down before I continued my announcement.

"I am thrilled to announce that the search is over." I smiled as the crowd erupted into an even more energetic celebration. "Rather than continuing with the Tournament, I'd like to announce the winner. He has worked hard to prove himself since we met the evening of the ball."

I glanced down to the princes. Frederick and Egan seem shocked, and Spencer's attempt to match their shock was lacking. He was certainly no actor, which made me smile.

"He proved himself worthy in the first round, and while I can't speak to how he'd have handled the other two events, I am confident that he will be the King you all deserve."

Egan's face was darkening. I checked my mental defenses and felt the wall. I worried we were wrong about Death not being able to get through those mental barriers. It was too late to change course now. Egan was shocked enough.

"I'm pleased to inform you that our next king, and my husband, will be Prince Spencer."

I offered a genuine smile as I looked around the crowd. So many celebrated, but some were upset and jeering. I looked back at the princes and saw Egan reaching for something in the folds of his shirt. I shouted to Spencer, trying to get words out, but no sound came out. He reacted, understanding my intention. He shoved Frederick to the side and then reached for his own dagger. Time seemed to slow as my fear for Spencer's safety overcame me.

Two castle guards restrained Egan's arms before any further

moves could happen. I felt relief, and the adrenaline slowed, hopeful that this meant there would be no show of magic.

Then Egan pointed at me and growled, "You, you are trash, filth. I should have ended you in that dining room like he told me!" Lightning shot across the air at me from his hand. His strike hit me in my stomach, knocking the wind out of me as I fell to my knees.

My emotions erupted, and before I could compose myself, pebbles rose in the air as I stood. I looked down, grateful to find the armor did it's job, even though the fabric burned at the impact site.

The ground shook.

Then gasps sounded all around me. I looked at the crowd to see what the gasps were for, and people were looking horrified, pointing out to the sea. I followed their reaction, and saw an island rising above the others, fire shooting into the skies above. The perfect blue sky marred by white and black smoke. The clouds grew rapidly, quickly covering the land, blocking the sun. Within minutes, ash started falling from the sky.

"Everyone, take shelter!" I heard lots of shouting all around me. Did Death do this?

I made eye contact with Egan.

"If you did this, if you killed my people, I will end your entire kingdom. Elthas doesn't deserve to survive." He swore his oath with so much vitriol that I could feel the cold black void of his soul.

Spencer reached me, standing in front to protect me. I felt frozen by all that was happening.

"You will never reach her," Spencer promised.

Egan replied, but castle guards, plain clothed soldiers, and villagers all swarmed between us, so I couldn't hear. People were rushing into the castle to take cover from the burning ashes falling from the sky. I coughed as Amyra grabbed one of my arms and Spencer took hold of the other as they guided me inside. Somewhere near me, I heard Ivy rushing us to get inside.

It took hours for the ash to slow down enough for people to return to their homes. The islands still had smoke billowing into the sky, but winds had shifted to blow it over open water. In all the chaos, Egan had escaped the guards who had him. Once we found that out, Father had the General and Guard Captain organize so that no one left the grounds without their knowledge. While the guards checked for Egan, Father had all of us shelter in Juniper's office all day into the evening. He hoped that by choosing her space, it would be unlikely for Egan to find me and carry out the plot. Ethan, Ivy, Amyra, and Spencer all joined us, and Juniper had the Priestesses assemble with us for added protection, for them and for us. Juniper's office, at the hall's end, simplified defense, and the cavern offered extra protection should anyone breach the door.

While waiting here, I used my gift to lift all the ash covering everyone, helping to clean them as best as I could.

"Juniper?" I asked, as I stood by the windows, watching the ash swirl out through the cracks in the glass. "Egan accused me of causing that… whatever that is. I don't know what even happened. Do you think I did it?"

Juniper's face told me everything I feared, but I still waited for her answer. She took a moment before talking.

"Yes, I felt the magic gathering and surging, and it came from you. You caused a fiery eruption, made the earth tremble, and caused *rivers of fire that reshape the ocean.* You are the Queen foretold, and Spencer is the King."

I looked around. Every time my eyes landed on a priestess, she thumped her chest and knelt before us. I looked at Father and saw pride as he lowered his gaze to offer me that same respect. I looked back out to the pillar of fire and ash spewing from Scoria Bay. "*She shall cause the land's heart to bleed flames into the sky and will herald a change in the realm itself.*" I whisper.

What do I do now? What change is coming?

CHAPTER 30

Ash fell from the sky for a full week. Since Zoya was the only other brown-eyed priestess in the city, she joined me, and we worked with the merchants and farmers to clear the ash from the fields and the open-air market every day. During these times, especially while out on the field, Zoya taught me everything she could about the prophecy. People commonly believed that our gods slept, but nobody ever shared the prophecy of their awakening. The history of the war was also incredibly vague and unhelpful, for being something that altered our way of life.

Spencer was busy too, learning from Emberly how to use his gifts to navigate diplomatic situations without people being aware. I learned only women received magical abilities before the war. Gods had told people that magic was an equalizer, to allow us a fighting chance when they tried to subjugate us. Anyone who knew that much wouldn't expect Spencer to have his gift. He learned how to hide it from those who know about magic and practiced using it without suspicion. The priestesses didn't know if his gifts meant that everyone in Elthas would have access to magic now.

I felt no small amount of satisfaction at the knowledge that the gods and goddesses wanted to avoid exactly the oppressive ways I secretly rebelled against. It helped me to feel more connected to them, and that, in turn, strengthened my ability to use magic.

Once the ash slowed to a level that Zoya could handle on her own, Father urged me to attend the following day's council meeting. He had been trying to navigate relations with the Council after making such an announcement without their input, but couldn't keep Lord Denenbaum and Lord Luther from demanding my presence. Until the coronation, they had the right to order me to attend their meetings when they wanted. Father was only just barely able to prevent them from sending royal guards after me, only because I was doing so much work to help preserve the crops and goods that our kingdom desperately needed.

So, I attended the Council meeting a week after I created that volcano. I took Spencer with me, too. I hoped Spencer could help me expect problems; it would be his first meeting with Lord Denenbaum, which might provide important insight into his connection to the God of Death and Prince Egan. He wouldn't pry into his mind. That's too risky. He can still find important information by reading his haze.

The morning of the meeting, I first headed to my mother's old office. The room remained as she had decorated it, and I almost regretted choosing it. It still smelled like her, and the pain from the grief almost felt too much. But no one knew I was using it, and Juniper has taught me the spell to check for ears, so we knew it was secure. I made a mental note to get Amyra and Ivy to help me redecorate the room. They'd handle the process with care and help me feel more comfortable in here.

Spencer was to meet me here, and he knocked on the door just as I wrapped up the spell to search for ears. Technically, we are supposed to have a chaperone, but I didn't much care about these traditions in the volcano's wake, as they protected archaic notions of a woman's value related to men. I may not have the same connection to the gods the priestesses did, but I felt it in my heart of hearts that they found this tradition useless, at least at this stage of betrothal.

As the door opened, I put the burning twigs out and tucked them into the box Juniper gave me. I glanced to the door to ensure it's just Spencer and offered him a smile as he closed it behind him.

"Are you ready for this?" He asked me. He quickly crossed the room to join me by the desk. I leaned into a hug from him, and as he released me, his hands naturally fell to my waist to keep me close.

"Zoya and I spent many hours talking about it all while we were alone in the fields, clearing them. I don't know how it will go, but I know what needs to be done."

I looked up at him. "The question is, are you ready? This won't be a polite, calm meeting. I need you to promise that you won't speak up or react unless I signal to you. I also need you to share with me if you sense any sign of alliance with Egan."

I hadn't talked to anyone about my plans for this meeting. I wouldn't be making friends and may even leave the meeting with enemies.

I felt Spencer inside my mind, looking for what's left unsaid. I didn't guard against his search, just stared up at him, waiting for his reaction. After a moment, he smiled.

"My Queen, I love you more every time I see how your beautiful mind works."

My breath hitched. He's never said he loved me before. I hadn't even had the time to stop and consider such a feeling. My mind raced, not sure how to respond. Spencer leaned down for a kiss. *'Don't worry about words with me. I will always have your back, even if you never match my feelings. I'm here to serve you, Lyla.'*

With his reassurance, I leaned into the kiss, the warmth of his lips sending a slow, melting heat through me. A hint of nutmeg and cinnamon lingered on his breath, rich and intoxicating, as if he had been savoring something forbidden.

Another knock on the door signaled our guards were ready to escort us down. I refused to navigate anywhere without them at this point. With Egan missing and no way of knowing whether Lord Denenbaum knew his whereabouts, the risk was too great.

Spencer and I ended our kiss, and he offered a smile with the same reassurance that his thoughts provided. I leaned into one more hug before saying, "Let's go start a fight."

CHAPTER 31

J ust walking into the meeting room was enough to start chaos before I even spoke. Besides the Council, I saw Father and Ethan present already and was grateful for their silent support as they sat in their respective seats. The rest of the Council struggled with this, choosing instead to shout at me. Spencer's apprehension was palpable, since this was his first invited meeting. I tried to offer the same mental reassurance he just provided me as I took my seat at the head of the table. I motioned to Spencer to take the one to my right hand, the one reserved for the King.

Then I sat quietly, waiting for the Councilors to stop their shouting, ignoring them until they calmed down. I knew they had a lot of issues to hash out with me right now, but that didn't mean I had to listen on any terms but mine. I fully intended to set the tone for how they would address their grievances with me going forward, among other things.

Eventually, they settled down, but most remained standing. I made a note that Juniper was sitting in her usual seat, with a smirk on her face, avoiding eye contact with me. I wondered briefly if she and Spencer were talking.

"Thank you for calming down." I started while still sitting. "Today's discussion will cover many issues, but I'd like to start by explaining my stance. I expect you will extend me the grace of listening without interruption."

I paused here, waiting for those standing to nod their agreement and sit down. Instead, Lord Denenbaum refused. He quickly became the last one standing. I turned all my attention to him to stare him down. He returned the stare, inviting me to call him out.

"Lord Denenbaum, you may take your seat."

He seemed a bit surprised to see me issue a directive instead of requesting his compliance. But he still stood. Father shifted into a position that allowed him to signal with his hand for an arrest, causing the royal guards in the room to shift into a slightly more defensive posture.

"With all due respect, Princess Lyla, we have a foreigner in the room. We cannot start the meeting until the uninvited guest leaves."

"We have no uninvited guests in the room. Prince Spencer is where he belongs."

Several of the Councilors shifted in their seats. Technically, I was out of order, since I wasn't queen yet. Tradition dictated that the one marrying into the position not attend these meetings until after their coronation. Tradition could find itself a comfortable grave to lie in, as I didn't intend to leave Spencer out of discussions related to our security.

"Princess Lyla, this is a most unusual circumstance, and we will not allow people not vetted through our military intelligence to attend this meeting." Lord Denenbaum had some absolute gall to use this specific excuse.

I raised an eyebrow. "You are not the one with the agenda for the meeting, Lord Denenbaum. I am. Prince Spencer is already aware of the issues I am about to discuss and has a higher clearance than you on these matters. He is going to be your king soon, whether you wish for it or not, so excluding him from this meeting is pointless. Now sit down, or else you may find yourself escorted out."

I stood, showing how serious I was on this matter. Lord

Denenbaum finally noticed the guards positioned to act and sat, conceding defeat.

I stayed standing as I continued.

"Again, thank you. A lot has happened over the last week, and much of it involved decisions I could not invite the council to discuss with me. These decisions stem from the discovery of a plot to take my life before the coronation."

I paused here, expecting some reaction, and knowing that this is a prime place for Spencer to check hazes and thoughts. I wished for Emberly to help him.

'*Lord Denenbaum is unsurprised by this news.*' I knew I could rely on Spencer to catch this key piece of information. Out of the corner of my eye, I noticed Spencer shift his head to get the attention of Juniper as I continued.

"After discussing this with General Kellen, we had decided that the information needed to be kept secret while his teams worked to gather more information. We had some suspicion that there was someone within this very Council who was working with the would-be assassin in this attempt, and we could not risk sharing with them."

Lord Greenhow, Amyra's father, stood. "Surely, Princess Lyla, you know who it is now? I don't see anyone missing."

I smiled at him, knowing that his outburst was out of genuine concern for me as his daughter's closest friend.

"I'm not at liberty to say, Lord Greenhow." I answered, offering a smile, and then I moved on.

"Over the last few months, I got to know all three princes well and found that Prince Spencer would be the one with which I'd work best to continue the peace and prosperity our kingdom had enjoyed. While I wish I could have presented this to you first, the General, the King, and I decided that this would put me at higher risk, as well as Prince Spencer. My decision to select him would not change with any more tournament events, so it was determined that they were unnecessary."

'*Denenbaum is getting angrier. His haze is darkening and swirling. Please watch him.*' Great. He was certainly involved. I motioned to Juniper, just subtly enough for Spencer to catch on. '*She knows too, and she says that he has no signs of controlling magic.*' I nodded. I was so grateful to have Spencer here for this.

"Now, I understand that you're upset that I cancelled the Tournament. However, it was necessary to ensure the safety of not just myself, but the people. The plot, as we understood it, could have involved a lot of civilian casualties and I decided that risking the lives of my people, and those visiting, was not worth the boost to our economy. I have full faith in our kingdom to strengthen the economy in other ways."

I looked at Denenbaum, and it didn't take Spencer's gift to see his anger seething just under the surface. His jaw clenched so tightly it might crack, and the deep lines on his aged face sharpened with barely restrained fury.

"There is one other concern I want to raise before I address questions. At the time of that eruption, Prince Egan was already reacting with terrible anger. Before he disappeared in the crowd, he made a clear and direct threat to Elthas, blaming me for the explosion."

I paused again, watching Denenbaum a bit more closely. While he was still quite angry, no surprise reflected on his face, despite the murmurs and gasps from the others. He must have known this, too. But did Egan tell him, or did someone else?

"If Prince Egan went home and told his king there is reason to blame us, I fear they will bring their navy to our city and kingdom and bring war to our doorsteps. I regret the loss of relations with Scoria Bay, but I also want you to know that my announcement was not the reason it soured. Prince Egan was one of the persons involved in the plot against me. The Generals are preparing our army for the possibility of war." I take a steadying breath before finishing my statement. "Thank you for listening. What concerns do you have?"

Father stood before anyone could ask a question. "Princess Lyla, I want to first say thank you for coming to share with us and address concerns about this council. Can you clarify how do you intend to handle the threat within the council?"

I nodded. "Yes, of course. I don't intend to clarify that

currently, given the circumstances. I will address this when the time is right."

I don't understand why Father would ask that. He knew the answer, and he knew I wouldn't share that here.

Lord Greenhow stood. "Princess Lyla, you said that Prince Spencer is already aware of this plot. Can you elaborate on what his role is?"

Was he questioning if Spencer was involved? Or Spencer's knowledge about Egan? Could he somehow know Spencer reads minds and could incriminate people? I glanced at Juniper. She didn't even look up from her notes, which I took to show my fears were a little out there. "Prince Spencer was present during Prince Egan's first attempt on me and his quick actions have prevented injury. He has since provided valuable information from the training they did together preparing for the first tournament event. He has been very useful in ensuring the success of our efforts to stay ahead of any attempts to harm me. And since he is to be king, I felt it right to have him join us and learn more about our meetings, effective immediately. He needs to learn about our ways as quickly as possible to allow us to respond to such outside threats."

Lord Greenhow nodded, satisfied with this answer. I looked over at Denenbaum. I expected more protesting from him if he was part of this plot, some type of acting to deflect any suspicions. He was keeping his head angled towards his notes but has a vaguely familiar glaze to his eyes. I turned to Spencer to get his attention.

'*What's wrong?*' He probed.

'*Can you get into Denenbaum's mind? Is he talking to someone?*'

Spencer shifted his focus. While he did that, I took one last look around the table. "Any further questions? I expected more."

"Yes, actually, Princess." Lord Luther stood up to address me, letting the disdain he had for me drip as he said the word princess. I looked towards him, bracing for trouble.

"Can you address the rumors that you were responsible for the attack on Scoria Bay?"

'*It's not good, Lyla. We need to go to the cave room.*' Spencer's voice caused me to pause before answering. His urgency and tone felt disturbing.

"I don't see how I could be responsible for a volcanic explosion near that kingdom when everyone could plainly see me standing on the steps of this very castle, telling people my intention to marry Prince Spencer. Are you not aware that volcanos are naturally occurring disasters?"

Juniper disguised her snort by rubbing her nose, while Father allowed his proud smile to show a moment longer than considered polite. I looked around the table one last time.

"Thank you for your time, Councilors. If there's no further questions about my decisions, then I will take my leave." As I turned to leave, Juniper, Father, Ethan, and Spencer stood to follow me. Whatever Spencer was about to share didn't seem promising.

CHAPTER 32

We were joined by all the priestesses in the cavern, which amplified my worries. I settled into my seat at the table, with Amyra on one side and Spencer on the other. Both offered their hand to me, and I held them together in my lap. The rest settled in, and once Juniper sealed up the door, Spencer didn't waste a moment with niceties.

"During that meeting, Lyla noticed Denenbaum had a glazed overlook. His mind was wide open, and I could hear a conversation. Well, sort of. I couldn't make out actual words, but I could sense the feelings. There was someone speaking to him, and he was responding. He felt fear, intense fear. And the other feeling I felt was anger, but not from him. The other's words held that. That was a male voice. I couldn't say it's the God of Death, but the power I felt," he trailed off, and his face twisted. "It wasn't good. If that's not a God, it's a powerful person."

An icy wave washed over me, and my skin turned to ice. I knew it was Death.

"Well, now we know. He's involved." Ethan offered.

"What do we do?" Amyra asked, panic lacing her voice. I squeezed her hand, using our language to say I love her and that it'll be ok. Her expression showed appreciation, but disbelief, when I looked up at her. I couldn't blame her; I didn't believe me either.

"We plan. We strategize." Juniper said in a determined tone. Her face reflected the strength we needed.

I inhaled deeply, drawing strength from her to lead us away from the panic. "If it wasn't a God, how far away could that other person have been, at most?"

Emberly answered, "Not much more than a room or two away. These walls act as a dampening agent, preventing long distance connections."

"So, then it's most likely Death?" My heart fell. "Do we know how close he has to be to enter our minds?"

"We have no clue. The Priestesses at the temple have found nothing to tell us from the past. For all we know, he could still be entombed, though it's more likely that he has been present in Scoria Bay, and maybe elsewhere."

"Do we know if Denenbaum has been to Scoria Bay?" I turned to Father for that answer.

"He was last there two years ago. He went for official business." Father replied.

"Did you send him, or did he volunteer?"

"I selected him. He didn't want to go and tried to make a case for another Councilor to go."

I nodded. "So, if Death is at Scoria Bay, it's safe to assume that's where they met, and he's been in contact with Denenbaum for the last two years."

I turned to Ethan. "How are things with you and Katelle? Do you think she's involved? Is she using you?"

He struggled to hide his emotions.

"I genuinely don't know." His voice was almost a whisper, reflecting the betrayal he felt from her. Juniper, who was sitting next to him, offers a comforting hand to his shoulder. He turned and offered her a small smile.

"I will end her if she is. No one hurts my brother and gets away with it."

He offered me a look of gratitude mixed in with heartbreak.

My nervous energy continued to rise. I stood up to pace. My emotions caused the flame on the torches to flare up.

"I can't do this anymore. We need to manage this. I hate living in fear of my life. Why in the blazing HELL is this goddamn God targeting me?" I turned to Juniper and Emberly. "Please, what can I do to end this?"

The plea kicked everyone into motion. We brainstormed, and we planned. I practiced my breathing to keep the magic at normal levels as each step of this plan fell into place. By nightfall, Denenbaum will be in one of our deepest dungeons, hopefully isolating him from the god. In a few days, Emberly would join one of the best interrogators to talk to him. They would also restrict the movement of his family and advisors. Emberly and Spencer will work to clear them one by one, using their abilities, and working with interrogators.

And Father and I would brace the kingdom for war.

CHAPTER 33

J ust a few days later, I met with Father, Juniper, Emberly, General Kellen, and General Simms in Kellen's office. Emberly and Simms had just finished interrogating Lord Denenbaum, and they were updating us.

"He revealed his connections, though he doesn't realize he did." Emberly stated. "He was not very talkative, but his mind was completely open."

General Simms interrupted. "Grubby bastard just kept taunting that I'd find nothing out. He really got on my last nerve, lucky to be alive."

I smiled before redirecting back to Emberly. "What did he share?"

Emberly sighed, clearly frustrated with Simms. "He provided quite the clear picture of meeting with the Priests of Bel when he was last at Scoria Bay, and the plot that the King and God of Death shared with him to murder the Queen and use Ethan to get to the throne. Scoria Bay wants this land, and they won't stop at anything for it."

"Do you know if he was the murderer, or did he just help the one who did?" Father asked. His face had tightened, his lips pressed into a thin line.

"He didn't direct his thoughts to that night, so I don't know yet. I know they planned to kill Lyla if Ethan wasn't the heir.

The God of Death stressed it was important to do that as soon as possible if Ethan wasn't heir."

"Are we able to trust his thoughts? What if he was intentionally misleading?" I asked.

A rapid knock sounded on the door, followed by royal guards entering without permission. Normally this would be an egregious error on their part, and the guard that spoke bowed to show his contrition as he interrupted. "Pardon me, we have an urgent matter at the front gate. A stranger, unable and unwilling to produce credentials, is demanding an audience with Princess Lyla. She calls her the Queen. She says that the Princess is expecting her."

Everyone turned to me, but I didn't know what was going on and shook my head slowly.

"I'm expecting no one. Did this woman travel with anyone? How big is her traveling group?"

"She came alone, on foot. She's also wearing peculiar clothes, not from around here." The guard answered.

I looked around at the others. "This is unfamiliar territory for me. I don't know what to do."

General Kellen spoke up. "Disarm her if she is armed and escort her into the meeting space next to the dining hall. Station four men inside and double up every door into the room. Have someone bring her warm food and water."

General Simms nodded, motioned to the guards to follow him, and left. The guards closed the door behind him.

"We should postpone Denenbaum's interrogation so that I can attend this meeting." Emberly announced. "We don't know who this is, and I will gather significantly more information than anyone else present."

"I agree. I will not enter the room until Emberly confirms it's safe. Send a guard for Spencer and for Zoya. Have them meet me in my chambers. If she's calling me a queen, then I need my king around, and Zoya can help defend against any potential dangers."

"Your chambers?" Father questioned.

"I am not dressed to meet a guest calling me a queen.

Amyra and Ivy will help me look the part while Emberly investigates."

Father smiled. "It's those details that will make you successful."

We stood and ended the meeting, agreeing to meet later.

❋

IN MY CHAMBERS, Amyra and Ivy helped me find a dress. We selected a honey hued dress with gold and brown embroidered ivy leaves around the bodice and down the upper half of the skirt. Amyra braided some of my hair to pull it away from my face while still leaving it flowing down my back. While she was working on my hair, Spencer and Zoya both arrived.

"The guards wouldn't tell us what's happening. Is everything ok?" Spencer asked, concern dripping through his tone.

"Yes, I'm sorry. They likely weren't told themselves. I was in a debrief from Denenbaum's interrogation. Someone walked up to the gates of the castle and asked for Queen Lyla. She told them I was expecting her. Emberly went to meet her right away while I presented myself more like a queen before going to meet this woman."

Spencer nodded, like this is a normal, everyday occurrence. "Getting used to these events?" Amyra teased.

He offered a small smile. "I wouldn't say I'm used to them, but they aren't phasing me as easily."

"Pardon, but why did you send for me?" Zoya asked.

"Truthfully, we don't know who she is, but having you to help with defenses will make it much safer to meet her. I need you." I didn't mean to sound so desperate, but with a magic wielding cult following the God of Death trying to kill me, it sometimes reached that level. Zoya nodded in understanding.

"What's the plan?"

I ran down what I hope would happen and asked Zoya and Spencer to enter the room with me. We came up with what we hoped was a plan to cover any likely reason for this person to be coming to me.

After Amyra fastened a tiara to my hair, we hurried down to the meeting room where they were holding this person. I noted the locations of the extra guards and paused at the door to double check my appearance while Spencer reached out to Emberly inside the room.

I watched as his eyes widened and his skin paled three shades, then whispered, "She says it's Mina."

"Mina? I don't know anyone by that name." I said, my nose wrinkling in confusion.

Zoya elbowed me. "Goddess of Peace of Order? Surely you know the names of the gods and goddesses?"

I felt my stomach twist as my jaw dropped. "Are you sure, Spencer? How does she know?"

He shook his head. "She didn't say, and now she's not replying. Her guard is up. We should do the same before we enter. Who knows what this could be?"

Nodding, I took three breaths to compose myself and then signaled to the guards to open the doors. I walked in with all the authority I could muster as the queen of this land. This person might have claimed to be a goddess, but until we knew it to be true, I would not offer deference.

As planned, Spencer and Zoya followed behind me, and the guards closed the door. The stranger and Emberly were sitting at a round table in the center of the room. Emberly was facing the door as we entered, and the stranger had taken a seat that had her turned away from us.

Emberly rose, offering a bow to me, as offered to a king or queen when they enter the room. This caused the stranger to push away from the table and turn her body to face us. She notably didn't stand. I stared at her and offered a look of disapproval.

"Ah, yes, finally, you are as you have appeared in my dreams, Queen Lyla." The stranger offered.

I shifted my gaze to Emberly, wondering if she would share anything before I spoke. She offered a subtle shake of her head. I returned my gaze to the stranger. "And you are?"

With that prompt, the stranger's lips turned up in a smile,

and she finally stood, slowly walking around the table towards me. "I had assumed your delegate had already informed you just a moment ago. I have been known by many names, but your people know me as Mina."

Mina wore a strange outfit including a skin-tight blue pants and a close-fitting gray shirt. She had on what looked like it could have been a light blue overcoat, but it stopped at her hips and held a hood. The coat lacked buttons. Her black hair was held back from her face, gathered into what looked like a pony's tail by a string with no tie or end.

"Ah yes, my dress. It is a bit out of fashion for your current era. Curious that your kind regressed this far in fashion since I was last here." Mina smoothed her coat down, then shoved her hands in the tiny pockets of her pants. "I suppose you have some spare dresses and the like around here that you could provide, so that I can fit in more easily. We have a lot of work to do to prepare you."

"Mina, is it? I'd like to invite you to sit and chat with me here. We don't understand the nature of your visit." I chose the seat closest to me, and Spencer helped to pull it out for me. Zoya sat between me and Mina, who also sat, while Spencer took the seat between Emberly and me.

Mina sighed, "Fine, we can sit here for now. Surely you know what I'm here for. These two look like priestesses. They must surely know the prophecy we shared to help you prepare for our arrival."

I reached for Spencer's hand under the table to help calm my nerves. I didn't know what to expect, but if this stranger spoke the truth and a goddess stood before me, then I was astonished.

"Yes, yes, I am the Goddess of Peace and Order. Calm your britches. It's not that shocking." Mina sighed again, rolling her silver eyes, seemingly agitated.

"I'm sorry, four months ago, I didn't know that magic actually existed outside of fairy tales, or this prophecy existed, much less was about—wait, I don't need to explain myself to you. You are just a stranger and have offered no evidence that you are who you claim to be."

Mina studied me intently for a bit. "Hm, fairly ok mind shielding for someone who's just started. I'll have to help you get stronger. I noticed you've already had the displeasure of meeting Death, and he's a pain in the ass to keep out. Oh shit, you went out of order. You were supposed to be crowned before you were strong enough to trigger that volcano. Oh, we've got to fix this asap."

I stood up from the seat indignantly. "Did you just dig through my mind? See my memories?"

My voice was barely a whisper, betraying me. I wanted to shout at her.

"Oh, you're one of those. Yeah, sorry, I'll ask next time." Mina's flippant attitude was just so infuriating.

"We will not be working together; I don't care who you are. You need to show some respect to the Queen. You think you're serving before I will entertain seeing you again." Anger felt good, but fear was bubbling at the surface, too. A part of me realized she was telling the truth, and I needed her to help me stay alive. Fear stopped me from allowing that vulnerability to show.

Spencer reached up to me, touching my arm as he stood. "Wait a second, Lyla. I know what she just did felt violating, but I think we need her."

"Don't worry. I can wait. She'll see she needs me in the next few days. I just need a room while I wait for her to calm down. Will one of you get one prepared?" Mina seemed entirely unfazed by my outburst. I wasn't sure if I should be grateful or even more annoyed. She scanned the others in the room, then pointed to Emberly. "You seem least necessary for the Princess's sense of safety. Get that room set up."

Mina turned back to me, dismissing Emberly, but Emberly stayed in her seat, waiting for me to show it's ok to leave. "And this is my turn to invite you to sit back down, Princess. You may be about to take the throne for this kingdom, but we all know that I outrank that. If you want to throw your authority around and demand respect, then you should show it when it's owed as well."

She waved her finger at the seat behind me. "Spencer, is it? Help the Princess sit down."

We both did as we were told. He placed a hand on my arm, offering grounding comfort. I turned to Emberly and nodded. She returned the head gesture and stood, but didn't leave the room yet.

"What is it you think you're here to do?" I asked, slowing my speech to keep my anger checked.

"I'm here to bring to life a new Goddess, of course. Are you not aware that this is the next step?"

I said nothing. I hadn't even considered that possibility. My mind raced. Why was she coming to me? What did it mean to bring a Goddess to life?

"Tsk, we need to help you work on your poker face." My face twisted at the unfamiliarity of the term poker.

"Oh, that's right, you all don't know the game. You need to learn to keep your emotions off your face." She sighed. "So much to teach you and such extraordinarily little time to do it. I wish you would have figured out this gift of yours sooner. Would have helped me do my job more easily. Ah well, some time is better than nothing. At least you timed it to give us the winter to prepare."

With that, she stood up and turned to the door. The guards shifted to stop her from leaving the room. Mina sighed. "Will you please decide, Princess? I'm exhausted and would like to bathe."

"Emberly, can you help coordinate a guest space for Mina? I will send Eliza over in a while for measurements for gowns." Emberly nodded and exited the room.

"Mina, I will also have you join me in my office for tea this afternoon. We will discuss what you intend to do. Please use this time to freshen up and rest." With that, I stood, and the others stood with me. We departed, leaving Mina in the room with the guards. Once the door closed, I glanced between Spencer and Zoya, then we simultaneously broke into a sprint.

We found Juniper in her office with Emberly already there. She had tasked a courtier with setting up Mina's room so she could also alert Juniper to the situation. By the time we arrived, Juniper had already confirmed she was the Goddess she claimed to be, using her connection to the air to sense her connection to magic. She was busy writing a letter to the Priestesses at the Temple to see if they could provide insight into what Mina may be here to do.

"Do you think it's really her?" I asked.

Emberly nodded. "I do. Her appearance fits the descriptions we have of her in our lore, and she spoke oddly enough to not be from this time or any of this country we know of."

Juniper's eyes lit up, "This confirms it. You two really are the fulfillment of the Prophecy. We can get so many questions answered, and she is going to help you make the changes we need."

She paused, studying my face. "You're not excited. What's wrong?"

I shook my head, sinking into a chair. "It doesn't feel right. Something is wrong. What does it even mean? What does it mean to bring life to a new goddess? What does it mean to reshape the world? What will she make me destroy?"

The door opened, and a guard announced, "His Majesty has arrived."

Juniper motioned to allow him in. As soon as the door latched, Father spoke, "Who was this visitor?"

"Mina, the Goddess herself." Emberly replied.

I could feel Father's emotions tense up. "What is she here for? Does this have to do with the God of Death?"

"She didn't say." My words sounded hollow.

"Lyla set up a meeting with her at tea, in the Queen's office." Spencer added.

Father sat down next to me, reached for my hands. I felt Spencer's hand rest on my shoulder. "Lyla, what's wrong?"

"She's here for the Prophecy. I caused that volcano, Father. I killed so many people because I can't control this magic. And now she's here to make me reshape the world. I don't want to kill anyone. Even if they want me dead, I don't want to destroy them. I don't know what to do. I don't know"- Tears fell, cutting me off, my breathing struggling to keep up. Through the tears, I saw all the dust and soil and furniture shifting.

'*Lyla, you're stronger than you know. You can do this. Take deep breaths for me, please.*' Spencer's voice in my head did help to calm me. I didn't stop crying completely, but my emotions did calm enough for my magic to settle. I freed a hand from Father's, reaching for Spencer's and offered him a small smile of gratitude.

Juniper shifted, going to her second room, and a handful of her courtiers come out to tidy up the mess I created. After they left, Father spoke again.

"When you were born, my sweet girl, I had a dream during those long restless nights in your infancy. This dream kept coming back, over and over. In it, the faces of Gods appeared, and they told me you are special, that you will change this kingdom in ways we couldn't even imagine. Each of them shared their plans, but alas, time and sleep have erased those from my mind. But, my dear, you were born to do great things. And you will do them, in your own time."

I felt my tears ease with his story. He'd never mentioned this before; I could have dismissed it as a lie, but his sincerity convinced me otherwise.

'*Your Father and Mother both have been preparing you all your life. You will be ready when the time comes.*' This was clearly Mina in my head, her voice carrying that same ethereal echo that the God of Death has, though her intrusion left a feeling of peace, rather than the disturbing unease that Death's voice carried.

I inhaled, closed my eyes, and straightened my back. "I know you are a goddess, and you can do what you will, but you need to stay out of my head, please. Uninvited guests in my conversations are unappreciated." I said this out loud, though I knew she could have heard it if it was only in my thoughts.

Juniper snorted and Emberly shared her smirk. "We will have to work hard on strengthening your mental guards. And your manners when talking to Goddesses." Emberly stated.

'*I will take your wishes under advisement.*' Mina's tone shared a similar hint of amusement.

I stood and shifted to the windows. The horses were out, despite the cold, and they seemed to enjoy their time in the pasture. Beyond them, I could see snow falling on the mountains and into the foothills between. Winter was here; snow would soon reach the city. I recalled Frederick sharing this summer how his elders worry that the snow may become permanent in Crystalford. The snow seemed to come earlier and earlier each year. Perhaps some of the change I could bring will help us avoid the freeze.

CHAPTER 34

L ater that afternoon, Amyra, Ivy, and I met with the event planners to plan the wedding. We had just five months to organize an event that draws several times more people than the Tournaments did. Eliza was already busy preparing a wedding dress that she promises would outshine all other dresses she's designed this year for me.

The first thing we discussed was where to hold the ceremony. my people held most weddings in the capital at the temple for Amata, the Goddess of love and fertility. It certainly made sense. It didn't feel right for me. I could only imagine promising myself to one person in that temple, and it was Amyra. Dedicating myself to Spencer there didn't feel right. Our marriage wasn't one for love, it was a political choice. Instead, I insisted on holding it in the temple for Mina. Since she's the Goddess for Peace and Order, this seemed like a good choice. Perhaps if I dedicated my marriage to peace, the threats Egan made could be harder to follow through on. Perhaps it would protect my kingdom from the recklessness I showed in not controlling my magic and causing such devastation to Egan's country.

I couldn't share all these reasons with the event planners, so it wasn't easy to convince anyone of this choice, but eventually, they relented.

Once that was in place, I stepped back from the rest of the choices. I allowed the planners, Ivy, and Amyra to discuss and debate the choices. Amyra's excitement with this was so palpable, it felt like she was planning her own wedding. Her excitement added to the guilt I feel. She insisted on being involved in this, and wanted to ensure it's the best day I could have, but how could it be, when I couldn't marry her? I tried to not let my guilt show, allowing Ivy and Amyra to make selections for the flowers, the color scheme, and even the food the reception after would serve.

'*Quit moping, you're getting married!*' Mina's voice shoved my thoughts aside.

'*I thought I told you to stay out of my head.*' I hoped my anger at her intrusion was palpable for her.

'*I told you I would take them under advisement. I did. And I will stay out once you can keep me out. You need to get stronger.*' Her brief lecture did not make me feel any happier, but I supposed I deserved it. At least with her around, we could know when I would finally keep Death out of my head.

'I know I'm not due for another thirty minutes, but I'm bored. I'll be coming now.'

'No! Wait. I don't need people to know who you are, not yet. Please let me end this meeting first.'

'*Too late!*' Her peppy tone was so irritating. With it, a knock sounded on the door of my office.

I rolled my eyes. "My apologies. It sounds like my next meeting has come early. Are we able to wrap up here?"

The lead planner shook her head. "No, we don't have enough information yet. Our next meeting won't be for two weeks, and we need to place orders before then. We really need the full meeting."

As she was protesting, Ivy was already heading to the door. I hadn't told her or Amyra about Mina being here, so she didn't know of this meeting yet. Her curiosity most certainly led her to opening the door and allowing Mina to enter.

"Oh, perfect, I love planning weddings. It wasn't my area of expertise back in the day, but I love a delightful party." Mina announced as she breezes past Ivy, leaving her at the door.

"Uh, wait, who are you?" Ivy stood there, not sure if she should close the door or ask a guard to come intervene.

"Sorry, Ivy, she's fine. She's the next meeting. She will sit over on the far couch and let us wrap this up, won't you?" I gave Mina a pointed glare, letting her know there wasn't room for debate. Mina smirked and took the seat I showed, but didn't stay quiet.

"Oh, I could, but I see you've chosen my temple for the wedding, and I would love to offer some insight."

"Your temple?" The planner raised her eyebrow. "I know the Priestesses at the temples, and you aren't wearing their clothes or the clothes of anyone I recognize."

"Ah, ok, thank you. I apologize; we will have to reschedule." I stood up.

"Ivy, please make room for my schedule in the next couple days to finish this meeting. We will meet for an hour."

I needed to set ground rules fast. And I needed to get Spencer in the room. He was supposed to join me for this meeting. I turned. "Amyra, I'm so sorry to ask this of you, but could you please retrieve Prince Spencer? He should be with Emberly."

Amyra nodded. "Of course, I will be back soon."

She stood, curtsied to me, and left. Seeing her use the formal curtsy like that felt jarring after I spent the meeting, wishing I could openly love her.

Ivy agreed to see the planners in the morning for scheduling, and they packed up their notes and leave as well. Once they had left, Mina moved to join Ivy and me at the table. "Well Princess, will you introduce me to your friend? Is she staying for this meeting too, or am I super top secret for even her?"

Ivy's eyebrows raised at her brazen tone. I grimaced, similarly not impressed by it, but ignored it. "Lady Ivy, this is Mina. She arrived this morning and is here to help me."

I watched Ivy's face, hoping I didn't need to explain too much. She didn't show any recognition of the name, unfortunately. "What a flimsy introduction. Princess, I thought you would have been better raised. I am not merely Mina; I am the Goddess of Peace and Order. Your Princess has awoken me, and I am here to help her fulfill the prophecy."

Ivy's eyes widened until I thought they might fall out. "I, uh, what? I'm sorry, I don't know the etiquette for meeting a goddess. Can I get you something to eat? Drink? Do you even eat or drink?"

Her reaction gave me pause. Before Mother died, I'd have been just as awestruck. What had changed? Who am I to find her presence annoying?

Mina smirked, saying, "No thank you. I mean, tea is nice if you intend to serve it, anyway. While I'm on this land, I need to eat, same as any other person." She turned to me and added, "You could learn a bit from this friend of yours."

My face blushed. "I will take your wishes under advisement." I didn't hide my smirk from my reply.

Mina barked a laugh. "You're feisty, an excellent trait for a future Queen. Be careful with that lip. Until you earn your respect with the other gods and goddesses, that type of attitude will get you into immense trouble."

"Other gods and goddesses? How many will join us?" I paled at the thought of having to host the entire court.

Mina smiled. "Oh, my sweet child, you shall meet them all as your training progresses."

I looked at Ivy, who looked just as shocked as I felt.

Amyra opened the door at that moment, arriving with Spencer. "Pardon my intrusion, here is Prince Spencer, as you requested. Shall I stay? I was unaware of this meeting." She bowed her head, waiting for my instruction.

"Amyra, please come sit and stay." Mina invited. Amyra straightened, closed the door, and chose a seat next to Spencer, who had sat next to me. "This little love triangle is quite intriguing. Tell me, Princess, why choose a husband when you clearly hold love for your girlfriend?"

I glanced to my left at both of them. Spencer sensed my hesitation and spoke for me. "Lyla must make some unfortunate choices to strengthen her claim to the throne. While she would love to declare her love for Amyra, her Council and other countries would question her judgment to shun the expectation to have a King and Queen ruling over Elthas."

Mina raised her eyebrow. "So, if you could set the rules, what would you do?"

I didn't want to hurt Spencer, but I also didn't want to lie. I panicked, trying to tell the truth without causing heartache. Eventually, I answered.

"Amyra would be my queen, if I had a real say in the situation."

I avoided looking at Spencer. I didn't want to know how that hit him. I wished I could see Amyra's face, though.

"Interesting," Mina replied. "And Amyra, what do you think of that?"

Amyra cleared her throat. "I have never considered this line of thought, because it's too foolish to daydream that way. I'm happy with what Lyla can offer me, and only want what's best for her, and for Elthas."

Mina tsked. "Such a political answer. You would love it, wouldn't you?"

I finally dared to look at Amyra, and found her staring at her lap, discomfort written all over her face. "Mina, what's the point of this line of questioning?" I demanded.

"Are you not intrigued by her answer?" Mina returned.

"No, she doesn't need to explain herself. As she said, this is fanciful, never going to happen. There's no point in wishing for the impossible."

Mina smiled. "Is it really impossible when you don't know yet what you can change?"

My breath hitched. Could I reshape the world to allow our kind of love to be lived out loud?

Mina started nodding. "Now you're really imagining it. Yes, you can change this. You could right now, but you would face a lot of resistance because your little priestesses have guarded the truth about you too much, and no one knows what you are tasked to do. What you will become."

"And what is it that I will become?"

"See? You saw the truth, you read it on that parchment, and you still don't know. There's so much to teach you and so little time left."

"As you've said already. Tell me, is the time limit because of the God of Death?"

"God of Death?" Mina seemed surprised by that. I started to question everything.

"Ye-yeah. There has been another who mind-speaks like you, all godlike in my head, who is the one that wants me dead. Isn't that why you're here? To help us confront him?"

Mina sat forward. "Tell me everything."

I recounted the last few months, the char marks on Mother and Frederick, the way Egan had been, the voice that spoke to me, every step leading up to the volcano.

Mina leaned back as I reached the end. "Hmm, I see. So that's why you woke me earlier than you should have."

"That's why I woke you earlier? I did nothing intentionally. I didn't want you to come here. I didn't want to potentially start a war with Scoria Bay. None of this was what I wanted. I just wanted to find my happily ever after with Amyra."

I might have just lost it a bit on Mina, but what did it matter? It wasn't like I could make things worse, right?

"Princess, your destiny was always to wake me. You are meant to bring a new way of life, not just to your kingdom, but to everyone. You could try running from your destiny, but I don't think you'd like that outcome. Would you like to see what happens if you choose to walk away?"

"I don't understand. How could I possibly see the outcome of a choice I wouldn't make?"

Mina stood up and walked around the table to me. With a loud screech, she dragged the chair across the stone floor behind her. She sat down next to me, pulling my chair out roughly so that I was knee to knee with her. She took my hands, then instructed, "Close your eyes. Drop your mind shields, let me in. Good."

Inside my head, a vision lit up the room. A blank, black

space took over my mind, and a feeling of nothingness overwhelmed me. I looked down and could see my body, as is, standing on nothing. I looked up, and Mina moved to stand in front of me, coming into existence from nothingness. "We are in an in-between space. I can take you through this space to show you what would have been if you had chosen at any point to give up the throne and run away with Amyra. No one will hear us, see us, or sense us. But don't try to change anything you see. You will have abilities to change things you don't yet have in your realm, and you will change fates you don't yet understand if you try. Are you ready?"

How could I be ready for anything with that kind of warning? I nodded anyway. She reached for my hand, and I took it. Suddenly we were in some type of tunnel, lights streaming past us in rapid speed, the motion making me feel so sick to my stomach. We stopped as fast as we started, landing in an alley I recognized out in town. I leaned against a wall and puked, grabbing a handkerchief to wipe my face after.

"You could have warned me about that."

Mina smiled, "And miss the fun of this? I'd never."

"For a Goddess of Peace and Order, I'm not feeling either." I replied.

"Of course not. You're in a future that your choices are created, not mine. Look around and learn what I'm trying to teach you."

I listened, tucking my handkerchief back in its pocket. While I recognized this alley, I recognized little. Homes were in such disrepair that many had wide holes into the living spaces. People were in torn, raggedy clothing. This made little sense. This was supposed to be one of the merchant districts, the one we took visiting dignitaries through to show how prosperous Elthas is.

"What happened?" I whispered as I hesitantly walked out to the main street to investigate more.

"You did. Instead of your people, you chose love. You ran away, choosing exile, instead of fighting to show your people a better way. Ethan had to rule, but he was never strong enough.

He got bullied by that horrible Council of yours, and that bastard Denenbaum got his way. That God you call Death called the shots from his own perch in Scoria Bay. All the kingdoms have fallen to ruin."

"Are you saying I can't have love in my life?" I couldn't let my country, or others, fall like this. "I have to give up my happiness for the rest of the world to have theirs?"

Mina placed a hand on my shoulder, causing me to turn to face her. I studied her face, her lips pressed into a faint, knowing smile, eyes soft with a sadness that wasn't hers to bear. "No, my Nivara, I want you to understand that you don't give up any of it. You fight for your love for Amyra, for your connection with Spencer and your people. You don't let anyone tell you what to do."

I nodded, looking around. "I never want my people to suffer while I hide. Running away was never in my plans, but I'll fight to avoid exile now. They will have to kill me if they want to take my throne from me."

I continued to walk the road that was supposed to be filled with the finest of wares, but I saw orphans begging, elderly huddling in doorways, barely alive, and so much destruction. Some buildings didn't have roofs, others were just shells. Stones crumbled in, like they were taken out by some massive force.

Mina smiled, "One exception, as I train you. It'll be easier if you let me lead and tell you what to do."

I turned to her and nodded. "I need you. This can't be allowed to happen. Tell me how to prevent this."

Mina grabbed my hand, and without warning, we were back in that tunnel of lights, moving so fast I could barely keep my footing. We dropped into the blank, black space, but thankfully I didn't vomit this time, as I fell to my knees, still so sick to my stomach.

"Please, never do that without warning again," I sputtered between bursts of dry heaving.

Mina laughed. "You'll get used to that one day. Until then, I'm going to get my fun where I can."

"Now, before I release you back to your body, you should

know while this felt like a half hour for us, it was just seconds for the others in the room." Mina cautioned me. I nodded. She shimmered into nothingness, and then I felt my spirit return to my body. Even though I went from weightlessness to feeling the full weight of my body, I felt better, lighter, being back to me. That entire experience was so weird.

"I hope to never have to do that again." I mumbled as I stood up to turn my chair back to the table. Spencer jumped up to help me with the chair. Once I was back in my seat, he moved to help Mina get her chair back in place as well.

"What just happened?" Amyra asked, her brows pinched and lips slightly parted, worry flickering in her eyes.

"I received the message loud and clear. I will fight for all that we deserve. Denenbaum, Egan, and the Priests of Bel don't deserve to win." I offered Amyra a steady gaze, my jaw set, chin lifted, and fire burning behind my eyes. I turned to Mina, "Let's go. How do I reshape this world?"

Mina laughed, clapping once, then slapped the table. "That's my girl. First things first, we got to get you on that throne. When's the wedding?"

"Spring equinox," Ivy volunteered.

"Oh no, that won't do. We need the wedding pushed up. Winter solstice should do. Make sure your coronation happens then, too. You probably need to get those planners back in here. They will not like that part."

"What? I couldn't ask them to plan that. That would be a logistical nightmare." I protested.

"You need to. By spring, Scoria Bay will make their move. You need to get these parts out of the way so we can focus on the war." Mina insisted.

She gave me a knowing look. Those buildings had crumbled because of this war. We lost. I nodded. "Ivy, you probably need to send that message to them. I guess clear the schedule for when they can meet next. I might need to just delegate all planning to you two."

Mina nodded. "Yes, if Amyra and Ivy could do that and leave you free to train with me, we'd be far more prepared.

Good idea. Ivy, just handle it without the Princess." She directed.

Ivy looked at me, confused. I confirmed what Mina had just ordered. "She's right. We can talk about any details during breakfasts or dinner, but it'll have to be out of my hands."

"Ok, I'd like to meet your priestesses. I need to know what's happening with magic around here. When do you see them next?"

"Tomorrow morning," Ivy replied. She always knew my schedule better than me.

"Excellent. I'll join you." Mina nodded. "About that Scoria Bay dealings. Who's handling that? I assume they aren't keeping a princess in the loop; I need to talk with the people in charge."

"Father, and the Army Generals." I replied.

"Ah, well, I'll meet with them tomorrow afternoon. Someone let them know to be ready?"

Amyra started scribbling a note. "She will," I replied.

"And you, Spencer, what's your role in all this before the coronation?"

I looked at Spencer, who stood frozen, his eyes wide and unblinking. "Uh, I have just been supporting Lyla and learning what I can when I can."

"Seriously? You're going to be king in two months. We need you learning faster, more. You'll be at that meeting in the afternoon." Mina nodded, as if that was all it took. And I supposed, as a goddess, she really could do that. Except that we can't let people know a goddess is awake and in the flesh, could we?

"I'm not sure that's that easy, Mina." I countered. "We can't just allow things to happen by your decree, if we are to hide that you're here. We can't just let the whole castle know you're here or else people will flock to the castle to demand an audience with you, hoping you'll fix their problems."

Mina sat thoughtfully for a moment. "You pose a good point, Lyla. You have good instincts. Spencer, you will join us. The outgoing king and Army Generals need to know I'm here, but I'll have them sign an NDA."

We stared at her blankly.

"What?" Our confusion confused her for a moment, before clarity reflected in her eyes. "Oh, you don't know what the NDA is. I'll have them swear to secrecy. They'll come up with a suitable cover for who I am. That's their job."

She always said the weirdest things. Once she was certain we understood her, she issued a bunch of orders.

"OK, now that there's a plan, Ivy, go get those planners up in arms again. Amyra, deliver that letter to whoever needs it. The two future rulers and I will spend the rest of the evening training. Uh, Amyra might want to send the priestesses who had been training them here. They'll probably love to learn more about how to prepare stronger magic wielders."

Ivy and Amyra left, and she turned to us. We were required to show our abilities. She asked what the most powerful thing was that I'd done, other than the volcano. She challenged Spencer with his shields and his ability to penetrate hers. We spent hours working on shielding until our minds felt scrambled. The daylight turned to dusk when someone knocked on the door. Spencer stood to check and found food delivered to us. We stopped to eat, discussing strategies throughout dinner. Mina shared details about the Last War that had been long forgotten. When Mina finished, we were all exhausted. It was well past our usual time to retire. Mina had assured me that her quarters were fit for her needs, and we agreed to meet in the morning with the Priestesses.

CHAPTER 35

Mina proved to be invaluable for every aspect of preparing for Scoria Bay to respond. Over the next couple weeks, scouts returned with information that confirmed that Scoria Bay was planning an offensive but would wait until the spring thaw to use their navy to attack. We had superior land forces, but they were definitely the stronger force on water. We prepared for our river to be breached and for them to reach the capital by summer. Father and the Generals had Spencer join them in planning since the coronation and wedding had been combined and scheduled for this winter. Father agreed to become a war advisor for us, to help ensure we had the best chance. He networked with our allies for reinforcements, and while many informed us they worried that directly supporting us with troops and ships would harm their relations with Scoria Bay, they agreed to support us in other ways. It was the best we could hope for, realistically.

The wedding planners were thoroughly upset with my decision, since it meant that the meeting Mina interrupted was useless. They had Ivy and Amyra ragged with all the details and never let them go a day without complaints about the timeline. I felt for all of them; it was certainly not my choice. But we couldn't just explain to them why, mostly because I didn't understand why.

Mina tried to teach me about what my role was to be, but I just couldn't wrap my head around it. She challenged me and helped me to find more effective ways of managing my magic through my emotions. I had fewer accidental releases, and more control. Using my connection to the earth to move large amounts became easier. We used that in our war preparations - I was to go help fortify the coastal towns in the late winter. I could move rocks larger than many of the merchant stalls with ease, so while it was not a grand plan to have me at the front near the expected start of the war, it was also the best way to ensure minimal loss of life. I insisted that Emberly and Zoya accompanied me to help with the effort, and to be there to remove me from danger with the speed of Emberly's magic. Mina also wanted to go in case we needed her. While I didn't understand all her powers, I knew it was the best plan for us, so we agreed. It's not like she would have listened to us telling her no, anyway.

We invited all our allies, and even a few we felt certain would ally with Scoria Bay, to the wedding and coronation. As we expected, nearly all accepted. People would fill the temple to the brim. We hired several artists to capture as many images as possible and planned for a larger section of journalists to share all the details they could. I couldn't remember a royal wedding as expected as this one. I didn't know if people just understood the gravity of what I was about to do with the world, without actually knowing, or if this was some kind of effort to be in Elthas before Scoria Bay took out the new king and queen.

Ethan had broken things off with Katelle during this time. She was incredibly upset at us for holding her father in the dungeons. I wish I could say I understood, and on some level I did, but I also couldn't understand how she could support someone who intended to kill me, a 20-year-old woman just barely starting life. Sure, a future queen, but still, I'm not that much different from her, just born with a different lot in life. Katelle sought refuge at her mother's estate to avoid the war. I was glad that she wasn't a loose thread in the castle.

About two weeks before the wedding and coronation, we

received a courier from Scoria Bay. He brought a letter to the gate, handed it to a guard, and ran off. The letter informed us that Scoria Bay knew about the wedding and was furious about not receiving an invitation. It seemed weird that they wanted to be invited when Egan left with such a threat. If we didn't have the intelligence reports telling us they were building up for war, we would have questioned the sincerity of his threat. Father determined this letter was designed to have us let our guards down for that day, so he ordered the strongest security possible for the entire capital city. It meant that we would have troops moving to the coastal cities in the period where we typically had the heaviest snowfalls, but it seemed wise to help prevent any surprise attacks from stopping the event. Father also wanted us to solemnize the wedding and transfer power quietly prior to the event, but I didn't like that idea, and Mina supported me in allowing the legalities to carry on the same day as we had planned.

The day of the wedding came, and I woke up long before the sun to prepare. I barely slept the night before. Amyra stayed with me that night, just as she had done nearly every night since they installed the warding spells. I had seen little of her since Mina showed up, other than when we slept next to each other. I ached for our days when we could just be together, giggling and sharing gossip about the various nobles staying in the castle and city. It felt like a lifetime ago. She had been almost as busy as me, working with the planners and learning more to control her magic. She could do some healing, which felt immensely fortuitous. Often, she would practice on me, healing my sore, aching body after grueling sessions with Mina. She worked often with Lettie, who was also a healer, to learn more about her gifts.

Amyra and Ivy were up and readying themselves for the day as I woke. They had my breakfast ready and informed me Eliza would be there shortly. I hurried through, eating what little I could and then moved to the bathing room to get ready. Once I was clean of any signs of Amyra and I spending the night together, Ivy and Amyra sat me down at my vanity to prepare my hair. They had quite the challenge with my hairstyle today, as they couldn't design it around a tiara. I would end the day with the official crown for the Queen of Elthas. They needed to design a hairstyle that could look stunning without hair accessories and under the crown. They chose well, using a series of braids that could then help fix the crown on my head when the time came. By the time they were done, my hair was covered in small braids that were pinned in diamond shapes, brought back to one larger braid down my back. They had left small bits to frame my face, which they curled using their fingers.

As they finished up, Eliza arrived with my dress. The dress was both my coronation dress and my wedding dress, so it was untraditional for both events, which felt so fitting for the change Mina promises I will bring.

As she pulled the dress out of the capsule, I felt floored once again by her ingenuity. She designed a perfect winter gown, woven from shimmering silver-blue fabric that caught the light like freshly fallen snow. The bodice is adorned with intricate embroidery of frost-kissed vines and delicate snowflakes, each stitched with glistening thread that mimics ice crystals. The off-the-shoulder sleeves are sheer, crafted from gossamer-thin fabric dusted with iridescent beads that resemble frozen dew. A dramatic, flowing cape of soft, translucent white tulle cascades from her shoulders, embroidered with a pattern that mimics frost creeping across glass. Tiny diamonds and pearls are scattered across the train, sparkling like icicles in the moonlight. The skirt is layered with delicate chiffon and velvet; the hem edged with a swirling pattern of icy filigree, as if winter's breath had traced its mark along the fabric.

"Eliza…" I whispered as I stared at her creation. "You've outdone yourself once more." I reached out to touch the dress. Eliza and Ivy helped me into it. After several minutes, I was finally facing my mirror and admiring the dress on me. It was then that Amyra came back into my sitting room from the bedroom. She was wearing her own dress, and it was so like mine. Where my coronation gown shimmered with regal opulence, hers was a softer reflection. It was no less breathtaking, but woven with understated elegance. The icy blue fabric hugged her frame, catching the light with a faint silver sheen, as if brushed by frost. Delicate embroidery traced the bodice in swirling patterns, subtle yet mesmerizing. Tiny pearl-like beads dusted the sheer, off-the-shoulder sleeves, glinting as she moved. The skirt flowed in layers of chiffon and velvet; the hem edged with an intricate frost pattern that mirrored my own. A soft, translucent cape draped from her shoulders, its edges scattered with crystals, like ice catching the light. In her dark hair, a silver hairpiece shaped like frost-laced vines rested in place—delicate yet unshakable.

She was beautiful. A quiet storm, standing at my side. As our eyes met, I knew I would never be alone in this.

I turned to Eliza, saying, "You didn't have to do that!"

Tears threatened to fall.

"No, but she wanted to," Ivy said. "She wanted you to know you will always have your love by your side, in all ways."

Amyra walked over to me, grasping my hands. We stared into each other's eyes; hers shimmering with magic; the color matching our gowns as if it was designed that way. "Wait, Eliza, did you match these to Amyra's eyes?"

I broke the stare to look at Eliza as she nodded. I turned back to Amyra, and we giggled, and for a moment, I felt like we were our past selves, ready to gossip about who was coming to the event.

It was in that moment that I wanted Mother here most, and a gentle wave of grief washed through me, knowing that I was only here in this moment because we lost her. This day was going to be difficult, in so many ways.

Ivy got dressed in her gown, a darker teal shade that closely matched Amyra's. The fitted bodice featured swirling silver embroidery, mirroring frost creeping over glass just as ours did. Off-the-shoulder sleeves draped in sheer fabric, dusted with tiny crystals that caught the light with every movement. The skirt cascaded in velvet and chiffon; its hem lined with delicate icy filigree. A matching silver hairpiece adorned her red curls, shaped like intertwining winter vines. She looked formidable, yet effortlessly elegant.

I was so impressed with how Eliza and her team pulled this off for us. They must've worked night and day to make these dresses look this stunning.

It was time for us to make our way to the temple. We planned to use underground tunnels to get there, both for safety reasons and to avoid revealing my appearance before the wedding ceremony. Courtiers walked with us through the tunnels, laying down long carpets just as we approached to keep our gowns clean from any of the dirt. Apparently, this was a tradition that the courtiers enjoyed doing for royal weddings. I tried to point out that I could take the dirt off when we arrived, but they insisted they be allowed this courtesy. I appreciated how they wanted to help make my day special and agreed.

We arrived at the room that hid us until the start of the ceremony. Shortly after, a knock sounded on the door. Ivy went to look and invited the person in. "Your Grace," she greeted him. "Wait, is that right? Or do I wait until after the coronation? I'm so sorry."

Father smiled, the first real smile I'd seen on his face since Mother died. "Technically, I'm still king until she completes the ceremony. But there is no worry for you, Lady Ivy. You'd have to face punishment from our future queen, and I suspect she has a soft spot for you."

"You're fine, Ivy, as always. But don't go abusing that," I teased.

Ivy curtsied after she shut the door.

"Lyla, you're so perfectly you, a dress to suit both occasions, while snubbing them each at the same time. This suits you and suits the change you'll bring us."

Father crossed the room as he complimented me. We were face to face, father and daughter, old king and new queen. I smiled, tears threatening to spill, and asked. "Have you come to offer your words of advice?"

"Don't get sick," Father teased again, showing his side as my parent, not my advisor or ruler. The role I hadn't really experienced from him in months. I giggled and reached to hug him.

"I just wish I could do this with Amyra, Father." I whispered. "I know why it couldn't be, but I wish it were different."

"Lylabug, once you are queen, you can make it different. Let's finish the war before we go making changes, but you can change the laws to allow you to openly embrace Amyra. If I make it through this war, I will help you make it happen." Father pulled out of the hug before adding, "You will bring this kingdom exactly to where it needs to be."

He stepped back and admired me again. "You were born for this. You will be my greatest gift to the world. I love you."

The tears spilled down my face as I smiled at him. "I will be only the Queen you helped me to become." I replied, dabbing at my face.

"Your Majesty, if I could just shoo you out of this room, so that Lyla doesn't destroy her look before the wedding starts?" Ivy asked, moving back towards the door to open it for Father.

"Yes, yes, of course. I will see you out there, Lyla." Father bowed to me as if he were my subject.

"I love you too," I replied, waving at him.

The door didn't even close before Ethan arrived, dressed in his standard black and white tuxedo. I snorted. "The same thing as always? Couldn't even get a different tie?" I teased.

Ethan bowed to me in that same reverent way that Father did. "My queen, I got a tie. I just missed my appointment to pick it up this morning."

Ivy pulled a tie out of her pocket, one that matched her dress. She helped Ethan put it on. Was there something between them? I had been so busy; I didn't even keep track of where Ethan had been for the last couple of months. What was happening?

She finished tying it on, and stuffed a square in his coat, then patted his chest. "Much better. Now you look like you belong."

"Uh, did I miss something here?" I asked, looking between the two.

Ethan and Ivy grinned at each other, then turned to me,

with Ivy saying, "You've missed precisely nothing, Lyla, I promise."

Somehow, I didn't believe that. But Ethan didn't give me a chance to question it. "Lyla, now that I'm properly dressed, can I offer my condolences?"

His smirk told me he was kidding, but I played along. "Condolences? What for?" I brought my eyebrows together in faux worry.

"For your freedom, my dear sister. You'll miss it so much." He hugged me and whispered. "I'm only kidding. I wish you years of happiness with Spencer, and let me know if he needs to be straightened. He might be my friend, but you're my sister and I will tolerate nothing below pure worship for you."

I giggled, hugging him back. "Of course, thank you."

He pulled out of the hug, holding my upper arms while I grasped at his forearms. "Lyla, you look absolutely stunning, and I can't state how much I am here for you in any way today."

"Want to take the crown later?" I offered, a knowing smirk on my face.

"But that." Ethan amended, laughing.

"Then what I need most from you is to have the most fun today, and to ensure I have a bit too." I smiled.

Ethan nodded. "Consider me the Fun Czar of the day. You will have the most fun I can dream up for you." He saluted me, causing all of us to laugh.

A door knock sounded, followed by the door opening. The planner entered and said, "It's time."

"That's my cue to get to my position." Ethan said as he rushed out the door.

I took one last glance at Ivy and Amyra. "Promise me you two will be by my side, not just today, but always?"

They nodded. "Of course, my Queen. I'll do anything for you." Amyra swore.

CHAPTER 36

W e left the room, entering the hallway towards the main worship area in the temple. I paused just before the doors, positioned so that no one could see when they open. Two attendants opened the doors, allowing Ivy, then Amyra, to walk through to their assigned places at the front of the temple. I paused for a few moments, listening to the quartet playing, waiting for the cue. When it sounded, I walked to the doors, pausing at the doorway. The crowded temple's worship space prevented me from seeing my destination at the front, despite the aisle created for my entrance. Two guards flanked me on either side in their fanciest of dress uniforms. There was no talking around them escorting me down the aisle, and at this moment, I appreciated not walking this alone.

I reached the altar when I saw he had also coordinated with Eliza to get an outfit to match mine.

Spencer stood at the top of the stairs, to the temple's altar just to my right, and for a moment, everything else faded. His midnight-blue frock coat rivaled the winter sky, silver embroidery catching the light like frost on glass. Beneath it, an icy blue brocade waistcoat gleamed, fastened with delicate snowflake buttons. A velvet-trimmed cloak draped over his shoulders, its fur edging adding to his quiet regality. Even his dark gloves bore intricate silver filigree, a subtle echo of winter's touch.

He had always been handsome, but tonight, he was breathtaking. Every detail of his attire complemented mine, as if we were carved from the same frostbitten moment. My heart stumbled, warmth rising in my chest despite the chill in the air. Spencer wasn't just dressed for the occasion; he was a vision of winter's quiet strength, and in that moment, I wasn't sure if I wanted to be crowned or simply fall into his arms.

His emerald eyes swirled with the warmth of his love, and his smile told me he was just as struck with awe at me as I was with him.

I finally noticed that Amyra was also standing at his level, just to my left. Both were watching me walk down the aisle, with no one else standing there. I climbed the stairs, and Ivy appeared from the front of the crowd to be sure my dress was properly situated once I stood there. I didn't know whether to face Spencer or if I should face them both, so I stood for a moment with my back to the crowd.

"I don't know what to do," I confessed in a whisper.

Spencer smiled. "For now, my queen to be, face me. We'll figure out the rest together."

I turned to face him, leaving Amyra slightly behind me.

Mina appeared, stepping through a shimmer of light rather than just crossing the altar to meet us. Her gown shimmered in pearlescent white with hints of silver and pale blue, flowing like a liquid light with every step. Intricate embroidery of olive branches and geometric patterns adorned the bodice and sleeves, symbolizing the harmony she upheld. A silver circlet crowned her moonlit hair, its luminous pearl centerpiece glowing softly as if infused with the very essence of peace and order.

I smiled at her, especially as I heard gasps from the crowd behind me. She shared a smile with me before addressing the crowd.

The air shimmered as the light coalesced around her, casting a serene glow over the temple's chamber. Gasps echoed throughout as Mina stepped forward, her very presence commanding reverence. She lifted her hands, a light glow of golden light emanating from them, and the murmurs fell into awed silence.

"Be still, and know me. I am Mina, Goddess of Peace and Order, the keeper of harmony, the weaver of fate's delicate threads. I have walked unseen among you, watching as this kingdom stands on the edge of change. And now, I stand before you, revealed, to bear witness to the union that will shape the days to come."

Her gaze softened as she turned toward Spencer and me, her voice both gentle and firm.

"Today is not only a joining of hearts, but a binding of destinies. A Queen and her chosen King, bound not by force, but by trust, by courage, and by love in its truest form. Under my guidance, their vows shall be spoken, and their fates intertwined as one. Let this be a moment of not only devotion, but of renewal—of hope, of promise, and of the balance that must always be upheld."

She extended her hands towards us, the light of divinity pulsing in her palms.

"Come forward, Lyla of Elthas. Come forward, Spencer of Vondalon. Let the gods bear witness to the bond you are about to forge."

Spencer and I joined hands and stepped forward. Mina went through the speech usually given, and I had to admit I lost focus. Every moment of surprise this morning has been so emotional, and I needed a moment to reflect. I had never imagined enjoying my wedding day, never thought I'd find a man I could trust so deeply like I do Spencer. Before long, I realized we were at the vows.

"Please face each other and share your commitment to each other now." We turned as directed.

Spencer shared his first, "Lyla, from the moment I saw you this summer, you were a force I could never turn away from. You are my North Star, the fire in the cold, the truth I never knew I needed. I vow to stand beside you, not as a shadow, but as your equal—through peace and war, through certainty and chaos. I will honor your strength, cherish your heart, and love you with a devotion as steady as the tides. You are my queen, my love, my home. And for as long as I breathe, I am yours."

Gods, the exact words that I needed to hear. The temple quieted, waiting for mine. I realized I didn't have any prepared, I never had time to write them, let alone memorize them. I took a breath, glanced at Mina in my peripheral, and then focused back on Spencer.

"Spencer, you see me as I am, not just as a ruler, but as Lyla. With you, I am not just bound by duty—I am free. I vow to lead with you, to fight beside you, to trust you with my heart and my kingdom. You are my safe harbor, my dearest friend, the steady hand I never knew I needed. Today, and always, I am yours, just as you are mine."

Mina cleared her throat. "Before we complete this cere-mony and cement the bond forever into eternity, I must invite one more person. Amyra, will you share your vows to these two, your future queen and king?"

My face flushed, and I felt my stomach twist in terror. I glanced down to the crowd, and saw Father smiling, and Juniper was nodding. They didn't plan this, did they? Did everyone know but me?

Amyra stepped down two stairs, then walked to stand in front of us, her back to the crowd. She smiled, just as Spencer spoke in my mind, '*No one knew this was happening. Mina is surprising all of us.*'

Mina also added, 'Don't worry, I shall address your council when they inevitably call their meeting to be angry about this. They can't subvert the will of the Gods, can they? Consider this my gift to you for all that you've done to show you are ready for this.'

With that, I breathed out a little shakily and focused on Amyra as she shared her vow.

"Lyla, Spencer, I stand here with you both, not just as your friend, but as your partner in all things. I vow to serve you, to protect the love shared, and to stand beside you in every trial that comes our way. My heart belongs to both of you, and I will cherish and honor our bond through all the years to come. Together, we will face whatever comes, and together, we will endure."

Mina threw her arms in the air, creating a subtle warm glow of light that surrounds us, as she announces, "As the will of the Goddess of Peace and Order is heard, so shall this union be. Lyla, Spencer, and Amyra shall forever more be joined as one, for this lifetime and throughout all others until the end of eternity."

Spencer and I shared the traditional kiss, and electricity filled me through to my core. He broke it quickly, and then we both immediately turned to Amyra and reached for her hands. She took one step up to be closer, and we all embraced. As we touched, the room erupted in a bright display of light, signaling the bond was accepted by the Gods. Such a display hadn't been seen in decades, not since Mother and Father's wedding.

"Forgive me, but I don't feel comfortable with a kiss in front of this crowd," Amyra whispered.

"We shall share it when it's right, as soon as we have a moment." I whispered back in understanding.

We broke free of the hug, and then the three of us turned to the crowd. Applause and cheers thundered throughout the chamber, so loud I was certain that the windows would shatter. Whatever consequences might have happened if we had done this without a Goddess as the presiding priestess, the people seemed to have forgotten.

Amyra moved to stand next to me, and I held hands with both of them as we accepted the applause.

After several minutes, the noise settled down. I knew this meant that the coronation was ready to begin. I glanced behind me and saw that a table was already placed behind us, and that the crowns, my scepter, and Father's ceremonial sword were placed on it.

Amyra let go of my hand and walked down the steps to join Ivy. This ceremony would only involve Father, Spencer, and me, as he passes the title to us, and then I grant him his new title of King Emeritus and Lord Regent.

Once the items were placed with care and the courtiers were out of the altar space, Father entered the altar. Mina seemed to have disappeared, completing her duties.

Father stood at the table and waited while Spencer and I turned and knelt to offer our respects. Father bowed his head and started whispering his prayer. We wouldn't be allowed to know what he said, but it's meant to be a prayer to ask for Mother's blessing from the beyond. Once he was done, his head rose, and I could see tears threatening to spill. We made eye contact, and smiled, realizing we both shared the wish that she was here with us. One tear dropped from his eye and landed on what was about to be my crown. When that tear landed, a small light flashed for a moment, a glow. Mother's blessing, I knew instinctively.

Then Father moved around the table to hand the items to us. The crowns were placed on us first. My crown, then Spencer's, to show that I was the one that inherited the throne by birth, while Spencer was the one to stand by my side and support me. These crowns were the heaviest and most intricate in the royal treasury, crafted to complement one another. Both were lined with rich blue velvet, their weighty golden filigree wrapping around the head in delicate, ornate patterns. Gems in every color of the rainbow adorned the filigree, catching the light with each movement. My crown was delicate, its design reminiscent of rose petals poised to bloom. Spencer's, more angular and square, reflected masculine strength but was no less dazzling, with gems intricately encrusted throughout.

Father carefully carried my crown over and held it over my head. "By the grace of the gods and the will of the people, I hereby crown you, Lyla, Queen of Elthas, to rule with wisdom, strength, and compassion. May your reign bring peace and prosperity to this land, and may you always uphold the dignity and honor of the crown. With this coronation, you are not only our sovereign, but the heart of our kingdom. Long may you reign."

He nearly shouted the last sentence, and the crowd behind us shouted it back to us. Father and I shared a smile as he placed it on my head.

He returned to the table, took Spencer's crown, and repeated the statement for him, "By the grace of the gods and the will of the people, I hereby crown you, Spencer, King Consort of Elthas, to rule with wisdom, strength, and compassion. May your reign bring peace and prosperity to this land, and may you always uphold the dignity and honor of the crown. With this coronation, you are not only our sovereign, but the heart of our kingdom. Long may you reign."

The crowd echoed his statement once more. Father turned and grabbed the scepter and sword. He handed them to us without fanfare. We stood as we accepted them, then turned to face the crowd, the newly crowned queen and king of these people. We held our hands, while Spencer held his sword in his outside hand, and I held the scepter. I made the speech to formally accept the role.

"May we forever serve you with the dignity and honor befitting the trust you bestow upon us. May we reflect the grace and wisdom you bestow upon us as your representatives. May Elthas endure through the ages, remembered for an era of prosperity, peace, and humility. I vow to be the queen you deserve, and that Spencer shall be the king this kingdom requires. Together, we shall lead with strength and compassion, for the future of our land."

The crowd erupted in another set of thunderous applause and cheers. Once quieted down, I called Father to us. He expertly moved around Spencer and knelt on the stairs before us. I thanked him for the decades of service that he provided our kingdom and wished him a long and happy retirement. I then blessed him with my scepter while naming him King Emeritus and Lord Regent. The crowd once again cheered for him, as he bowed and accepted his new titles.

Amyra and Ethan moved to join us, to walk behind us as we walked down the aisle and out of the temple.

Once outside the temple, we met the crowd of people who

couldn't be inside. They cheered thunderously when they saw us in our crowns. Spencer had sheathed the sword, but the scepter had no convenient way to carry it. I met Amyra's eyes, quietly beckoning her to my side, even though I couldn't take her hand.

We reached the top of the stairs leading to the square where people were gathered. I noticed the uniformed guards sprinkled through the crowd and along the fringes. They were the only ones not openly cheering, but I could still sense their excitement, even if they couldn't display it while in uniform. I hoped I could be the ruler these people needed me to be.

A formal announcement declared Spencer and I crowned, and our marriage union to include Spencer, Amyra, and me. The crowd cheered as if that was completely expected. We all grinned, waving to the crowd. After a few moments, a royal guard instructed us to step back from the steps and guided to the underground tunnels to return to the castle.

We had only barely enough time to get back to the castle and get ready for the reception later today.

CHAPTER 37

The schedule called for our arrival just as the reception's cocktail hour ended. We would be the last to be announced upon arrival for the evening.

While waiting for the announcers to be ready for us, Amyra turned to Spencer and me, and said, "That was truly the hardest secret to keep. Mina promised she would allow me to join the union, but that it was to be a gift to you two, so I couldn't tell you. I had known since almost the day she arrived we would get this."

She was grinning from ear to ear.

I returned the smile. "Amyra, I had never known you to keep a secret like that from me. You've always been the one ready to share everything you know. But that was truly the best gift you two could offer, and I'm so glad you did."

It was at this moment, in a quiet, dimly lit hallway awaiting our entrance to the reception, where we shared our first kiss. She leaned in, and her honeyed raspberry taste enveloped me as I returned the kiss. Though my eyes were closed, I could sense that same light flashing around us; the gods accepted our union. I placed my hands on her waist, deepening the kiss. I wished to touch more, but I didn't want to ruin her hair. Finally, we broke apart, and I glanced at Spencer, intending to pull him towards us.

His eyes had widened, and he studied us. "Your hazes, they merged fully." He whispered in awe. "Can you stand apart?"

We obliged, stepping two steps back from each other. His eyes darted between us, taking in what he could see. "Wait, Lyla, you must have mine within yours also. You embody an entire scene of a mountain stream, with the emerald grass and trees and the brown sandy shores and the crystal blue water. I've never seen anyone's haze so clearly. Amyra, yours is missing something..."

With that, he leaned in and shared his kiss with her. The two of them didn't hold back, with Spencer dipping her as they kissed. They had the same flash of light, a small one, but one all the same. Once they broke apart, Spencer took a couple of steps back, and within a moment, a satisfied smile crossed his face.

"There, your haze is now identical to Lyla's. I've never seen this before. But then, I've never seen a union blessed by a goddess."

The band sounded the cue for us to make our grand entrance. I looked at my two partners, offered my hands to each of them, and when they took my hands, we turned and walked as one through the doors to be announced as Queen, King Consort, and the Crown Princess of Elthas.

I had gotten what I wanted, and so much more. I married my girlfriend, I guess now she's my wife, and gained a King that would rule Elthas at my side, not as the man I must serve, but as the man who supports me and defers to me.

The reception carried on so quickly. We had so many well-wishers from all of our nobility and our visiting dignitaries coming to us and congratulating us for such a moving ceremony and coronation. Even Lord Luther treated Amyra royally, as if having her at my side had never been illegal.

Amyra's father approached us, tears in his eyes. "I knew, even though you two could never tell me, I always knew. And I'm so glad that you can live freely as you are. I couldn't have hoped for a better daughter-in-law, and son-in-law."

Amyra hugged her father, grateful for the support. She whispered in his ear, but I couldn't hear it. Whatever it was, it caused Lord Greenhow to cry a little. Once she pulled away from him, I held out my arms and asked, "May I?"

"For my queen, anything you wish," he replied before hugging me.

He then whispered, "Welcome to the family. I will always cherish you as my own."

After we pulled away, he turned to Spencer and offered a handshake. Spencer pulled him into a hug, and they exchanged words privately as well.

"I must keep moving. You have so many people to speak with this evening," Lord Greenhow bowed as he stepped away. He quickly disappeared into the crowd as we greeted others.

The announcement for dinner was soon made, and we proceeded to the dais. They set up the royal chairs, placing a smaller third chair at the table so Amyra could sit with us. I made a mental note to commission a third for her, and to amend the throne room for her to join us when we needed to hold court as well. We took our seats, and the food started coming out.

As we were enjoying the main course, a commotion came from the back of the hall, where the main entry was. A man in a blue marching uniform with Scoria Bay insignia rushed through, reaching the dais. He handed me a paper before any of the guards could reach him. As they reached him and wrestled him into a position to drag him away, he shouted, "Please, I need to stay and receive the Queen's response. This is urgent and can't wait another moment."

I nodded to the guards holding him, and they forced him to kneel at the bottom of the stairs. I broke the seal and opened the letter. As I read, Spencer and Amyra both leaned over to read with me. I reached the end of the letter and looked up at the courier.

"All hail Bel!" He shouted.

He then started choking and convulsing. The guards let go

of him, unsure of what to do. We all watched in horror as the man paled, unable to breathe. He choked his last breath out, and before his body could fall, it turned to ash. The dust that was once a man drifting eerily in the air before it simply vanished.

AFTERWORD

Thank you, truly, for reading.

When I wrote in the dedication that this was a love letter to anyone who's ever been told to sit down, stay quiet, or follow the rules for their own good — I meant it with my whole heart. That line shaped every page of this story. And if it resonated with you... I hope you felt that love in every choice Lyla made.

We're living in a world where obedience is still too often mistaken for virtue — where conformity is rewarded and those who dare to love differently, lead boldly, or speak too loud are told to hush or hide. But Lyla didn't. And maybe you won't either.

This book was always about more than court politics and forbidden kisses. It's about burning down the lie that you have to be what the world demands, instead of who you truly are.

And still — Lyla's story is just beginning.

In *Toll of the Crowned Flame*, the heat only intensifies. You'll finally get answers to the questions I know are burning you up right now: Why did Lyla start with immense power, even before she understood what it meant? How did Egan go from awkward and overlooked... to dangerous and calculating? What does Lyla *really* want from Spencer, and can she let herself love him without losing herself? What's going on with Ethan, and why

245

did he walk away from Katelle without a word? What did that letter say?

Some loyalties will shatter. Some hearts will surprise you. And some fires were always meant to spread.

If you're craving even more, I wrote "The First Spark," a bonus chapter that shows exactly how Lyla and Amyra's slow-burn romance first caught fire. It's all yours when you join my newsletter at www.oliviatildon.com. If you've already read it, still join, as I plan to share more bonus scenes, other updates, and special events for members of the revolution.

See you on the other side of the flame.

With love and fire,
Olivia Tildon

ABOUT THE AUTHOR

OLIVIA TILDON (they/she) writes queer romantasy for rebels with soft hearts—readers who crave defiant love, layered magic, and characters who change the world by choosing themselves. A mother of twins navigating a military divorce, Olivia rediscovered writing during a season of upheaval, solitude, and impossible choices. Without a budget or a blueprint, she taught herself to publish and poured everything she had into stories that reflect the quiet power of authenticity.

A queer author drawn to stories about chosen family, forbidden love, and becoming who you were never allowed to be, Olivia builds worlds where identity is power and love is an act of defiance. Without a budget or a blueprint, she taught herself how to publish and built a career from the ground up, pouring that grit and vulnerability into every page.

Her work is driven by the belief that small, brave choices can be revolutionary—and that stories still have the power to heal, awaken, and set us free.

Want more magic?

Download *The First Spark*, a free prequel to *Iris of the Crowned Flame*, by signing up for the newsletter. Get early access to new books and behind-the-scenes lore, and join a growing rebellion of romantasy readers.

Find Olivia online at www.oliviatildon.com and on social media @olivia.tildon

ALSO BY OLIVIA TILDON

The *Oracles of the Gelid* series

Toll of the Crowned Flame (Book 2)

The next book in this series is coming soon, and will follow Nymbria's story.